MARGERY ALLINGHAM

More Work for the Undertaker

VINTAGE

10

Vintage
20 Vauxhall Bridge Road,
London SW1V 2SA

Vintage is part of the Penguin Random House
group of companies whose addresses can be found at
global.penguinrandomhouse.com

 Penguin
Random House
UK

This edition reissued in Vintage in 2016

First published in Vintage in 2007

First published in Great Britain by William Heinemann in 1949

penguin.co.uk/vintage

A CIP catalogue record for this book is available
from the British Library

ISBN 9780099506072

Typeset in India by Thomson Digital Pvt Ltd, Noida, Delhi

Printed and bound in Great Britain by Clays Ltd, St Ives plc

Penguin Random House is committed to a sustainable future
for our business, our readers and our planet. This book is made
from Forest Stewardship Council® certified paper.

VINTAGE MURDER MYSTERIES

With the sign of a human skull upon its back and a melancholy shriek emitted when disturbed, the Death's Head Hawkmoth has for centuries been a bringer of doom and an omen of death – which is why we chose it as the emblem for our Vintage Murder Mysteries.

Some say that its appearance in King George III's bedchamber pushed him into madness. Others believe that should its wings extinguish a candle by night, those nearby will be cursed with blindness. Indeed its very name, *Acherontia atropos*, delves into the most sinister realms of Greek mythology: Acheron, the River of Pain in the underworld, and Atropos, the Fate charged with severing the thread of life.

The perfect companion, then, for our Vintage Murder Mysteries sleuths, for whom sinister occurrences are never far away and murder is always just around the corner . . . .

To all old and valued clients this book is dedicated with respect and apologies for unavoidable delay in delivery of goods.

CONTENTS

Every character in this book is a careful portrait of a living person, each one of whom has expressed himself delighted not only with the accuracy but with the charity of the delineation. Any resemblance to any unconsulted person is therefore accidental.

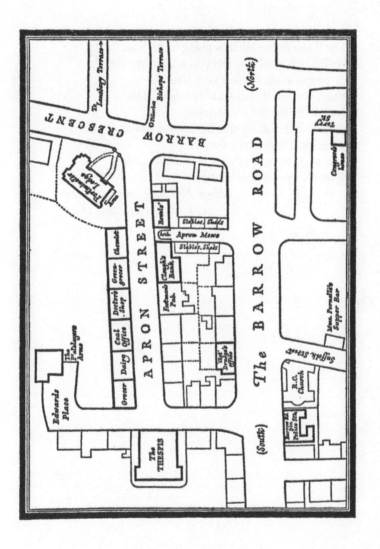

(North)

BARROW CRESCENT

Landing Terrace →

O'Rorke

Bishops Terrace

Prothero's Lodge

APRON STREET

Bennie's

Stables, Sheds

Apron Mews

Arch.

Stables, Sheds

Chemist

Green-grocer

Doctor's Shop

Coal Office

Clough's Bank

Dairy

Grocer

Podmore's Pub

The Prioligers Arms

Café Douglas Office

Edwards Place

The THESPIS

Terry St.

Conynge's House

The BARROW ROAD

Suffolk Street

Mrs. Permilla's Supper Bar

R.C. Church

Barrow Rd. Police Stn.

(South)

Now listen to the tale I'm going to tell you.
You'll laugh until you feel you want some breath,
For people often think it very funny
When you tell them of a vi-hi-o-lent death!
More work for the Undertaker,
Another little job for the Tombstone Maker,
At the local cem-e-tery they've
Been very, very busy on a brand new grave:
He won't be cold this winter!

Music Hall song sung by the late
T. E. DUNVILLE, *circa* 1890

CHAPTER 1

Afternoon of a Detective

–

'I found a stiff in there once, down at the back just behind the arch,' said Stanislaus Oates, pausing before the shop window. 'I always recollect it because as I bent down it suddenly raised its arms and its cold hands closed round my throat. There was no power there, fortunately. He was just on gone and died while I clawed him off. It made me sweat, though. I was a Sergeant Detective, Second Class, then.'

He swung away from the window and swept on down the crowded pavement. His raincoat, which was blackish with flecks of grey in it, billowed out behind him like a schoolmaster's gown.

His eighteen months as Chief of Scotland Yard had made little outward difference to him. He was still the shabby drooping man, who thickened unexpectedly at the stomach, and his grey sharp-nosed face was still sad and introspective in the shadow of his soft black hat.

'I always like to walk this bit,' he went on with gloomy affection. 'It was the high spot of my manor for nearly thirty years.'

'And it's still strewn with the fragrant petals of memory, no doubt?' commented his companion affably. 'Whose was the corpse? The shopkeeper's?'

'No. Just some poor silly chap trying to crack a crib. Fell through the skylight and broke his back. That's longer ago than I care to think. What a lovely afternoon, Campion. Enjoying it?'

The man at his side did not reply. He was extricating himself from a passer-by who had accidentally cannoned into him on catching a sudden glimpse of the old Chief.

The main stream of bustling shoppers ignored the old detective, but to a minority his progress was like the serene sailing of a big river fish from whose path experienced small fry consider it prudent to scatter.

Mr Albert Campion himself was not unknown to some of the interested glances but his field was smaller and considerably more exclusive. He was a tall man in the forties, over-thin, with hair once fair and now bleached almost white. His clothes were good enough to be unnoticeable and behind unusually large horn-rimmed spectacles his face, despite its maturity, still possessed much of that odd quality of anonymity which had been so remarked upon in his youth. He had the valuable gift of appearing an elegant shadow and was, as a great policeman had once said so enviously, a man of whom at first sight no one could ever be afraid.

He had accepted the Chief's unprecedented invitation to lunch with reservations and the equally unlikely proposal that they should go and walk in the park with a stiffening of his determination not to be drawn into anything.

Oates, who usually walked fast and spoke little, was dawdling and presently his cold eyes flickered upward. Mr Campion, following their gaze, saw that it rested on the clock over the jeweller's two doors down. It was just five minutes past three. Oates sniffed with satisfaction.

'Let's have a look at the flowers,' he said and set off across the road. The Chief leading the way had seen his goal. It proved to be a nest of small green chairs arranged cosily at the foot of a giant beech which made a tent of shadow over them. He crossed towards them and sat down, wrapping the tails of his coat over his knees like a skirt.

The only other living creature in sight at the moment was a woman who sat on one of the public benches which flanked the gravel path. The full sunlight poured down on her bent back and on the square of folded newspaper in which she was so engrossed.

She was just within normal vision. Her small squat form was arrayed in an assortment of garments of varying length, and as she sat with her knees crossed she revealed a swag of multicoloured hems festooned across a concertina'd stocking. At that distance her shoe appeared to be stuffed with grass. Wisps of it sprouted from every aperture, including one at the toe. It was warm in the sun but she wore across her shoulders something which might once have been a fur, and although her face was hidden Campion could see elf-locks peeping out from under the yellowing folds of an ancient motoring veil of the button-on-top variety. Since she wore it over a roughly torn square of cardboard placed flat on her head the effect was eccentric and even pathetic, in the way that little girls in fancy dress are sometimes so.

The second woman appeared on the path suddenly, as figures do in the bright sunlight. Mr Campion, who had nothing else he wished to think about at the moment, reflected lazily that it was gratifying to see how often Nature employs the designs of eminent artists and was happy to recognize a Helen Hopkinson. She was perfect, the little feet, the enormous bust, the tall white hat, half wine-glass, half posy, and above all the ineffable indication of demure ingenuousness in every curving line. He became aware of the Chief stiffening at his side at the instant in which the shining figure paused. The coat, which some ingenious tailor had evolved to give a torso like a jellybag the inoffensive contours of a jug, hesitated as it were in mid-air. The white hat turned briefly this way and that. The small feet fluttered to the side of the woman on the seat. A tiny glove moved forth and back, and then she was in mid-path again, walking on with the same self-conscious if unsteady innocence.

'Ha,' said Oates softly as she passed them, and they saw her face was pink and virtuous. 'See that, Campion?'

'Yes. What did she give her?'

'Sixpence. Possibly ninepence. It has been a shilling.'

Mr Campion looked at his friend, who was not by nature flippant.

'A purely charitable act?'

'Utterly.'

'I see.' Campion was the most polite of men. 'I know it's rare,' he said meekly.

'She does it nearly every day, somewhere about this time,' the Chief explained unsatisfactorily. 'I wanted to see it with my own eyes. Oh, there you are, Super . . .'

Heavy steps on the grass behind them came closer and Superintendent Yeo, most just if most policemanlike of policemen, came round the tree to shake hands.

Mr Campion welcomed him sincerely. The two were very old friends and had that deep liking for each other which springs up so often between opposite temperaments.

Campion's pale eyes became speculative. Of one thing he was now certain. If Oates had taken it into his grey head to play the goat, Yeo was not the man to waste an afternoon to humour him.

'Well,' Yeo said with glee, 'you saw it.'

'Yes.' The Chief was thoughtful. 'Funny thing human greed. The exhumation must be reported in that paper if it's at all recent, but she's not reading it unless she's learning it by heart. She hasn't turned it over while we've been here.'

Campion's lean chin shot up for a moment and then he bent again over the piece of stick with which he was doodling in the dust.

'Palinode case?'

Yeo's round brown eyes flickered at his Chief.

'You've been making it interesting for him, I see,' he said with disapproval. 'Yes, that's Miss Jessica Palinode sitting over there, Mr Campion. She is the third sister and she sits on that particular seat every afternoon, rain or shine. To look at she's what we used to call a "daisy".'

'And who was the other woman?' Campion was still intent on his hieroglyphics.

'That was Mrs Dawn Bonnington of Carchester Terrace,' Oates intervened. 'She knows it's "wrong to give to beggars" but when she sees "a woman who has had to let herself go" she

4

just can't resist "doing something". It's a form of superstition, of course. Some people touch wood.'

'Oh give it to me straight,' grumbled Yeo. 'Mrs B. walks her dog here on fine afternoons, Mr Campion, and seeing Miss Jessica always sitting there she formed the opinion, not unnaturally, that the poor old girl was down and out. So she made a habit of slipping her something and she was never snubbed. One of our chaps observed the incident was pretty regular and walked over to warn the old thing against begging. As he came up to her he saw what she was doing and he admits quite frankly that it put him off.'

'What was that?'

'A crossword puzzle in Latin.' The Superintendent spoke placidly. 'They run one in a highbrow weekly alongside a couple of others in English, one for adults and one for children. The officer, who is highbrow himself, bless his heart, does the one for kids, and he recognized the page as he approached. It shook him to see her slapping the words in and he walked past her.'

'Ah, but next day when she was only reading a book he did his stuff,' put in Oates, who sounded happy, 'and Miss Palinode gave him a fine comprehensive lecture on the ethics of true politeness, and half-a-crown.'

'He doesn't admit the half-crown.' Yeo's small mouth was prim but amused. 'However, he had the sense to find out her name and where she lived and he had a quiet word with Mrs Bonnington. She didn't believe him – she's that kind of woman – and ever after she's had to do her little act when she's thought no one was looking. The interesting thing is that he swears that Miss Palinode likes the money. He says she waits for it and goes off livid if Mrs Bonnington doesn't come. Well, does it attract you, Mr Campion?'

The third man straightened his back and smiled half in apology, half in regret.

'Frankly, no,' he said. 'Sorry.'

'It's a fascinating case,' Oates said, ignoring him. 'It's going to be one of the classics of its kind. They're such difficult interesting people. You know who they are, don't you? When I was a boy even I heard of Professor Palinode, who wrote the essays, and his wife the poetess. These are the children. They're queer brainy people, all boarding privately in what was once their own home. They're not easy people to get at from a police point of view, and now there's a poisoner loose among 'em. I thought it was right down your street.'

'My street has developed a bend,' Campion murmured apologetically. 'Where are your young men?'

Oates did not look at him.

'Well, young Charlie Luke is the DDL in charge,' he explained. 'He's old Bill Luke's youngest. You'll remember Inspector Luke. He and the Super here were mates in Y Division. If young Charlie is what I think he is, I don't see why he shouldn't pull it off – if he has help.' He looked at the younger man hopefully.

'We'll give you all the dope anyway,' continued Oates. 'It's worth hearing. The whole street seems to be in it, that's such a funny thing.'

'I do apologize, but you know, I fancy I've heard most of it.' The man in the horn-rimmed spectacles considered them unhappily. 'The woman who owns the house they all live in is an old variety artiste called Renee Roper. She's an acquaintance of mine. In fact she once did me a very good turn a long time ago when I was having fun and games with some ballet stars. She came to see me this morning.'

'Did she ask you to act for her?' They spoke together and he laughed.

'Oh, no,' he said. 'Renee's not your bird. She's just upset at having a murder or two – is it two yet, Oates? – on her nice respectable hands. She invited me to be her star boarder and tidy it all up for her. I felt a lout having to turn her down and as it was I listened to the whole harrowing story.'

Well!' The Superintendent was sitting up like a bear, his round eyes serious. 'I'm not a religious man,' he said, 'but do you know what I'd call that? I'd call it an omen. It's a coincidence, Mr Campion, you can't ignore it. It's intended.'

The thin man rose and stood looking out across the sunlit grass to the bundle on the seat and to the flowers beyond her. 'No,' he said sadly. 'No, two crows don't make a summons, Super. According to the adage one needs three for that. I've got to go.'

CHAPTER 2

The Third Crow

—

One crow means danger; two, strangers; three, a summons.

On the brow of the rise the thin man paused in his stride and looked back. Below him the scene was spread out in bright miniature, as if it were under the dome of a glass paper-weight. There was the shining grass and the rod of the path, and beyond, no larger now than a puppet, the untidy figure with the mushroom head, a blurred mystery on the dark seat.

Campion hesitated and then drew from his pocket one of those midget telescopes. When he put it to his eye the woman rushed towards him through the sunny air and he saw her for the first time in vivid detail. She was still bent over the paper on her lap, but in an instant, as if she were aware he watched her, she raised her head and stared full at him, apparently into his eyes. He was much too far away for her to have seen the telescope or even that he faced in her direction. Her face startled him.

Under the ragged edge of cardboard which showed clearly through the centre parting of the veil it blazed with intelligence. The skin was dark, the features fine and the eyes deep-set, but the outstanding impression he received was of a mind.

He moved his glass away hastily, aware of his intrusion, and quite by chance became the witness of a minor incident. Behind the woman a boy and a girl had appeared between the bushes. They had evidently come upon her unexpectedly and at the precise moment in which they swung into the bright circle of Mr Campion's seven-leagued-eye the boy started and caught the girl round the shoulders. They retreated stealthily, walking backwards. The boy was the elder, nineteen or so, and possessed all that clumsy boniness which promises size and weight. His untidy fair head was bare and his pink worried face ugly and pleasant. Campion could see his expression clearly and was struck by the concern in it.

The girl was a little younger and his fleeting impression of her was that she was oddly dressed. Her hair silhouetted against the burning flowers shone with the blue-black sheen of poppy centres. Her face was indistinct, but he was aware of round dark eyes alive with alarm, and, once again to surprise and capture him, he received the same indefinable assertion of intelligence.

He kept his glass upon them until they gained the sanctuary of the tamarisk clump and vanished, leaving him curious. Yeo's remark that his intervention in the Palinode affair was 'intended' nagged like a prophecy.

All that week coincidences had occurred to keep the case before his mind. The chance glimpse of these two youngsters was the latest of the baits. He found he wanted to know very much who they were and why they were so afraid of being seen by that unlikely witch on the public bench.

He hurried away. This time the ancient spell must not be permitted to work. In an hour he must telephone the Great Man and accept with gratitude and modesty the great good fortune his friends and relations had engineered for him.

He was crossing the street when he caught sight of an elderly limousine with a crested door.

The great lady, a dowager with a name to conjure with, was waiting for him with the small side window down as he came up and stood bareheaded in the sun before her.

'My dear boy,' the thin voice had the graciousness of a world two wars away, 'I caught sight of you and made up my mind to stop and tell you how glad I am. I know it's a secret but Dorroway came to see me last night and he told me in confidence. So it's all settled. Your mother would have been very happy.'

Mr Campion made the necessary gratified noises but there was a bleakness in his eyes which she was too experienced to ignore.

'You'll enjoy it when you get there,' she said, reminding him of something someone had once lied about his prep school. 'After all, it is the last remaining civilized place in the world and the weather is so good for children. And how is Amanda? She'll fly out there with you, of course. She designs her own aeroplanes, doesn't she? How clever girls are these days.'

Campion hesitated. 'I'm hoping she'll follow me,' he said at last. 'Her work is not unimportant and I'm afraid there may be a great many loose ends to be tied up before she can get away.'

'Indeed?' The old eyes were shrewd and disapproving. 'Don't let her delay too long. It's vital from a social angle that a Governor's wife should be with him from the first.'

He thought she was going to leave him with that, but another idea had occurred to her.

'By the way, I was thinking of that extraordinary servant of yours,' she said. 'Tugg, or Lugg. The one with the impossible voice. You must leave him behind. You do understand that, don't you? Dorroway had quite forgotten him but promised to mention it. A dear faithful creature can be very much misunderstood and do a great deal of harm.

'Don't be foolish,' her blue lips moulding the words with deliberation. 'All your life you've squandered your ability helping undeserving people who have got themselves into trouble with the police. Now you have the opportunity to take a place which even your grandfather would have considered suitable. I'm glad to see it happen. Good-bye, and my warmest congratulations. By the way, have the child's clothes cut in London. They tell me the local style is fanciful and a boy does suffer so.'

The great car slid away. He walked on slowly, feeling as if he were dragging a ceremonial sword, and was still in the same state of depression when he climbed out of a taxi at the entrance to his flat in Bottle Street, the cul-de-sac which runs off Piccadilly on the northern side.

The narrow staircase was as familiar and friendly as an old coat, and when his key turned in the lock all the warmth of the sanctuary which had been his ever since he left Cambridge rushed to meet him like a mistress. He saw his sitting-room in detail for the first time for close on twenty years, and its jungle growth of trophies and their associations shocked him. He would not look at them.

On the desk the telephone squatted patiently and behind it the clock signalled five minutes to the hour. He took himself firmly in hand. The time had come. He crossed the room quickly, his hand outstretched.

The note lying on the blotter caught his eye because a blue-bladed dagger, a memento of his first adventure which he was in the habit of using as a paper-knife, was stuck into it, pinning it to the board. The sensational trick annoyed him, but the frankly experimental type used in the letter heading and a certain spontaneity in the advertisement matter caught his attention and he bent down to read.

COURTESY * SYMPATHY * COMFORT in transit
JAS BOWELS & SON
(The *Practical* Undertakers)

Family Interments
12 Apron Street,
w3.

'If you're Rich, or count the Cost,
We Under stand there's Someone lost.'

Dr to
MR MAGERSFONTEIN LUGG,
c/o A. Campion, Esq.
12a Bottle Street,
Piccadilly, w

Dear Magers,

If Beatty was alive which she is not more's the pity as you will be the first to agree she would be writing this instead of me and the Boy.

We was wondering this dinner time can you get your Governor if you are working for the same one and this reaches you, to give us a bit of a hand in this Palinode kickup which you will have read of in the papers.

Exhumations as we call them in the Trade are not very nice and bad for business which is not what it was before all this.

We both think we could do with the help your chap could give us with the police etc. and might be useful ourselves to someone *not in the blue* if you see what I mean.

Without disrespect bring him along for a bit of tea and a jaw any day as we do not do much after three-thirty and will do less if this goes on as it may between ourselves.

Remembering you very kindly and all forgotten I hope.

Yours truly,

Jas Bowels

As he raised his head from this engaging document there was a movement from the inner doorway behind him and the floor shook a little.

''Mazing cheek, ain't it?' Magersfontein Lugg's lush personality pervaded the room like a smell of cooking. He was in *deshabillé*, appearing at first sight to be attired as the hinder part of a pantomime elephant, and was holding out in front of him a mighty woollen undervest. The 'impossible voice' to which the great lady had referred so recently was after all only a matter of taste. There was expression and flexibility in that rich rumble which many actors might have sought to imitate in vain.

'Wot a 'orrible man too. Bowels by name and Bowels by nature. I said that when she married 'im.'

'At the actual wedding?' inquired his employer with interest.

'Over me one 'alf of British champagne.' He appeared to recall the incident with satisfaction.

Campion laid a hand on the telephone.

'Who was she? Your only love?'

'Gawd, no! My sis. 'E's my brother-in-law, the poor worm shoveller. 'Aven't spoke to 'im for thirty years nor thought of 'im till this come just now.'

Campion was startled into meeting the eyes of his ancient companion, a thing he had not been able to do for some few weeks.

' 'E took it as a compliment.' The beady eyes peered out from their surrounding folds with a truculence which did not hide the reproach or even the panic lurking there. 'That's the kind of bloke Jas is. Come my little trip inside, 'e be'aved as though I'd took 'im with me, sent back me wedding present to Beatt with a few questions not in the taste you and me is accustomed to. I wrote 'im clean off my slate. Now 'e pops up, says by the way me sis is dead some time, which I knew, and asks a favour. It's a coincidence, that's all. Would you like me to go outside while you do your bit of telephonin'?'

The thin man in the spectacles turned away from the desk.

'Is this a put-up job?' he inquired briefly.

The place where Mr Lugg's eyebrows may once have been rose to meet the naked dome of his skull. He folded his vest with great deliberation.

'Some remarks I do not 'ear,' he said, achieving dignity. 'I am just puttin' my things together. It's all right. I've got my advert wrote out.'

'Your what?'

'My advert. "Gentleman's gentleman seeks interesting employment. Remarkable references. Title preferred." That's about it. I can't come with you, cock. I don't want to see meself an international incident.'

Mr Campion sat down to re-read the letter.

'When exactly did this arrive?'

'Late post, ten minutes ago. Show you the envelope if you're suspicious.'

'Could old Renee Roper have put him up to it?'

'She didn't marry our Beatt to 'im thirty-five years ago, if that's what you mean.' Lugg was contemptuous. 'Don't be so nervy. 'E's only a coincidence, the second you've 'ad over this Palinode caper. Don't you get excited, though. There's no need for it. What's Jas to you anyway?'

'The third crow, if you're interested,' said Mr Campion and, after a while, began to look quietly happy.

CHAPTER 3

Old-fashioned and out of the ordinary

—

THE D.D.I. was waiting in the upstairs room of the Platelayers Arms, a discreet old-fashioned drinking house in one of the more obscure streets of his district.

Campion met him there at a few minutes after eight, as the Superintendent promised he should. Over the telephone Yeo had sounded relieved and pleased.

'I knew all along you'd never resist it,' he said cheerfully. 'You can't change your spots. It's something in a man's character which draws him to a certain type of happening. I've seen it scores of times. You've been sent by heaven, let alone Headquarters, to the family Palinode. I'll get on to Charlie Luke at once. You'd better meet him in that pub they use in Edwardes Place. You'll take to Charlie.'

And now, as he came up the wooden stairs and entered the varnished cabin which overhung the huge circular bar, Mr Campion's pale eyes rested on Bill Luke's boy. The D.D.I. was a tough. Seated on the edge of the table, his hands in his pockets, his hat over his eyes, his muscles spoiling the shape of his civilian coat, he might well have been a gangster. There was a lot of him, but his compact and sturdy bones tended to disguise his height. He had a live dark face with a strong nose, narrow vivid eyes, and his smile, which was ready, had yet a certain ferocity.

He got up at once, hand outstretched.

'Glad to see you, sir,' he said and conveyed distinctly that he hoped to God he was.

The Divisional Detective Inspector is in sole and complete charge of his own territory until something happens inside it which is so interesting that his Area Superintendent at the Yard feels it his duty to send him help. To that help, despite his superior knowledge of the district, he is always liable to find himself second-in-command. Campion sympathized.

'I hope it's not as bad as that,' he said disarmingly. 'How many Palinode murders have you actually got on your hands so far?'

The narrow eyes flickered at him and he saw that the man was younger than he had supposed, thirty-four or five at the most, sensationally young for his rank.

'First, what will you drink?' Luke thumped the humpbacked bell on the table. 'We'll get Ma Chubb safely out of earshot and I'll give you the full strength.'

The licensee waited upon them herself. She was a quick-eyed, quick-moving little person with a politely worried face and grey hair coiled into intricate patterns under a net.

She nodded to Campion without looking at him directly and trotted out with the money.

'Well now,' said Charlie Luke, his eyes snapping and the trace of a country inflexion creeping into his voice, which was as strong and pliant as his shoulders, 'I don't know what you've heard so far but I'll rough it out as it's come to me. It began with poor little old Doctor Smith.'

Campion had never heard before of this particular Doctor Smith but suddenly he was in the room with them. He took shape like a portrait under a pencil.

'A tallish old boy – well, not so very old, fifty-five, married to a shrew. Overworked. Over-conscientious. Comes out of his flat nagged to a rag in the mornings and goes down to his surgery – room with a shop front like a laundry. Stooping. Back like a camel. Loose trousers, poking at the seat as if God were holding him up by the centre buttons. Head stuck out like a tortoise, waving slightly. Worried eyes. Good chap. Kind. Not as bright as some (no time for it) but professional. Old school, not old school tie. Servant of his calling and don't forget it. He starts getting poison pen letters. Shakes him.'

Charlie Luke spoke without syntax or noticeable coherence but he talked with his whole body. When he described Doctor Smith's back his own arched. When he mentioned the shop front he squared it in with his hands. His tremendous strength, which was physical rather than nervous, poured into the recital, forcing the facts home like a pile-driver.

Campion was made to share the doctor's scandalized anxiety. The man talked like an avalanche.

'Show you the file of filth later,' he said. 'This is just the outline.' He was off again, vigorous muscular mouth pumping out the words, hands rubbing them in. 'Usual scurrilous stuff. Had a psycho on them. Says of course probably female, but very experienced sexually and not as uneducated as one would think from the spelling. They accused the doc of conniving at murder. Old lady called Ruth Palinode murdered, buried, no questions asked, doc to blame. Doc gets wind up slowly. Feels patients may be getting the same letters. Chance remarks seem to mean more than they were ever meant to. Poor old blighter starts thinking. Goes over old woman's symptoms. Frightened to hell. Tells his wife, who uses it as a handle to torment him. He gets in nervous state, has to go to brother medico, who makes him call us in. The whole thing's passed to me.'

He took a breath and a gulp of whisky and water.

' "Good God, boy!" he says to me, "it may have been arsenic. I never thought of poison." "Well, Doc," I said to him, "it may have been wind. Anyway it's worrying somebody. We'll find out and that'll settle it." Now we go to Apron Street.'

'I'm with you,' said Mr Campion, trying not to sound breathless. 'That's the Palinode house, is it?'

'Not yet. Got to get the street roughed in. Street important. Narrow little way. Small shops either side. Old Brotherhood chapel, now the Thespis Rep Theatre, highbrow, harmless, one end; Portminster Lodge, the Palinode house, the other. The district's gone down like a drunk in thirty years and the Palinodes with it. Now a dear old variety gal turned lodging-house keeper owns their house. Mortgage fell in, she inherited, her own place got bombed, so she moved over with some of her old boarders and took the Palinode family in her stride.'

'Miss Roper's an old acquaintance of mine.'

'Is she, though?' The bright eyes widened from slits to diamonds. 'Then you can tell me something. Could she have written the letters?'

Campion's brows rose up behind his spectacles.

'I don't know her sufficiently well to say,' he murmured. 'I should have guessed that she was the last person in the world not to have signed her name.'

'Oh, so should I. I love her.' Luke spoke earnestly. 'But you never know, do you?' He thrust out a great hand. 'Think of it. Woman alone, happy life gone, nothing but drudgery, boredom, hatred very likely of toffee-nosed old scroungers. Perhaps they turn on the "my good woman" when it's her perishing house.'

He paused. 'Don't think I blame her,' he said with simple earnestness. 'Everybody's mind has its dregs. As I see it, it's the circumstances which stir 'em up. I'm not shooting at the poor old blossom, I just want to know. She might have wanted to turn the whole gang of 'em out and not known quite how to do it, or she might have fallen for the doc and wanted to hurt him. She's old for that, of course.'

'Anyone else?'

'Who might have written 'em? About five hundred. Any one of the doc's patients. He's got a very funny manner when that basket of a wife of his has been at him, and they're all ill to start with, aren't they? Now there's the street. I can't take you through it house by house or we'll be here all night. Drink up, sir. But I'll give you the smell of it. There's a grocer's and ironmonger's on the corner opposite the theatre. He's a country chap gone Cockney fifty years ago. He runs his place as if it were a trading post somewhere. Tick unlimited. Gets into trouble, keeps the cheese too near the paraffin and hasn't been the same man since his wife died. He's known the Palinodes all his life. Their father helped him when he was starting and but for him some of them would starve at the end of a quarter, I fancy.

'Next door to the grocer is the coal office, he's new. Then we come to the doc's outfit. Then there's the greengrocers. They're okay. Big family of girls. Paint all over their faces and dirt all over their hands. And then, Mr Campion, there's the chemist.'

He had been keeping his voice down but the strength of it even when suppressed was liable to set the panelling vibrating. The sudden silence as he paused was grateful.

'Chemist of interest?' encouraged his listener, who found himself fascinated by the performance.

'Pa Wilde would be interesting if he was only on the pictures,' said Charlie Luke. 'What a shop, eh! What an emporium! Ever heard of *Old Ma Appleyard's Dynamite Cough Cure and Intestine Controller*? Of course you haven't, but your grandpa used to bung himself up with it, I bet. And you can still buy it there if you want to, in the original wrapping. He's got dozens of little drawers of muck, smell of old lady's bedroom enough to knock you back, and old Pa Wilde in the middle of it looking like auntie's ruin with his dyed hair, collar like this' – he strained his chin upwards and made his eyes bulge – 'little black tie, striped trousers. When old Joey and Pantaloon Bowels dug up Miss Ruth Palinode and we all stood round in the cold waiting for Sir Doberman to get his damned jars loaded, I must say I started thinking about Pa Wilde. I don't say he administered whatever it was but I bet it came from there.'

'When do you expect the analyst's report?'

'We've had a provisional one. The final isn't till tonight. Promised for midnight. If it's something that could only have been criminally administered, we wake up the undertakers and dig up the brother right away. I've got the order. I hate that job. All stones and stinks.'

He shook his head as a wet dog does and took a drink.

'That's the eldest brother, I take it? The eldest of them all?'

'Yes. Edward Palinode, age sixty-seven at the time of his decease, which was last March. What's that, seven months? Let's hope he's settled. It's a damp old cemetery, ought to be done away with.'

Mr Campion smiled. 'You've left me at the shady chemist's,' he said. 'Where do we go? Straight into the Palinodes' house?'

The D.D.I. considered. 'May as well,' he agreed with unexpected reluctance. 'On the other side of the road there's only that old blighter Bowels, the bank, which is a small branch of Clough's, the entrance to the Mews, and the worst pub in the world called the Footman's. Righto, sir, now we come to the house itself. It's on the corner, same side as the chemist. It's enormous. It's got a basement as I told you. It's shabby as a camel and on one side it's got a little sand and laurel yard of a garden. All cats and paper bags.'

He paused. Some of the enthusiasm had gone from him and his angled eyes watched Campion gloomily.

'I tell you what,' he said with sudden relief. 'I can show you the Captain now, I expect.' He got up softly and with that cautious gentleness peculiar to the very powerful lifted down a large framed poster advertising Irish whiskey which occupied a centre position on the inner wall. Behind it was a small glazed window through which a prudent landlord might obtain a clear overhead view of the whole of the public part of his house. The partitions which formed the various bars radiated from the central counter like the spokes of a wheel, containing segments of crowd. The two men stood well back, their heads together, and peered down.

'There he is.' Charlie Luke's murmur was like the roll of distant artillery. 'In the saloon. Tall old boy in the corner. Green hat.'

'Talking to Price-Williams of *The Signal*?' Campion had caught sight of the finely moulded head of the most astute of all crime reporters.

'Pricey hasn't got anything. He's bored. Look at him scratching,' said the D.D.I. softly. It was the voice of the fisherman, experienced, patient, passionately interested.

The Captain proved to be a soldierly figure. He was approaching sixty, a slender Edwardian drying into old age very gently. Hair and tiny moustache were cut so short that their colour was indeterminate, neither fair nor grey. Campion could not hear his voice but he guessed it was pleasant in accent and depreciatory in tone. He also guessed that his hands were mottled on the back like the skin of a frog, and that the chances were he wore a discreet signet ring and carried visiting cards.

It struck him as amazing that such a man should have a sister who affected a piece of cardboard and a motoring veil as a head-covering, and he said so. Luke was apologetic.

'Sorry. Ought to have told you. He's not a Palinode. He just lives in the house. Renee brought him with her from her other place. He was her pet boarder there and has one of the better rooms now. The name is Alastair Seton, the rank is Regular Army, out of which he was invalided. Heart, I fancy. His resources amount to something like four pounds fourteen per week. But he's a gentleman and does his best to live like one, poor old devil. This is his secret pub.'

'Oh, dear,' said Mr Campion. 'This is where he comes when he mentions casually that he has an important business interview, I suppose.'

'That's it.' Luke nodded appreciatively. 'The interview is with Nellie and half a pint. He's enjoying this flare-up in spite of himself. One side of his mind is bloody outraged that he should be brought into contact with anything so sordid, but the other half is tickled to death by the excitement.'

There was silence between them for a moment. Campion's gaze wandered over the crowd.

Mr Campion took off his spectacles and spoke without turning round.

'Why don't you want to talk about the Palinodes, Inspector?'

Charlie Luke refilled his glass and presently looked over it, his eyes unexpectedly frank.

'I can't, as a matter of fact,' he said.

'Why?'

'Don't understand 'em.' He made the admission like the prize pupil confessing ignorance.

'How do you mean?'

'Just that. I don't understand what they say.' He sat back on the table and spread out his muscular hands. 'If it was only a foreign language I'd get an interpreter,' he said, 'but it's not. It isn't even that they won't talk. They talk for hours, they like talking. But when I come away from them my head is buzzing, and when I read the verbatim report I keep sending for the stenographer to see if he's got the words right. He doesn't know, either.'

There was a pause.

'Er – long words?' suggested Mr Campion diffidently.

'No, not particularly.' Luke was not offended. He seemed mainly sad. 'There's three of them,' he said at last. 'I can tell you that. Two dead, three alive. Mr Lawrence Palinode, Miss Evadne Palinode, and the baby, Miss Jessica Palinode. She's the gal who gets presents in the park. None of them have any money to speak of and God knows why anyone should kill 'em. They're not barmy, though. I've made that mistake already. It's no good, sir, you'll have to see 'em yourself. When are you moving in?'

'At once, I thought. I brought a bag with me.'

The D.D.I. grunted. 'It's good news to me,' he said seriously. 'There's a man on the door but he knows you by sight. Name of Corkerdale. Sorry I can't give you a line on these people, Mr Campion, but they're old-fashioned and out of the ordinary. It's not a phrase I like but it sums 'em up.'

He bent over his glass and patted his stomach.

'I've got to the stage when as soon as I think of 'em I feel a bit faint. I'll send you word of the analyst's report as soon as I get it.'

Mr Campion finished his own drink and picked up his suitcase. A thought occurred to him.

'By the way, who is the girl?' he inquired. 'Young, dark-haired. I hardly saw her face.'

'That's Clytie White,' said Luke calmly. 'She's a niece. There were six Palinodes once. One got away and married a doctor who took her to Hong-Kong. On the voyage out the boat went down and they were both nearly drowned, and the baby was born while her Ma was still wet with sea-water. Hence the name. Don't ask me more than that. It's what I've been told. "Hence the name".'

'I see. Does she live with Renee, too?'

'Yes. Her parents sent her back, which was lucky because they were both killed later. She was a little kid then. She's only eighteen and a half now. She works as an office girl at the *Literary Weekly*, licks the stamps and sells the review copies. As soon as she can type she's going to write.'

'And who is the boy?'

'With a motor-cycle?' The words were uttered so violently that Mr Campion jumped.

'I didn't see one. They were in the park.'

The end of the sentence faded. Charlie Luke's still youthful face had grown several shades darker and his triangular lids were drawn down over his bright eyes.

'A bullpup and a stray kitty, that's what they are,' he said sulkily, and then, looking up and laughing suddenly with a self-depreciatory grace which was wholly disarming, he added, 'such a dear little kitty. Hasn't got its eyes open yet.'

CHAPTER 4

You Have to be Careful

—

CAMPION passed quietly to the stairhead, whence he could see down through a bright-barred window to the heart and soul of Portminster Lodge.

There was Renee, looking much as he had seen her for the first time nearly ten years before. She was in profile, leaning across a supper table talking to someone he could not see. Miss Roper's age might still have been 'about sixty', although in all likelihood she was some eight or nine years older. Her small figure was as compact, if not quite as curved, as in the days when she was kicking up her heels on the provincial stage, and her hair was still a wonderful if unlikely brown.

She was in her receiving costume, a fussy multi-coloured silk blouse tucked tightly into a neat black skirt, not too short. She heard Campion when he was half-way down the area, edging his way through a booby-trap of milk bottles. He caught a glimpse of her face with the tip-tilted nose and far too prominent eyes turned sharply towards the window before she hurried to open the door a foot or so.

'Who is it?' The words ran up the scale like a cue for song. 'Oh, it's you, ducky.' She was human again but still more or less before footlights. 'Come in, do. This is good of you, I appreciate it and I shan't forget it. How's your mother? Nicely?'

'As well as can be expected.' Mr Campion, who had been orphaned some ten years, fielded the catch as neatly as he was able.

'I know. Well, we mustn't grumble.' She patted him on the shoulder, possibly in approbation, and turned back into the room.

It was a typical basement-kitchen of the ancient sort, a place of pipes and unexplained alcoves, with a stone floor. A certain gaiety had been achieved by the display of some hundreds of theatrical photographs of all periods covering half the walls, and there were bright rag rugs on the matting.

'Clarrie,' she rattled on, still with the same false brightness, 'I don't think you've met my nephew Albert. He's the one from Bury. The *nobby* side of the family, dear. He's a lawyer and one does so need one at a time like this. His mother wrote and said he'd help me if I wanted him to, so I sent her a wire – didn't tell you in case he didn't come!'

She lied like the staunch old trouper she was and her laugh was pretty. It welled up fresh and young from a heart nothing had aged.

Mr Campion kissed her. 'Glad to get here, Auntie,' he said, and she blushed like a girl.

The man in the plum-coloured pullover, who had been eating bread and cheese and pickled onions with his stockinged feet tucked over the chair-rail, got up and leaned across the board.

'Pleased to meet you,' he said, thrusting out a carefully manicured hand. His nails were misleading. So was the flash of gold in his smile, and the shock of dry fair hair, now receding somewhat drastically in a cascade of ordered crimps. His deeply-lined face was kindly and a pattern of common sense had been battered into its second-rate good looks. The pink and brown striped shirt which showed in the V of the pullover had small darns at the sides where the points of the collar had worn holes.

'My name's Grace,' he went on, 'Clarence Grace. I don't suppose you've heard of it.' The tone was not even wistful. 'I did a season in Bury.'

'Ah, that was Bury, Lancs, dear,' Renee put in quickly. 'This is Bury St Edmunds, isn't it, Albert?'

'That is so.' Mr Campion managed to sound both regretful and apologetic. 'It's very quiet down there.'

'Still, he has to understand the law down there, just the same as anywhere else.' Renee was valiant. 'Sit down, ducky.

I expect you're hungry. I'll find you something. We're in a bit of a hurry, as usual. It's a funny thing, but I never seem to get done. *Mrs Love!'*

The final summons, uttered in a sort of musical scream, brought forth no response and Campion had time to protest that he had already fed.

Rene patted his shoulder again as if it were the situation she was jollying along. 'Sit down and have a drop of Clarrie's stout while I get on with your bed. *Mrs Love!* The others will be in soon, or at least the Captain will. He's got a dinner on tonight, with an old flame, I fancy. He'll go straight to his room. He doesn't really like the kitchen. If you hear the front door, that's who it is. After that you boys will have to help me with the trays. *Mrs Love!'*

Clarrie lowered his feet gently to the matting.

'I'll fetch her,' he said. 'What about the kiddo? She ought not to be out this time of night.'

'Clytie? Yes.' Renee glanced at the clock. 'Quarter past eleven. She *is* late, isn't she? I shouldn't worry if she was my daughter, but I don't like real innocence, do you, Albert? You never feel safe with it. But you shut up, Clarrie. No tale-telling, mind.'

The man paused with a hand on the doorknob.

'If I tell that old jar of smelling salts anything, it won't be about her niece, ducks,' he said cheerfully, but his face was working and in the second before he turned away they caught an uneasy flicker in his big indeterminate-coloured eyes. Renee waited until he closed the door before she said, 'It's nerves. But he'll get another job.' She spoke defensively, as if Campion had questioned it. 'I've seen many worse than Clarrie in the provinces, I have really.' And then, almost in the same breath but with a startling change to genuine intensity, 'Tell me, Mr Campion, *are they going to dig the other one up?'*

He glanced down at her with affection.

'Cheer up,' he said. 'It's not your funeral. Honestly, I don't know.'

She looked small and old. Little networks of red veins had appeared through the powder on her cheekbones and over the bridge of her nose.

'Oh, I don't like it.' She spoke softly. 'Not poison. I keep all the food locked up, you know. I try not to let it out of my sight until it's eaten. You can drink the stout, that's safe. My old girl has just brought it in and we opened it together, Clarrie and I.'

Suddenly it was all there before him, as if she had taken the lid off a cauldron, all the horror which she had been concealing under her valiant small-talk. It spread out over the bright room like an evil cloud, blotting out all the other reactions, the excitement, the interest, the avid curiosity of police, public and Press.

'I'm glad you've come,' she said. 'I knew you would. You're a sport. I shan't forget it. Now, these sheets must be aired by this time. *Mrs Love!*'

'Want me, miss?'

An ancient voice from the doorway was followed by a deep satisfactory sniff as a little old woman in a bright pink overall came shambling in. She had a high colour, vivid sky-blue eyes which despite a certain rheumy mistiness possessed a definite twinkle, and a thinly covered little poll bound with a snood of pink ribbon. She paused in the doorway, regarding Campion with interest.

'Yer nephew?' she shouted. 'Eh? I see the likeness. I say I see the likeness.'

'I'm glad,' Miss Roper bellowed back. 'We'll make his bed now.'

'Make 'is bed?' Mrs Love sounded as if the idea had occurred to her. Her eyes were inquisitive. 'I've done yer porridge. I say I've done yer porridge. Put it in the 'ay-box and turned the padlock on it. Key's 'ere till you want it.' She patted her lean bosom.

Clarrie, who had followed her in, began to laugh rather helplessly, and she turned on him, looking, thought the fascinated Campion, exactly like a kitten which has been dressed up as a doll.

'You laugh.' The hoarse London voice might have come from the top of the building. 'But you can't be too careful. I say you can't be too careful.'

She turned to Campion and caught his eye with a gleam which was wholly feminine.

''E don't understand,' she said, shrugging a shoulder at the actor. 'Some men don't. But you 'ave to mind if you want to keep above ground. I'm only 'ere because my friends think I'm at the pub. 'E says I'm not to come getting meself talked about and mixing with the police and that, but I couldn't let 'er down so I come at night. I say I come at night.'

'That's right, the old sport comes at night.' Renee giggled but there was a catch in her voice.

'I come with 'er from the other 'ouse,' roared Mrs Love. 'Otherwise I wouldn't be 'ere. Not me, no fear! Too dangerous.'

Having achieved one effect, she shot out for another.

'Still got me evenin' doodah on.' She waggled her ribbon at Clarrie, who touched an imaginary hat to it, making her laugh like an evil child. ''E's my second string,' she said to Campion. 'I say 'e's my second string. These 'ere the sheets? Got any piller-cases? I done me floor. I say I done me floor.'

She shuffled out with the warm linen, her heels dragging sadly. Renee followed her with a second armful.

Clarrie Grace sat down again and pushed a glass and bottle at the visitor.

'They'd censor a comic who did her on the halls,' he remarked. 'All of eighty and still brimful of what it takes. Works like a navvy, too. Can't stop in case she falls down dead. Renee and her do all the chores between them. How she's loving this business, God, how she's loving it!'

'A case of one woman's poison being another woman's meat?' suggested Mr Campion foolishly.

Clarrie paused, his glass half-way to his mouth.

'You could use that,' he said seriously. 'I often hear people say things they could use. Of course, though, you're a solicitor, aren't you?'

'That makes it more difficult,' murmured Mr Campion.

Clarrie Grace laughed. He had a delightful smile when he was genuinely amused and a hideous one for more polite or professional purposes.

'You know,' he began conversationally, 'Renee's been a pal of mine ever since I was a nipper, and somehow I can't see you being her nephew. I should have heard of you before. I must have. She's one of the very best, Renee is.' He hesitated. 'Don't tell me if you don't want to. Live and let live. I've had that on my hatband all my life. I mean I'd never be surprised by anything. You can't afford it in my profession and I daresay it's the same in yours. Surprise costs money, that's what I say. Your old man wasn't really her brother, was he?'

'Only in a manner of speaking,' said Mr Campion, thinking, no doubt, of the brotherhood of man.

'Now that is rich.' Clarrie was delighted. 'That's wizzo. *I* shall use that. That can't be wasted. "In a manner of speaking" – you're a laugh! You're going to cheer us up.'

His nerviness appeared to have evaporated.

'Keep up your strength,' he said, indicating the glass. 'They can't get at the bottled stuff.'

'Who?'

'The family. The Pally-allys upstairs. Roll me over, you don't think Renee or I . . . or even the Captain, excuse my glove – that's what I call him, "excuse my glove" – have been going in for chemistry, do you? My dear, if we had the brains we haven't the initiative, as the queens say. We're the regulars. We're all right. We've known each other for donkeys' years. It's the Ally-pallys, that's certain. But they can't get at the beer. Have one with the seal unbroken.'

Since his honour appeared to demand it, Mr Campion took some stout, which he disliked.

'I should hardly think there was much danger of indiscriminate poisoning,' he ventured diffidently. 'I mean, what are the facts? An old lady died a couple of months ago and for reasons best known to themselves the police have dug her up again. No one knows yet what the findings of the public analyst will be. The inquest hasn't been resumed. No, I don't think there's anything to show that everyone in the household is now in danger, I really don't. Until the police made this move you can't even have thought of poison.'

Clarrie set down his beer. 'My dear old boy, you're a lawyer,' he said. 'No offence, mind you. You don't see the situation in a human light, that's all. Of course we're all in danger! There's a killer about, isn't there? No one's been hanged. Besides, what about the old boy? – the brother, the first one.'

He was waving his manicured hand with the big masculine knuckles like a baton.

'He died, didn't he, last March? The police are going to have him up next. It stands to reason. I for one shan't be satisfied if they don't.'

Campion was not at all sure that he followed the other's exact process of thought, but he was extraordinarily convincing, at least in tone. Clarrie appeared gratified by this tacit acceptance of his argument.

'You'll find him bunged to the brim with muck,' he said flatly, 'just like his sister. I say the old Ally-pallys are all in it together, that's my theory.' He was very serious. 'It'll hit you in the eye. You wait till you see them.'

Mr Campion stirred. He had begun to tire of this formula.

'I realize they're eccentric,' he murmured.

'Eccentric?' Clarrie stared at him and got up. For some unexplained reason he appeared insulted. 'Good lord, no,' he said, 'not eccentric. They're all number eight hats and very quite-quite. Eccentric? Not unless brains are eccentric. They're a very good family. Their old man was a sort of genius, a professor. Letters after his name.' He let this intelligence sink in and then went on earnestly, 'Old Miss Ruth – that's the one who's been done in – wasn't up to the family standard. She was going a bit. Used to forget her own name and take her plate out in public and that sort of thing generally! Thought she was invisible probably. I think the others just got together and talked it over and –' he made a gesture. 'She couldn't make the grade,' he said.

Campion sat looking at him for a considerable time. Gradually the unnerving conviction seized him that the man was perfectly sincere.

'When could I meet one of them?' he said.

'Well, you could go up now, ducky, if you cared to,' said Renee as she appeared from an inner kitchen, a tray in her hands. 'Take this up to Miss Evadne for me. Someone's got to do it. Clarrie, you can do Mr Lawrence tonight. Take him a kettle and he can mix it himself.'

CHAPTER 5

A Little Unpleasantness

—

IT occurred to Mr Campion as he stumbled up the unfamiliar staircase that Miss Evadne Palinode, even when considered as a possible poisoner, went in for a strange assortment of evening beverages. He was bearing her a small tray on which were clustered a cup of chocolate-coloured patent milk food, one glass of hot water, a second of cold, a ramekin case filled with castor sugar or alternatively salt, a tot glass filled with something horrible resembling reconstituted egg, a tin marked 'Epsom Salts' with the 'Epsom' crossed out, and a small greasy bottle labelled unexpectedly, 'Paraffin, Household'.

The interior of the house, what little he could see of it, was a surprise.

The staircase had been designed in pitch-pine by someone who was getting back to simplicity but not all at once, for at intervals a discreet bunch of hearts, or possibly spades, appeared fretted in the solid woodwork. The steps were uncarpeted. They wound up two floors, following the four sides of a square well, and were lit from above by one inadequate bulb hanging from a ceiling rose intended to sprout a candelabrum. Solid eight-foot doors arranged in pairs lined the walls of each landing.

Campion knew where he was going, since he had had his way explained to him in endless detail by all three of the excited souls downstairs.

Treading carefully, he approached the single window the first landing contained. He paused to glance out of it. The contours of the sprawling house stood out against the washed-in backcloth of the lamplit street, and as his glance rested on one promontory, nearer to him and more curiously shaped than the rest, part of it moved.

He stood quite still, his eyes growing slowly more accustomed to the light. A moment later a figure appeared almost on a level with him and very much nearer than he had expected, so that he guessed that there was some sort of platform – the roof of a bay window perhaps – directly below the window.

It was a woman on the roof. He caught a brief but clear glimpse of her as she passed through the shaft of light. His startled impression was of finery of some sort, a white hat with a mighty bow on it, and a bright scarf wrapped high round a small throat, Regency fashion. He did not see her face.

By holding his breath he could just hear her moving and he wondered what on earth she was doing. If she was burgling she was certainly taking her time about it. Campion was venturing a half-step closer when a piece of drapery passed once over the window. There was no repetition of this, but the rustling noises continued. Presently, after a long pause, the sash began to rise.

He took the only cover which presented itself and crouched down on the second step from the top, where, hugging his tray, he leaned close to the solid screen of the balustrade. The window moved silently and from where he knelt some feet below it he had a direct upward view of the widening aperture.

The first thing to appear was a pair of new shoes, very high-heeled. A small thin hand, not too clean, placed them gently on the window-ledge. The white hat followed and after that a flowered dress, folded carefully and tied up in a parcel with the scarf. Finally a rolled-up pair of stockings was set atop the pile.

Campion awaited the next development with interest. In his experience the reasons for which people entered houses by an upstairs window were as many and diverse as those for which they fall in love, but this was the first time he had known anybody to disrobe before doing so.

The owner of the garments appeared at last. A slender leg, now muffled in a thick drab stocking, came cautiously over the sill and with the silence of long practice a girl slid gently on to the landing. She was a queer dowdy figure, clad in an old-fashioned costume which the unenlightened might have miscalled 'sensible'. A hastily donned skirt, grey and shapeless, hung limply from a narrow waist, and a dreadful cardigan in khaki wool half hid a tuckered saffron blouse which might just have been worn without actual offence by a woman four times her age and bulk. The black silk hair by which he recognized her was once more hanging in a straight bob. It was untidy and all but obscured her face.

Miss Clytie White again, changing on the roof this time. Rescuing his tray, Mr Campion rose to his feet.

'Been on the tiles?' he inquired affably.

He had expected to startle her a little but was entirely unprepared for the effect of his sudden appearance. She froze where she was and a tremor ran through her as if she had been shot. There was something horrible about her arrested movement and he thought she was going to faint.

'Look out,' he said abruptly. 'Put your head down. It's all right, don't worry.'

She caught her breath audibly and shot a nervous glance all round her at the closed doors. Her anxiety reached him and held him for an instant. She put her finger to her lips and then, snatching up the clothes, rolled them frantically into a large unwieldy bundle.

'I'm very sorry,' he said quietly. 'It's terribly important, is it?'

She thrust the parcel behind the curtain and put her back against it before she faced him, her huge dark eyes looking steadily into his own.

'It's vital,' she said briefly. 'What are you going to do about it?'

Campion became aware of her charm. Charlie Luke had indicated it. Clarrie too, now he came to think of it, had betrayed interest. It was certainly there, a shaft of animal magnetism like a searchlight held inexpertly by a child. It was strange, because she was not beautiful, at any rate in these appalling garments, but she was desperately alive and wholly feminine and her intelligence was obvious.

'It's hardly my affair, you know,' he said, treating her as if she were older. 'Won't you consider it didn't occur? I've met you on the stairs, that's all.'

Her relief was so evident that he was reminded how young she was.

'I'm taking this to Miss Evadne,' he said. 'She is on this floor, isn't she?'

'Yes. Uncle Lawrence is down there in the study, near the front door. That's why –' she broke off – 'I didn't care to disturb him,' she said mendaciously. 'You're Miss Roper's nephew, aren't you? She told me you might be coming.'

She had a pretty voice, very clear, with a hint of pedantry in her enunciation which was not unpleasant, but at the moment it was unsteady and the nervousness was flattering and engaging.

At this point the white hat, which had been set on top of the incriminating bundle, lost its balance and rolled out from behind the curtain to lie at her feet. She snatched it up, caught him smiling, and blushed violently.

'A charming hat,' he said.

'Oh, do you think so?' She gave it one of the most pathetic glances he had ever seen. There was wistfulness there and a sort of awe shot through with honest doubt. 'I wondered once or twice,' she said. 'On me, you know. People stared. One couldn't help noticing it.'

'It's an adult hat,' said Mr Campion, avoiding patronage by stressing his respect.

'Yes,' she said briskly. 'Yes, it is. Perhaps that was it.' She hesitated and he was aware of her impulse to tell him a great deal more about it, but at that moment somewhere in the house a door closed. It was a long way away, but the sound seemed to touch her like an enchantment. She faded and grew prim while he watched, and the white hat slid stealthily behind her back. They both listened.

It was Campion who spoke first.

'I shan't say anything,' he insisted, wondering why he felt so certain that she needed such reassurance. 'You can rely on me. I mean it.'

'If you don't I shall die,' she said, and spoke so simply that she startled him. There was an enchanted princess fatality in the remark and no trace of histrionics. But there was force there too, a disquieting element.

While he was still looking at her she turned swiftly and, with grace unexpected in such an inexperienced young person, swept up the secret bundle and ran off on light feet down the landing, to vanish through one of the tall doorways.

Mr Campion gripped his tray and advanced on his objective. His interest in the Palinode family was becoming acute. He tapped on the centre door under the archway in the recess where the stairs began again. It was solid and well fitting, very reminiscent of the door of the headmaster's study.

While he was listening for the summons from within it opened abruptly and he found himself looking into the worried eyes of a dapper little man of forty or so in a dark suit. He smiled a nervous salutation at Campion and stood aside.

'Come in,' he said. 'Do come in. I'm just going. I'll let myself out, Miss Palinode. Most good of you,' he murmured to the newcomer, a remark which although civil was without explanation. He squeezed by as he spoke and went out, closing the door behind him, leaving the other man just inside the room standing on the mat.

Campion hesitated a moment, looking about him for the woman who had not replied. At first he thought there was no sign of her. He was in a rectangular room at least three times the size of a normal bedchamber. It had a lofty ceiling and three tall windows at the narrow end which faced him, but the general impression he received was of gloom. The furniture was vast and dark and so plentiful that there was scarcely room to move between it. He was aware of a canopied bed, far away to his right, and there was certainly a concert-grand piano between him and the windows, but the dominant note was of austerity. There were few hangings and no carpets save for a rug by the fireplace. The plain walls housed a few reproductions which, like those outside, were in sepia. There were three glazed bookcases, a library table, and at least one mighty double-sided pedestal desk upon whose cluttered surface stood the reading lamp which provided the only light in the room. No one sat beneath it, however, and he was still wondering where to set the tray when a voice comparatively close to him said distinctly: 'Put it here.'

He caught sight of her at once and realized with a shock that he had mistaken her in the half light for a coloured blanket thrown over an armchair. She was a large flat woman in a long Paisley gown who wore a small dull red shawl over her head, while her face, which was not very different in colour, was creased and mottled until it merged into the chair's own rust-and-brown brocaded velvet.

She did not move at all. He had never seen any living thing, save a crocodile, quite so still. But her eyes, which now peered up into his own, were for all their smudgy whites bright and intelligent.

'On this little table,' she said, but she did not attempt to point it out to him or to draw it closer to her side. She had a clear authoritative voice, educated and brisk. He obeyed it at once.

The little table proved to be a very fine pie-crust affair on a slender three-footed leg, and its contents struck him as peculiar enough to remember although he thought little of it at the time. There was a squat bowl of everlasting flowers, very untidy and somewhat dusty, and two small apple-green glasses also containing tufts of these wiry blooms. Beside them was a plate with an inverted pudding-basin over it, and a small antique handleless cup holding a minute portion of strawberry jam. Everything was the least bit sticky.

She let him fiddle with this bric-à-brac and get the tray into position without helping him or speaking, and continued to sit watching him with friendly amused interest. He smiled himself as it seemed ungracious not to, and her observation took him by surprise.

> *Herdgroom, what gars thy pipes so loud?*
> *Why bin thy looks so smicker and so proud?*
> *Perdy, plain Piers, but this couth ill agree*
> *With thilk bad fortune which aye thwarteth thee.*

Mr Campion's pale eyes flickered. Not that he minded being addressed as 'Herdgroom', or even 'plain Piers', although this last seemed a little unnecessary, but he happened to be fairly well up in George Peele at that moment, having been moved to read him only the evening before in search of the name which had been tantalizing him.

'"*That thwarteth me, Good Palinode, is fate,*"' he said, continuing the quotation as accurately as he could remember it. '"*Y-born was Piers to be unfortunate.*"'

'*In*fortunate,' she corrected him absently, but she was pleased if surprised and became at once not only more human but startlingly more feminine. She let the red shawl slide back to reveal a fine broad head on which some sparse coils of grey hair were neatly pinned. 'So you're an actor?' she said. 'Of course. I ought to have known. Miss Roper has so many friends from the stage. But,' she added with graceful ambiguity, 'they're not always the sort of actor I know best. My stage friends are more your own kind. Now tell me, out of a shop?'

She produced the piece of slang as if it were a Greek tag of which she was a trifle proud.

'I'm afraid I haven't acted for some considerable time,' he began cautiously.

'Never mind, we must see what we can do.' She spoke without looking at him. Although remaining remarkably still in her chair she had fished out from down the side of it a small notepad covered with tiny and beautiful handwriting. 'Ah,' she went on, glancing at an inner page, 'now let me see what you've brought me. A cup of Siepe Rite? Yes. The eggie? Yes. The hot water?

Yes. The cold water? Yes. The salts, the sugar, and – ah, yes, the paraffin. Splendid. Now, tip the egg into the Siepe Rite – yes, go on, straight in, stir as you go, don't spill it, I dislike a dirty saucer. Are you ready? Now.'

No one had spoken to Mr Campion with such authority since his infancy. He did what he was told and was mildly surprised to see his hand tremble. The chocolate beverage took on a dangerous hue and some nauseating flotsam appeared on its surface.

'Now the sugar,' commanded the elder Miss Palinode. 'That's quite right. Hand the cup to me and keep the spoon, for if you've mixed it rightly I shall not need it. Stand the spoon in the cold water, that's what it's for. Leave the tin where it is beside the hot water, and put the paraffin in the fireplace. That's for my chilblains.'

'Chilblains?' he murmured. The weather was comparatively warm.

'Chilblains the month after next,' explained Miss Palinode placidly. 'Proper treatment now will prevent chilblains in December. That's very nicely done. I think I must ask you to my theatrical afternoon next Tuesday. You would like to come, of course.'

It was not a question and she gave him no time to let it grow into one.

'It may lead to something but I can't promise. The repertory theatre is overcrowded this year, but I'm afraid you know that.' Her smile was very kindly.

Campion, mildest of men, began to feel an uncharacteristic need to assert himself, but he remained cautious.

'I believe there is a small theatre near here, isn't there?' he ventured.

'Indeed there is. The Thespis. A very hard-working little troupe. Some of them are quite talented. I see every play except the rather unworthwhile things that they have to put on to try to draw the crowd, and once a month they all come here to a little conversazione and we have some amusing talk.' She paused and a shadow settled on her fine old face. 'I did wonder if perhaps I should put it off next week. We've had a little awkwardness in the house. I expect you've heard of it. But on the whole I think I shall carry on as usual. The only difficulty is those wretched newspapermen, although I'm afraid that they bother my brother far more than they do me.'

She was sipping her fearful beverage very noisily, arrogantly, Mr Campion reflected, as if she felt she were privileged to give certain small offences. Yet she was still attractive and remarkably impressive.

'I think I saw your brother as I came in,' he began, and broke off, she looked so horrified. However, she mastered her irritation and smiled. 'No, that was not Lawrence. Lawrence is – a rather different person. No, one of the pleasant things about this house is that one never need go down to the street. The street comes to one. We have been here for so long, you see.'

'I heard that,' he murmured. 'All the tradespeople call in person, they tell me.'

'The tradespeople visit downstairs,' she corrected him, smiling. 'The professions come up. That's so interesting, isn't it? I have always thought that Social Stratification would make a very jolly second subject if one wasn't so occupied already. That was little Mr James, our bank manager. I always get him to come over when I have any business. It's very little trouble for him. He lives above the bank, which is just across the road.'

She sat there, florid and gracious, while her pleasant intelligent glance rested upon his face. His respect for her grew. If Charlie Luke was right and she had next to no money, her capacity for extracting service was quite remarkable.

'When you came in,' she observed, 'I wondered if you were one of the reporters. They do such peculiar things. But as soon as you capped my little piece of Peele I knew I was wrong.'

Campion doubted that argument but said nothing.

'This little unpleasantness we are experiencing now,' she began magnificently, 'has made me think about the extraordinary curiosity of the vulgar. I use that word in its proper Latin sense, of course. I've been playing with the idea of writing a monograph on it. You see, the interesting point as it occurs to me is that the higher or more cultivated the subject the less the curiosity. Now that would appear to be a contradiction, wouldn't it? Is it a question of parallel taboos exerting their restraints or is it actual? What do you think?'

Of all the possible aspects of the Palinode case this was one which had so far escaped Mr Campion's attention, but he was spared the effort of making an answer by the sudden opening of the door. It shuddered back against the wall and a tall, shambling figure, wearing very strong spectacles, appeared on the threshold. It was evident that this was the brother. He was tall and big-boned like his sister and possessed her wide head, but he was a far more nervous subject and his jaw was underhung and finer. Both his hair and clothes were coarse and dark and untidy, and his thin neck, surprisingly more red than his face, stuck out from a wide soft collar at a sharp forward angle. In both hands, carrying it before him as if he were pushing his way with it, he carried a thick volume which bristled with paper markers. He peered at Campion as if he were a stranger encountered in the street whom he thought he recognized, but on discovering he did not he swung past him and confronted Miss Evadne, saying in a queer honking voice which sounded goose-like and unreliable, as if he seldom used it:

'The heliotropium is still out. Did you know?'

He seemed so upset about it that Campion might have received an entirely false impression had he not remembered that Clytie White had been born in, or nearly in, the sea. The name was a classical one and he guessed that the original Clytie was probably a daughter of Oceanus. He fancied that he recollected that one of the daughters of the sea god was changed, after the habit of nymphs, into the plant heliotropium. He was not sure but the odds seemed very good on heliotropium being the family or pet name of Clytie White. It was all a little literary but not impossible.

He was congratulating himself when Miss Evadne said easily:

'No, I did not. Does it matter?'

'Of course it does.' Lawrence was irritable. 'Aren't you forgetting the daisies which never blow?'

Campion was elated. Once again he recognized the reference. It came out fresh from a forgotten locker in his mind.

> *While to this day no grass will grow*
> *Where she lies low.*
> *I planted daisies there a year ago*
> *That never blow.*
> *You should not loiter so.*

Goblin Market. Christina Rossetti. The wise sister cautioning the silly sister about staying out late in questionable company.

Lawrence Palinode seemed to be speaking fairly practically, if in a curious vernacular. Although deeply sympathetic towards Charlie Luke if he had been taking evidence in the patois of this particular country, Campion was relieved. If the Palinode 'family language' consisted of references to the classics, a good memory and a comprehensive dictionary of quotations should go quite a long way.

Miss Evadne disillusioned him.

'That's all very well,' she said to her brother. 'Have you performed a Cousin Cawnthrope?'

Mr Campion's heart sank. He recognized in that remark the one unbreakable code known to man, the family allusion.

The effect of the words on Lawrence was surprising. He looked bewildered.

'No, no I haven't, but I will,' he said, and strode out of the room, leaving the door wide open.

Miss Evadne handed Mr Campion her empty cup, presumably to save herself the trouble of bending forward to set it down. She had not altered her position since he had entered the room, and it went through his mind that she might possibly be hiding something behind her. It did not occur to her to offer him any sort of thanks or to ask him to sit down.

'My brother is extremely clever,' she remarked, her clear even voice caressing the words. 'Of its kind a most ingenious mind. He prepares all the crossword puzzles for the *Literary Weekly* in his spare time, although his real work, which will be completed in a year or two now, is on the Origins of Arthur.'

Mr Campion's brows shot up. So that was it. Of course, the man had talked in crossword puzzle clues with an occasional unsolvable family reference thrown in. He wondered if they all did it, and if so, how often.

'Lawrence has so many subjects,' Miss Palinode continued. 'Of us all he has always been the least exclusive in his interest.'

'Among which he includes horticulture, no doubt,' said Mr Campion pointedly.

'Horticulture? Oh, yes.' She laughed gently as she took the allusion to the heliotropium and the daisies. 'Including horticulture, but only on paper, I'm afraid.'

Mr Campion was informed. The obscurity had been deliberate. It occurred to him that the Palinode family did little that was not deliberate. Meanwhile a certain amount of muttering had reached them from the passage, not all of it amicable. Now a door closed sharply and Lawrence reappeared. He looked crestfallen.

'You were quite right,' he said. 'I ought to have Cawnthroped. By the way, I've got this thing for you. I've worked it out. As I've always said, the foreign wheat was completely witless.'

He put the book in her lap as he spoke, but avoided her eyes. She let her big soft hands close round it, but she was annoyed.

'Does it matter now?' she reproved him gently, and added, smiling a little as if she were making a bitter little joke, 'After all, the sheaves are gathered.'

'Foreign wheat – alien corn – Ruth?' reflected Mr Campion. Well, Miss Ruth Palinode, or part of her, poor lady, was at this moment in Sir Doberman's laboratory. He arrived at that point in time to hear Lawrence catch his breath.

'All the same I had to test it. You will allow that?' he was saying fiercely to his sister.

As he turned away his thick lenses focused on Campion standing a few feet from him, and suddenly, as if in apology for ignoring him so long, he gave him the sweetest and shyest of smiles. Then he went quietly out, closing the door gently behind him.

Campion collected the tray and, as he bent to take it up, he caught sight of the title of the book on Miss Palinode's Paisley-covered knees. The markers bristled from it like so many tapers.

It was *Ruff's Guide to the Turf.*

CHAPTER 6

Bedtime Story

—

MR Campion sat straight up out of sleep, turned on his elbow and waited.

'There's a light-switch by your side, ducky,' said Miss Roper's voice softly. 'Turn it on. I've got a letter for you.'

He found the button, noted his watch on the bedside table said forty-five minutes past two, and glanced up to find her already half-way across the room, looking like a travesty of something out of the lesser chapters of his youth. She wore a gay little happi-coat, over pink fairy-wool pyjamas, and a lace-and-ribbon boudoir cap. Moreover, in her arms, were a syphon, a bottle of Scotch, half full, and two large tumblers. The blue envelope was lightly caught between her knuckles. The note was on official police paper, but was written in longhand apparently by a hasty-tempered schoolboy.

Dear Sir, *re Ruth Palinode, deceased.* Sir Doberman's report to hand 0.30 hours this morning. Organs contain two-thirds grain hyoscine in available material, indicating much larger dose. Probably administered in form hyoscine hydrobromide but no evidence to show if taken subcutaneously or by mouth. Normal medicinal dose one-hundredth to one-fiftieth grain.

Re Edward Bon Chretin Palinode, deceased. Proposed have up pronto. Belvedere Cemetery, Wilswhich N. 4.0 a.m. approx. Cordial invitation extended, no offence taken if you cut it.

C. LUKE, D.D.I.

Campion read the document through twice and folded it. He decided once again that he liked Charlie Luke. Proposed to have Edward up pronto, did he? What a dear chap he was. Well, he could have his exhumation, and good digging.

At this point Miss Roper handed him a glass half full of dancing amber.

'What's this for? To steady my nerves?'

To his dismay her hand wobbled. 'Oh, dear,' she said, 'it's not bad news, is it? A policeman brought it and I thought it was probably your licence, and you might be lying here worrying about it.'

'My what?'

Her kind foolish eyes wavered in embarrassment.

'Well, I don't know,' she said defensively. 'I thought you might have to have a paper or something, to protect yourself if – if –'

'If I got poisoned?' he inquired, smiling at her.

'Oh, the whisky's all right,' she said, mistaking him promptly. 'Take my dying oath it is. I've had it under lock and key. Well, you have to these days anyway, don't you? But I have and, see, I'm going to have mine.'

She settled herself daintily on the extreme edge of the end of his bed and took a sizeable swig. Campion sipped his own but with less enthusiasm. He was not a whisky drinker and indeed by custom drank little of anything in bed in the middle of the night.

'Did the policeman wake you?' he said. 'I'm sorry. There was no great urgency.'

'No, I was about, you know.' She spoke vaguely. 'I want to talk to you, Mr Campion. First of all, you're sure there's not bad news in that letter?'

'Nothing that wasn't expected,' he said truthfully. 'I'm afraid we shall find that Miss Ruth was poisoned, that's all.'

'Well, of course she was. They didn't wake us up to tell us that, I hope.' She spoke comfortably. 'That's the one thing we are sure of, unless we're all going to look bloody fools. Now look here, Mr Campion, I want just to tell you this. I'm absolutely on the level with you. I'm more than grateful to you and you really can trust me. I shan't keep anything back. I mean that, see?'

It was a protestation which could have appeared suspicious from anyone else but was here curiously impressive. Her small red bird's face was serious under her sportive cap.

'I didn't think you would,' he assured her.

'Oh, I don't know, there are little things one keeps to one's self. But I won't. Now I've got you here I'll play fair with you.'

He laughed at her gently. 'What's on your conscience, Auntie? Your young woman who changes on the roof?'

'On the roof. So that's how she does it. Little monkey.' She was surprised and it would seem relieved. 'I knew she took them off somewhere because last week Clarrie caught sight of her in the Bayswater Road all dolled up, and I met her coming in the same night in her old clothes. I did so hope she didn't do it – well, in front of anyone. She's not that kind of a girl at all, poor kiddie.'

It was not quite clear if her pity bubbled up at this particular deficiency of Miss White's, or at some more general weakness.

'You like her?' he suggested.

'She's a pet.' The old woman's smile was tickled as well as kind. 'She's had such a dreadful upbringing. These poor old folks don't understand girls. How can they? Now she's head over heels in love and she's like a bud unfolding. I've read that somewhere, haven't I? I was going to say it doesn't sound like me. But she is. Thorny, you know, but with a little bit of pink just showing. Clarrie says the boy is very nice with her. Frightened to touch her, if you ask me.'

'Is he very young too?'

'Oh, quite old enough. Nineteen. A great bony fellow in one of those fair-isle pullovers shrunk till he looks like a skinned rabbit. I think he must have chosen those new clothes of hers. She's paid for them of course. But she wouldn't know how to buy herself a bathing dress. From what Clarrie said, the whole outfit sounded to me like a boy's idea.'

She took another sip and giggled.

'He said she looked like a cross between the chorus and washing day. Plenty of frills, I expect, and everything a bit too tight. That's a boy all over. On the back of the bike, too. So dangerous!'

'Where did she find him?'

'God knows. She never mentions him. Blushes whenever she hears a petrol engine, and thinks nobody knows.' She paused. 'I can just remember being like that,' she said with a ruefulness which was delightful. 'Can't you? Ah, you're not old enough. It'll come back to you one day.'

Sitting up in bed with his drink, hearing the small hours tick away, Mr Campion rather hoped it wouldn't. But she was off again, bending forward now with delicate earnestness.

'Well, dear, as I was saying, there is just one little thing that's been going on for a long time and I feel I ought to mention it just so you don't go rooting it out and being surprised . . . Hullo?'

The final word was directed towards the door, which had opened quietly. A slender soldierly figure clad in a solid blue-cloth dressing-gown of wonderful cut and braiding had appeared on the threshold. Captain Alastair Seton stood hesitating. He was covered with embarrassment and extremely apologetic.

'I do beg your pardons,' he said, betraying just the accent but a slightly deeper voice than Campion had envisaged. 'I was passing the door and thought the room was unoccupied. My – er – attention was caught by the shaft of light.'

'Go along with you, you smelt it,' said Renee, laughing. 'Come along. There's a tooth-glass over there. Bring it here.'

The newcomer smiled with an innocent mischief which was wholly disarming. 'Something to mother,' reflected Mr Campion, and he looked sharply at Miss Roper. She was pouring the whisky, a neat two fingers, obviously a ration.

'There,' she said. 'Now, it's quite a good thing you've come because you can tell Mr Campion exactly how it was that Miss Ruth was taken ill. You were the only one who saw her except the doctor. Keep your voice down. We're in committee and anyway this bottle won't last if anyone else comes in.'

She was turning it into a party, showing off and covering up at the same time. So this was her secret. It seemed highly respectable.

The Captain settled himself comfortably in a fumed-oak armchair shaped like a nordic throne.

'I didn't kill the lady,' he said, smiling shyly at Campion as if he hoped he was going to be liked.

'You didn't know her, Albert,' said Renee hastily, as if she were afraid to let go of the situation. 'She was a great big woman, larger than the others, and she wasn't quite so clever. I know what Clarrie thinks but he's wrong.'

'Strange as that may appear,' murmured Captain Seton into his glass and laughing a little spitefully, as a cat might.

'They didn't kill her because of that, anyway,' she went on, ignoring him. 'They were all very angry with her, I know, but it wasn't because she wasn't clever. She was ill, poor woman. The doctor told me that nearly two months before she died. "If she doesn't take it very easy she'll have a stroke, Renee," he said, "and that'll mean more work for you. She'll go like her brother did."'

Campion sat up. 'Mr Edward died of a stroke, did he?'

'So the doctor said.' Miss Roper put suspicion and a warning into the words and her head was held on one side like a robin's. 'Still, we don't know about him, do we? Well, on the day she died Miss Ruth went out early with her shopping bag. There'd been a bit of a barny the night before because I heard them all shouting at her in Mr Lawrence's room. No one seems to have seen her until she came in about half past twelve. I was in the kitchen, the others were out, but the Captain here met her in the front hall. Now you go on, love.'

The Captain cocked an eye at the endearment and his narrow mouth twitched.

'I saw she wasn't well,' he said slowly. 'One could hardly miss it. She was shouting, for one thing, don't you know.'

'Shouting?'

'Talking very loudly.' He dropped his own pleasant voice on the words. 'She was crimson in the face, waving her arms

49

about and staggering. Since I happened to be there I did what I could, naturally.' He sipped his drink reflectively. 'I took her down to the sawbones next door. We made a pretty pair, I can tell you. Heads popped out of every window in the city, or so it seemed to me.' He laughed at himself, but there was still a trace of resentment lurking in his eyes.

'Very embarrassing, but all the same a noble act,' said Campion.

'That's what I say,' put in Renee eagerly. 'It was nice of him, wasn't it? Didn't call me or anything. Just quietly did the right thing. That's like him. And the doctor was there, you see, but he didn't help.'

'No, no, my dear, it wasn't quite like that.' With an apologetic glance at the man in the bed, the Captain hastened to counter some earlier complaint. 'I must be reasonably honest. What actually happened was this. As we came roaring up the street like a copper and a female drunk we found the sawbones on the point of locking up his surgery. With him he had some great lout of a fellow who, to add to the general discomfort, was in floods of tears. They were dashing off to officiate, as far as I could understand, at a birth' – he paused and added, 'of some sort.'

It was clear that the scene was returning to him with some vividness and he was viewing it with sour amusement.

'There we all were,' he said, 'on the doorstep. I was looking ineffectual, clutching my old green hat which I probably resemble. The doctor was tired and worried by the intimate symptoms the lout was relating. My lady friend, who was wearing her spring costume – a sugar-sack sari over a flannel petticoat I fancy, Renee?'

'It was obviously two dresses, dear, not a petticoat. They all wear funny clothes. They're above clothes.'

'Miss Ruth was beneath these,' said the Captain grimly. 'As more and more safety-pins came adrift, so that much became alarmingly obvious. Well, anyway, there she was, shouting all these figures . . .'

'Figures?' demanded Campion.

'Yes, figures. She was the mathematical one of the family. Didn't Renee tell you? The police keep asking me "What did she say?" and all I know is that it sounded like figures. She couldn't articulate, you see. That's how I knew she was ill and not merely mad.'

'The doctor ought to have taken her in,' said Renee. 'He's a busy man, we know, but –'

'Oh, I see his point of view.' Captain Seton was being obstinately fair. 'I do admit I thought his behaviour extraordinary at the time, but I was harassed myself, God-dammit. No, he realized that she was as near her own home as made no difference and he thought she'd had a stroke as he'd predicted. He took one look at her and said to me: "Oh, dear. Yes, yes, indeed. Yes. Take her to her room and wrap her up. I'll come the moment I can." Mind you,' he added, directing his queer self-deprecating smile at Campion, 'by this time the weeping lout, who was a good foot broader than either of us and possibly thirty years younger, was making it exceedingly plain that the doctor was coming with him and not me. He said so with considerable force, as I recall. At any rate I gave way and escorted my titubant doxy, who was now frothing at the mouth, through the crowd which had begun to collect, and up to her room. I placed her in the one chair which did not contain books, tucked a pile of old clothes over her, and slunk down to the kitchen for Renee.'

'Where he stirred the saucepan I had on the stove, while I went up to her,' said Miss Roper, smiling at him with deep affection. 'He's a good old boy.'

'Whatever they say,' finished the Captain for her, and his eyes met hers provocatively and laughed.

'You drink up and don't be so greedy for praise,' she said. 'Well, Mr Campion, when I got up to her she seemed to be dozing. I didn't like the way she was breathing but I knew the doctor was coming, and I thought I'd better let her rest, so I put another blanket round her and came away.'

The Captain drained his glass with a sigh. 'Next time anyone looked at her she was dead,' he said. 'Very little trouble to anybody, except me, of course.'

'Oh, don't make it sound so awful!' The pink bows on Miss Roper's cap quivered. 'I caught Miss Evadne, Mr Campion, just as she was coming in, and we went up together. That was nearly two in the afternoon, I suppose. Miss Ruth was still asleep but she was making a terrible noise.'

'Was Miss Evadne helpful?' inquired Campion.

Renee met his eyes. 'Well, no,' she said. 'Not more than you would expect of her. She spoke to her sister, but when the poor woman didn't wake she looked about the room and picked up a book from one of the shelves, read a little bit, and then told me to send for the doctor as if I hadn't thought of it.'

'When did he come?'

'Well, it was nearly three. He had to go home after the baby was born. He said it was to get cleaned up, but I think it was to explain to his wife why he was late for his meal. Miss Ruth was dead then.'

There was silence for a moment before the Captain said:

'He certified a thrombosis. After all, it was what he expected. One can't blame him.'

'Yet somebody did.' Campion made the remark and was surprised to find them both immediately on the defensive.

'People *will* talk,' said Renee as if he had censured her. 'It's human nature. Any sudden death makes a lot of stink. "Quick, wasn't it?" they say, and then "Weren't you surprised? Nerves of iron, haven't you?" Or, "Perhaps it's a blessed relief to you." It makes me sick.' Her small face was flushed and her old eyes angry.

The Captain rose and set down his tooth-glass. He was a little pink round the gills himself.

'At any rate I did not kill the vulgar trollop,' he said with suppressed venom. 'I had words with her, I admit it, and I still feel I was within my rights, but once and for all I did NOT KILL HER!'

'Shush !' Renee quietened the military voice with the firmness of her authority. 'Don't wake the house, dear. We know you didn't.'

The Captain, thin and compact in his Edwardian robe, bowed to her and then to Campion, and even from him the gesture was theatrical.

'Good night,' he said stiffly. 'Many thanks.'

'There.' The old woman let the door close behind him before she spoke. 'Silly old fool. Now all that'll have to come out, I suppose. He's highly strung to begin with and a single drink puts him right on his dig.' She paused and regarded her adopted nephew dubiously. 'It was only because of the room,' she said. 'Old people are like children. They get jealous. I gave him a nice room when we came here and Ruth always wanted it. She said she'd had it as a child and when she found she couldn't get any change out of me she had a go at him. That's all there was to it. Really, I'm not lying. It was too footling to mention.'

She looked so guilty that he laughed at her.

'How long did the feud last?'

'Too long altogether,' she admitted. 'All the time we've been here. It blew up and then cooled down and then started again. You know how these things do. There was nothing in it and although he has said dreadful things about her he was the first to do what he could for her when he saw she was ill. He's like that. A sweet old Flick when you know him. I'd go bail for him any day.'

'I'm sure you would,' he agreed. 'By the way, is that the awful secret you were going to uncover?'

'What! Me and the Captain?' She threw back her head and her laugh was full and deep with amusement. 'My dear,' she said with cheerful vulgarity, 'we've lived in the same house for nearly thirty years. You don't want a detective to find out any secret there. You want a time-machine! No, I was going to tell you about the coffin cupboard.'

The sleepy Campion was taken off his guard.

'I beg your pardon?' he said.

'Of course it may not *be* coffins.' Miss Roper tipped a tea-spoonful of spirit into her glass, added a ladylike splash, and continued airily: 'It may be anything in that line.'

'Bodies?' he suggested helpfully.

'Oh no, ducky.' Her tone was reproving but she was quite ten years younger after her laugh. 'It may be simply wood or perhaps those nasty little trestles they use. I've never seen inside. Never had the chance. They always come at night, you see.'

Campion roused himself. 'Suppose you tell me what you're talking about.'

'I'm trying to.' She sounded plaintive. 'I've let one of my cellars – the little ones leading off the area round by the front door and not actually in the house at all – to old Mr Bowels the undertaker. He asked me as a special favour and I didn't like to refuse him as it's always as well to keep in with people like that, isn't it?'

'In case you want a quick box-up at any time? Well, you know best. Never mind, go on. When did all this happen?'

'Oh, years ago. Months, anyway. He's very quiet. Never makes any trouble. But I thought you might find it locked and get it open and wonder if the things inside were mine, whatever they are. It might look funny, I mean.' She was perfectly serious and her eyes, grey and round, met his own placidly. 'I thought you might possibly hear him and his son down there tonight, as a matter of fact,' she said.

'Is he here?'

'If he isn't he soon will be. He popped in when you were up with Miss Evadne to say I wasn't to be nervous if I heard him moving about between three and four. He's a very thoughtful man. Old-fashioned.'

Mr Campion ceased to hear her. Charlie Luke had surely said that the exhumation of Edward Palinode's body was fixed for four a.m., but that was at Wilswhich Cemetery. He wondered if he was quite awake until the explanation occurred to him.

'Of course! They didn't bury him,' he said triumphantly.

'Not Mr Edward. Bowels and Son didn't. No.' She looked troubled. 'Oh, there was a fuss about that! Mr Edward had put it in his will, the thoughtless old man. Didn't care how much he hurt people's feelings. The dead don't. But there it was, all written out. "Having spent grim nights in an abominable cellar listening to the menacing roll of guns and the thunderbolts of enemy attack, with the man Bowels watching me and mentally measuring me up for one of his gimcrack carrion-caskets, I declare that should I die before him, which I would have him know I doubt, I will not have my body interred by him or any member of his insignificant firm." '

Her imitation was not unskilled and she finished with a gesture.

'I got it off like a part,' she explained. 'It seemed so wicked.'

Her audience appeared delighted.

'A man of character,' he observed.

'Pompous old idiot.' She spoke with feeling. 'He was full of smarty ideas and had no manners, even in his grave. He lost the family their money, being so clever. Well, there you are, my dear. If you hear any thumping it's just the undertaker.'

'The ultimate reassurance,' said Campion, and he got out of bed and into a dressing-gown.

'Are we going to have a look?' She was so complacent about it that it occurred to him that it might have been her object from the beginning. 'I've never liked to spy on him,' she murmured confidentially, 'because there was no excuse and anyway you can't see from my room. It's three or four months since he came last.'

In the doorway Campion paused.

'How about Corkerdale?' he demanded.

'Oh, we needn't worry about him. He's asleep in the kitchen.'

'What?'

'Now, Albert,' she used his christian name with daring, he felt, 'don't be unreasonable and don't do anything to get the poor man into trouble. It was my idea. I didn't want him to run into Bowels. "Everybody's in," I said, "and it's the inside you're watching. You come and sit down in a comfortable chair in the warm." Of course he came. I haven't done anything wrong, have I?'

'Only demoralized a good man.' Mr Campion sounded cheerful. 'Come on. Like to lead the way?'

They went softly along the wide landing and down through the house, which was only comparatively silent. The Palinodes slept as they lived, with a fine disregard for the rest of the community. From one room a thunderous sound of snoring reminded Campion that brother Lawrence's goose-like voice had probably an adenoidal explanation.

On the ground floor Miss Roper paused. The man behind her stopped but his attention had been caught, not by a sound but by an odour. It crept up from the basement, a thin coil of appalling affront. He sniffed and smothered a cough.

'Good heavens, what is it?'

'Oh, that's all right. That's nothing. That's only cooking.' She was deliberately offhand. 'Can you hear them?'

There was a noise, he heard it now, very far off and muffled, a lumping, scraping sound suggesting hollow wood.

Although there was nothing of the charnel house about the alarming odour from the lower floor, the effect of it in conjunction with the sound was eerie. He started when she touched him.

'This way,' she whispered. 'We'll go in the drawing-room. There's a window there just above the cellar door. Keep close to me.'

The drawing-room door swung open quietly enough to admit them to a vast shadowy room, faintly lit by the subdued glow of a single far-away lamp outside on the corner of Apron Street.

The bay window taking up most of one end was cut square at the top by the sharp line of a Venetian blind. The noise was much nearer now and as they waited a flicker of light appeared at the bottom of the centre pane.

Campion made his way cautiously through an archipelago of furniture and peered over the final barrier, a set of empty fernpots wired together on a stand.

The coffin appeared suddenly. It swung up vertically on the other side of the glass as someone hoisted it from below to get it clear of the open cellar door. Renee sucked in her breath in a silent scream as she saw it, and at the same moment Campion switched on the torch which hitherto he had thought it wisest not to use.

The broad white beam lit the casket like a searchlight. The sinister headless shape of the thing was made infinitely more repellent by the smoothness and blackness of the wood. It shone like a piano, broad, important and silky with veneer.

The dust-sheet which had been covering it had fallen back and the wide brass name-plate faced them nakedly. The lettering was so bold and legible that its message might have been shouted through a megaphone:

EDWARD BON CHRETIN PALINODE
Born September 4, 1883
Died March 2, 1946

In the silent airless room the two stood staring at it until it heeled gently over and out of sight, while the sound of careful footsteps reached them clearly from the narrow chasm below.

CHAPTER 7

The Practical Undertaker

—

A face as broad and blandly pink as a gammon rasher looked into Mr Campion's own from the area's well. In the arc of the torch beam the man appeared large and solid, with wide shoulders and the breast and belly of an ox. Beneath his hard black hat his hair was white and curling, and his heavy chins rested on a glistening starched collar. The general effect was as imposing as a fine new marble tombstone.

'Good evening, sir.' His tone was brisk but subtly deferential and a thought knowing. 'We did not disturb you, I hope?'

'Think nothing of it,' murmured the torchbearer magnanimously. 'What are you doing? Stocktaking?'

A gleam of friendly white appeared from two large teeth and a very round mouth.

'Not exactly, sir, not exactly, although there are likenesses. It's all perfectly in order. All above . . .'

'Ground?' suggested the thin man helpfully.

'No, sir. Board, I was going to say. It is Mr Campion I'm addressing, isn't it? I'm Jas Bowels, at your service any time of the night or day, and this is my son, Rowley boy.'

'Here, Dad.' Another face rose into the circle of light. Mr Bowels Junior's hair was black and his expression was slightly more alert than his father's, but otherwise he was one of the most aggressively legitimate sons Mr Campion had ever seen. Two or three puffs from the bicycle pump of the years would, he felt, render the two identical.

There was a brief unsatisfactory pause while they stood looking at one another. For once Campion was unhelpful.

'I'm just taking her across,' remarked Mr Bowels Senior unexpectedly. 'We hire the cellar, you see, sir, and I've had her in there a month or so while we was full up over the road. Now, I thought, what with one thing and another – the police and that – I'd better get her back home. Looks better. You'll understand, being a gentleman and used to these things.'

It occurred to Mr Campion just in time that the pronoun was complimentary, as in ship.

'She looks a very fine affair,' he said cautiously.

'Oh, she is, sir.' Jas betrayed pride. 'A very special job. One of our de-luxe types. Me and the boy call her the Queen Mary when we're talking among ourselves. It's not too much to say that any gentleman who *is* a gentleman would be proud to be buried in it. It's like going below in your own carriage. As I always say when asked for an opinion, it's the last thing you do so you may as well do it right.'

His blue eyes smiled innocently as he spoke.

'It's a pity people are so ignorant. You'd think they'd like to see a lovely job like her going across the road at any time, but no, they don't like it. It worries them, so I've got to nip her over when there's no one about.'

Mr Campion was growing cold.

'Yet the man whose address is on the label had other views?' he suggested.

The small eyes did not waver but the pink face deepened in colour, and a rueful smile, which was infinitely confiding, twitched the ugly little mouth.

'Ah, you saw it,' he said. 'I'm caught and I may as well admit it. I'm caught proper. He saw your name-plate, Rowley boy. He's very fly, is Mr Campion. I ought to have known that from all I've heard from your Uncle Magers.'

The idea of Mr Lugg being anybody's uncle was sufficiently unnerving, but the compliment and the flattering flicker of the eyelids as it was ventured was definitely unpleasant. Campion waited.

The undertaker let the silence go on a fraction too long. Then he sighed.

'Vanity,' he said superbly. 'Vanity. You'd be surprised how often I hear that in church, and yet it don't seem to have done me the good it might. Vanity, Mr C., that's what that there name-plate shows you. The vanity of Jas Bowels.'

Mr Campion was diverted but not beguiled. He said nothing and laid a restraining hand on Miss Roper, who had taken breath for speech.

Jas saddened. 'I'll have to put it to you,' he said finally. 'There was a gentleman in this house once that me and the boy took a real fancy to. Am I right, Rowley?'

'As you say, Dad.' The younger Mr Bowels spoke with emphasis but there was frank curiosity in his eyes.

'Mr Edward Palinode.' Jas spoke with real relish. 'A lovely name for a headstone. He was a fine figure of a man too, something like meself. Broad, you see, and wide at the shoulders. They always make a beautiful coffin.'

The clear eyes regarded Mr Campion thoughtfully rather than with speculation.

'I loved that man, in a professional way. I don't know if you can understand that, sir?'

'In a glass darkly,' murmured Campion and could have cursed himself. His tone had betrayed him and the undertaker grew faintly more wary.

'It isn't easy for one man to see another's professional pride. It's an artist's pride, really,' he continued with dignity. 'I used to sit in the lady's kitchen here and listen to the bombs dropping, and to keep me mind at peace I'd think of work. I'd look at Mr Edward Palinode and I'd think "If you go before me, Mr Palinode," I'd think, "I'll do you a treat, I will," and I meant it.'

'Dad did mean it,' put in Rowley suddenly, as if Campion's silence was getting on his nerves. 'Dad's a craftsman, that's what Dad is.'

'That'll do, boy.' Jas accepted the tribute and threw it lightly aside. 'Some people understand these things and some people don't. What I'm coming to, Mr C., is something you *will* understand. I did wrong, and in a way I made a fool of meself. Pure vanity, that's what it was.'

'I'll take your word for it,' conceded Campion, who was shivering. 'You're trying to tell me you made it on speculation, I take it?'

A happy smile lit up Mr Bowels's face and for the first time his eyes looked shrewd and alive.

'I see we can talk, you and me, sir,' he said, dropping the comedy performance like a cloak. 'I've had old Magers all the evening and I thought, "Well, anyone who employs you must know what's what," I thought, but I wasn't sure, you see. Yes, of course, I made it on spec. When Mr Palinode died I took it for granted we should get the order. In fact I started on me masterpiece when he was first took ill. "The time's come," I said. "I'll start on it and if you ain't ready it'll keep." I didn't realize how long.' He laughed with genuine amusement. 'Vanity, vanity. I made it on appro and the perishing old blighter wouldn't have it. It's a laugh, really. He'd seen me watching him, see?'

It was a creditable performance and Mr Campion regretted the necessity to mar it.

'I thought these things were made to measure?' he ventured.

Jas was equal to the occasion. 'So they are, sir, so they are,' he agreed heartily. 'But we old experts, we know within a little just from looking. Matter of fact, I made it to fit meself. "You're no bigger than what I am," I said, thinking of him. "If you are you've deceived me and you'll 'ave to 'ave a tuck in you." She's a lovely job. Solid oak, veneered ebony. If you'll come over to the shop in the morning, sir, I'll show her to you in the light.'

'I'll see her now.'

'No, sir.' The refusal was gentle but adamant. 'Neither torchlight nor the narrer passage would do her justice. You'll excuse me, sir, but I couldn't do it, not if you was the King of England. I can't bring it in the house either, because some of the old folks might come down and that wouldn't be the thing at all. No. You'll excuse of us tonight and in the morning I'll have her all shined up. And you'll not only say, "She does you credit, Bowels," but I wouldn't be surprised but what you'll add, "Put her on one side, Bowels. She'll suit me one of these days," you'll say. "If not for meself, for a friend." '

The face was smiling, the eyes merry, but there were tiny beads of sweat under the hard brim of the black hat. Campion watched with interest.

'It wouldn't take me a moment to come down,' he said. 'Believe me, I buy things much more easily at this time of night.'

'Then we won't impose on you, sir.' Jas was brisk. 'Take her along, boy. We've got to get across the road while it's dark, sir, if you'll excuse us.'

He was behaving admirably. There was no panic, no undue haste. Only the sweat betrayed him.

'Is Lugg with you?'

'He's in bed, sir.' Once again the blue eyes were child-like. 'We sat up talking and filling our glasses, mentioning his sainted sister, my late wife, sir, and poor old Magers he got quite overcome. We put him to bed and let him rest.'

Knowing Mr Lugg's alcoholic capacity to be as considerable as his emotional range was limited, Mr Campion was surprised. He controlled it, however, and made a last probe.

'I've got a man in the house,' he began. 'He ought to be on duty. At least let me tell him to give you a hand.'

The undertaker revealed his mettle. He hesitated.

'No, sir,' he said at last. 'It's kind of you. It surely is. But no, sir. Me and the boy are used to it, you see. If it wasn't empty, now, well, that'd be another story. But there's only the weight of the wood to carry. Good night, sir. We feel it's an honour to have met you. See you in the morning, I hope. You'll excuse me for being so personal, but if you stand by that open window in your thin robe, sir, well. I'll be seeing you when you won't be seeing me, if I make meself plain. Good night, sir,' and he faded quietly into the darkness.

'He's a very good man,' whispered Miss Roper as she closed the window on the two figures bumping their way gently up the area steps. 'He's thought very highly of in the street, but I never feel I can get to the bottom of him.'

'Ah,' murmured Mr Campion absently, 'I wonder what he's got in the bottom of the Queen Mary?'

'But, Albert, that was a coffin. There wasn't a body in it.'

'Wasn't there? Perhaps just a little foreign body,' said Mr Campion with considerable cheerfulness. 'And now, Auntie, since we appear to have overcome any initial shyness and can speak from the heart, the stink coming up from your basement can no longer be ignored. Come on, darling, tell me the truth, what's cooking?'

'Go along with you!' It was typical of Renee that it was the endearment which she heard most clearly. 'It's only old Miss Jessica. It pleases her and doesn't hurt anybody else. But I won't have it in the daytime, because she gets in the way and really there is a smell. It's worse than usual tonight.'

Campion looked apprehensive. Miss Jessica, as he recalled, was Cardboard Hat, of the park, and, recollecting some of Yeo's more intimate details of her habits, he hardly liked to think of the possibilities which came into his mind.

'You've got a fine old menagerie here, haven't you?' he said. 'What is she doing?'

'Making little mucks,' said Miss Roper casually. 'I don't think they're quite medicine. She lives on them.'

'Eh?'

'Don't be silly, dear. You're making me feel quite jumpy. We've had our bit of excitement tonight. That name on the coffin gave me quite a turn until Mr Bowels explained. You would think Mr Edward wouldn't have disappointed him. He didn't have a very good one either, but I didn't say so. There's no point in hurting people, is there, when a thing's done and the bill's coming in.'

'To return to Miss Jessica,' Campion sounded chastened, 'are you telling me she's distilling?'

'No she's not, not in my house.' She flared with indignation. 'That's illegal. I may have had a murder in the house but that doesn't mean I'm going to set up as a law-breaker generally.'

Her squeaky voice shook with irritation. 'The poor old girl is a bit of a crank, that's all. She believes in New Food, and so on. I let her go her own way, although she does make me wild when she wants to eat grass and send her rations to the people who tried to kill her two or three years ago. "You do what you like," I say to her, "but if you want to feed the hungry there's your own brother downstairs with every bone sticking out through his homespun. Give it to him and save postage." She says I'm "doomed to insularity".'

'Where is she? May I go and see her?'

'Dear, you can do what you like. I told you that. She's annoyed with me at the moment because she thinks I'm a Philistine which I am, so I shan't come with you. She's quite harmless and the cleverest of the three in one way. At least she can look after herself. You go down. You can find her. Follow your nose.'

He grinned and turned his torch on her.

'All right. Go and get your beauty sleep.'

She patted her lace cap straight at once.

'I need it, do I? Oh, you're laughing. You are a naughty boy! Yes, all right. I'll leave the blooming place to you, ducky, loonies and all. I'm fed up with the lot of them. See you in the morning. Be good and I'll bring you a cupper in bed.'

She trotted off, a ghost of a warmer world, leaving him alone in the cluttered room. His nose led him to the top of the basement stairs and there almost dissuaded him. Miss Jessica might have been tanning, the atmosphere was so remarkable. He went quietly down into the reasty dark.

The stairs ended in the nest of doors, one of which was ajar. It led, as he remembered, into the main kitchen in which he and Clarrie Grace had sat talking earlier in the evening. Now it was in darkness, but the sound of regular snoring from the stoveside chair announced that Detective Officer Corkerdale was impervious both to a sense of duty and partial asphyxiation.

The air was very thick and the uppermost odour was strange as well as unpleasant. It was a whiff of 'dragons' lair'; strange and awful.

A sound from behind the door on his right decided him. He thrust it open cautiously. The room was unexpectedly large, one of those vast back kitchens for which past generations of great feeders had found use. It was stone-floored and white-washed, but unfurnished save for a rough wooden table built out from a wall. On this was a gas ring, two oil stoves and an astonishing array of treacle tins, most of which appeared to be in use as cooking utensils.

Miss Jessica Palinode, clad in a butcher's overall, was at work there. She spoke without looking round and before he realized she had heard him.

'Come in and close the door, if you please. Don't disturb me for a moment. I shan't be long.'

It was a fine clear educated voice, more incisive than her elder sister's, and once again he was pulled up by the family's remarkable authority. He also noticed a return of the half-childish sense of alarm which he had first experienced when she had looked up as he watched her through the miniature telescope. Here was a real witch if ever there was one.

Without the cardboard hat her elf-locks flowed freely and not entirely unattractively. He waited in silence and she went on stirring her brew in the treacle tin over the gas ring. With some relief he discovered she was not omniscient but had merely mistaken him for Corkerdale.

'Now I know perfecty well that you should be on guard in the garden,' she remarked. 'Miss Roper took pity on you and let you into the kitchen. I shan't tell on you and I shall expect you not to tell on me. I am not doing anything reprehensible, so your immortal soul, as well as any hopes you may have of promotion are not in jeopardy. I am merely doing my cooking for tomorrow and the next day. Do you understand?'

'Not entirely,' said Mr Campion.

She turned round at once, looked at him with the shrewd intelligence he had noticed in her before, and went back to the tin.

'Who are you?'

'I am staying here. I smelled something and came down.'

'No one warned you, I suppose? The inefficiency in this house is quite extraordinary. Well, never mind. I'm sorry if you were disturbed. Now you know what it is you can go back to bed.'

'I don't think I shall rest,' said Campion truthfully. 'Can I help?'

She considered the offer seriously. 'No, I don't think so. All the rough work is done. I do that first, and then one handwashing does. You can wipe up later, if you like.'

He took refuge in the child's resort of merely waiting. When she decided that her tin had boiled long enough she took it off and turned down the gas.

'It's not very difficult, and as a recreation I find it amusing, even,' she remarked. 'People make a drudgery of feeding themselves. Either that or it's a rite with them, something holy before which everything else must give way. That's very ridiculous. I make it a relaxation and I get on very well.'

'I see you do,' he said. 'You're very alert. That doesn't suggest improper food.'

She glanced at him again and smiled. It was the same ineffably sweet and disarming smile with which her brother had favoured him. There was grace in it and true intelligence. He felt she had suddenly and rather unfairly become a friend.

'That's very true,' she said. 'I'd ask you to sit down if there was anything to sit on. But these are Spartan times. What about that pail, if you turned it over?'

It would have been churlish to refuse such an offer, although the knife-sharp rim in conjunction with his thin dressing-gown produced between them a new form of torture. When he was settled she smiled on him again.

'Would you like a nice cup of nettle tea?' she said. 'We'll have one in a minute. It's quite as nice as yerba maté and very good for one as well.'

'Thank you,' Campion looked more optimistic than he felt. 'I don't quite understand, though. What are you *doing*?'

'Cooking.' She had a laugh like a nice girl's. 'It may seem peculiar to you that I have to do it in the middle of the night in my own home, but there's an excellent explanation for that. Have you heard of a man called Herbert Boon?'

'No.'

'There you are, you see. Hardly anybody has. I should not have done so myself but I happened to find his book on a stall. I bought it and read it and it's made my life possible. Isn't that remarkable?'

Since she seemed to expect a reply, he made the prescribed polite noise.

Her eyes, which were of an odd colour, a brownish-green with a hard line round the irises, regarded him with positive excitement.

'I find it fascinating,' she said. 'You see, the title of his book is so cheap and so crude that on first sight one discounts it. It's called *How to Live on One-and-Six*. Now, this was written in nineteen-seventeen. Since then the index figure has risen. It still sounds miraculous, doesn't it?'

'Almost incredible.'

'I know. And yet, this is the delightful part, it only sounds absurd because it's earthy.'

'I beg your pardon?'

'Well, material and commonplace. Now, take *A Joy For Ever*, or *Creative Evolution*, or *Civilization and its Discontents*, aren't all those absurd titles if taken as literally as you are taking *How to Live on One-and-Six*? Of course they are. It occurred to me at the time because I was most anxious to know how to live on a very small sum. It's all very well to have an intellect and to entertain it, but one must first ensure that one can maintain the machine.'

Mr Campion stirred uneasily on his pail. He felt that, intellectually speaking, he was having a conversation with someone at the other end of a circular tunnel, and was in fact standing directly back to back with her. On the other hand, of course, it was possible that he had become Alice in Wonderland.

'Everything you say is undeniably true,' he said cautiously. 'Do you do it?'

'Not quite. Boon lived in a district slightly more rural. Also, of course, he was simpler in his tastes; something of an aesthete, which I am not. I am my mother's daughter, I am afraid.'

Campion remembered the celebrated Mrs Theophila Palinode, poetess of the sixties, with some surprise. He saw the likeness now. This dark vivid face burningly alive with the quest of the sweetly impracticable, had once smiled out at him from the frontispiece of a little red volume on his grandmother's chest of drawers. Miss Jessica was exactly like her, had her elf-locks been curled into ringlets.

Her clear forceful voice interrupted him.

'I do nearly,' she said. 'I'll lend you the book, It answers such a lot of people's problems.'

'I should think it might,' he said sincerely. 'Dear me yes. What's in there, may I ask?'

'In *this* tin? The thing that's been smelling rather is over there; it's embrocation for the grocer's knee. But this is broth of sheep's jawbone. Not the whole head, that's too expensive. Boon says "two under-jaws for a farthing" but then he lived in the country and in slightly different times. The modern butchers are very unhelpful.

He sat looking at her in shocked astonishment. 'Look,' he said, 'is this necessary?'

A slow, hard expression spread over her face and he realized he had disappointed her.

'Do you mean am I so poor that I have to live like this, or are you merely inquiring if I am mad?'

This exact diagnosis of his precise state of mind was disconcerting. Her swift intelligence was quite as frightening as it was attractive. It occurred to him that honesty was not so much the best as the only policy.

'I'm sorry,' he said humbly. 'I don't really understand at all. You must let me see the book.'

'I will. But you must understand that, like all important informative books, its appeal, its true appeal, is to a desire of the emotions. I mean if you do not want most terribly to

understand a certain kind of love, then you will not get the best
out of Plato's Banquet. In the same way, if you do not want to
live more cheaply than you dare to hope, you will not get the
essence out of Herbert Boon. He may disgust and bore you.
Do I make myself plain?'

'I think perhaps you do,' he said seriously.

His glance wandered over the depressing array on the table
and back again to her clever, proud face. She was the younger
sister by some ten or fifteen years, he guessed.

'Are treacle-tin saucepans Boon's idea too?' he inquired.

'Oh yes. I'm not practical myself. I simply obey the writer
implicitly. It may be that is why I am successful, more or less.'

'I expect that is so.' He looked so worried that she laughed
at him and another few years slid off her age.

'I have less money than the others, not because I am the
youngest, but because I trusted my elder brother Edward to
invest the greater part of my inheritance.' Her tone was primly
Victorian. 'He was a man of ideas and in one way he was more
like my mother and myself than are Lawrence and my elder
sister Evadne, but he was not very practical. He lost all our
money. Poor man, I am very sorry for him. I will not tell you
my exact income now, but it is counted in shillings and not in
pounds. Yet, by the grace of God and the perspicacity of Herbert
Boon, I am not a poor woman at all. I use the intelligence I
possess to live in my own way. You may think it is a very odd
way, but it is *my* way, and I do no one any harm. Now do you
think I'm a crank?'

The word shot out at him and pinned him. She was waiting
for an answer.

Campion was not without charm himself. His smile was
disarming.

'No,' he said. 'You're a rationalist. I might not have guessed
that, though. This is the tea, is it? Where do you get the nettles?'

'Hyde Park.' She spoke casually over her shoulder. 'There are
lots of weeds – I mean herbs – there, if one hunts for them. I
made a mistake or two at first. You have to be exact, you know,

with plants, and I was quite ill several times, but I've mastered it now, I think.'

The man on the upturned pail looked dubiously at the grey beverage which steamed in the small jam-pot she had handed him.

'Oh, that's all right,' she said. 'I've been drinking that all the summer. Taste it, and if you can't bear it I shall understand. But you must read the book. I should like to think I'd made a convert.'

He did his best. It tasted like death.

'Lawrence doesn't like it either,' she confessed, laughing, 'but he drinks it. And he drinks the yarrow tea I make. He's very interested but he's more conventional than I am. He doesn't really approve of my having no use for money, although I don't know what he'd do if I had, for he's none.'

'Yet you like sixpences,' murmured Campion. He spoke not without thinking, but despite himself, as if she had bewitched him into it. From her triumphant expression he realized with amazement that she had.

'I made you say that,' she said. 'I know who you are. I saw you there today under the tree. You're a detective. That's why I'm talking to you so frankly. I like you. You're intelligent. Isn't it interesting how one can will people to speak? What is it, do you think?'

'Dictatorial telepathy, perhaps.' Campion was sufficiently shaken to take a sip of nettle tea. 'Do you will the stout party to give you the sixpences?' he ventured.

'No, but I never refuse them. She enjoys it so. Besides, they're very useful. That's rational too, isn't it?'

'Utterly. To return to your more magical powers, can you see behind you?'

He thought he had foxed her but she followed after a moment's consideration.

'You're talking of Clytie and her young man who smells of petrol,' she announced. 'Well, I knew they were there today. I heard them whisper. But I didn't look round. They were both playing truant from their jobs or pretending to be on some errand. They'll both get dismissed.' She shot a purely human and naughty look at him. 'I may have to lend them my book. But Boon doesn't say how to feed babies. That might present a difficulty.'

'You're a very odd woman,' said Mr Campion. 'What are you doing? Showing off?'

'I wonder,' she said. 'I hadn't thought of that, but it's possible. On the other hand, I am very sympathetic towards Clytie. I was in love myself once, and only once. It was platonic for a very good reason, but it wasn't, if you understand me, a Banquet. Really hardly a picnic. I was encouraged to make my little intellectual advances and then I discovered that the pleasant intelligent man was using them to torment his wife, with whom he must obviously have been physically in love since otherwise he would hardly have bothered. Being rational but not suicidally generous, I withdrew. However, I am still sufficiently feminine to be entertained by Clytie. Is all this helping you, do you think, to find out who poisoned my sister Ruth?'

For a moment he did not look up but sat staring at the ground.

'Well,' she said,' 'is it?'

He raised his head and looked into her face, so full of wasted beauty and wasted cleverness.

'You must know,' he said slowly.

'But I don't.' She seemed surprised herself by the admission. 'I don't. My magical powers are not very remarkable. Everyone who lives alone as much as I do becomes supersensitive towards the behaviour of the people they meet. Still, I assure you I have no idea who poisoned Ruth. I may as well admit I am not ungrateful to him. You will find that out, so I may as well tell you.'

'She was very trying, was she?' he said.

'Not very. I hardly saw her. We had very little in common. She was more like my father's brother. He was a mathematician of genius and went a little mad, I believe.'

'Yet you're glad she's dead?' He was deliberately brutal because he was afraid of her. She was so nice and yet such a terrifyingly and indefinably wrong thing.

'I had cause to fear her,' she said. 'You see, the Palinode family is in the position of the crew of a small castaway boat. If one member drinks all his allotted share of water – she was not an alcoholic, by the way – the rest must either watch him die of thirst or share, and we haven't very much to share, even with the assistance of Herbert Boon.'

'Is that all you're going to tell me?'

'Yes. The rest you can find for yourself. It's not very interesting.'

The thin man in the dressing-gown rose to his feet and put down his jam-pot. He towered over her. She was very small and the rags of attractiveness hung round her like dead petals. His own not insensitive face was passionately grave, the question in his mind appearing much more important than any murder mystery.

'Why?' he burst out uncontrollably. 'Why?'

She understood him at once. A touch of colour came into her grey face.

'I have no gifts,' she said gently. 'I am dumb, as the Americans say so penetratingly. I cannot make, or write, or even tell.' And then as he blinked at her, trying to comprehend the enormity of the thing she was saying, she went on placidly: 'My mother's poetry was mainly very bad. I have inherited a modicum of my father's intelligence and I am able to see that. She wrote one verse, though, which has always seemed to me to say something, although I daresay many people would find it nonsense. It goes:

> "*I will build me a house of rushes,*
> *Intricate; basket-work. Through the stems the wind rushes*
> *Inquisitive, light-fingered. It torments, its breath crushes.*
> *I shall not notice it. I shall be busy.*"

You wouldn't like any more of that tea, I suppose?'

It was half-an-hour before he got back to his room and he went to bed shivering. The book Miss Jessica had lent him lay on his coverlet. It was ill-printed and impossibly dog-eared, with a crudely stamped cover and end-papers crowded with long out-dated advertisements. He had opened it at random and the passages which he had read still hung in his mind as he closed his eyes.

CURDS (the residue of sour milk often left by ignorant housewives in bottle or can). These may be made more palatable by the addition of chopped sage, chives, or, as a luxury, watercress. I have myself, for I am not a heavy feeder, existed very comfortably on this mess, taken with a little bread, for days together, varying each fresh day's dish by the incorporation of a different herb.

ENERGY. Conserve energy. So-called scientists will tell you it is no more than heat. Use no more of it, then, than you need at any one time. I estimate an hour's sleep to equal one pound avoirdupois of heavy food. Be humble. Take what is given you, even if the gift is contemptuously offered. The giver is rewarded in his own soul be he virtuous or merely ostentatious. Be calm. Worry and self-pity use up as much energy (ie., heat) as deep thought. Thus you will be free and no burden to relatives or the community. Your mind will also be lighter and more fit for the contemplation and enjoyment of the Beauties of Nature and the Conceits of Man, both of which are inexpensive luxuries the intelligent can freely afford.

BONES. The large and nutritious shin-bone of an ox can be purchased for one penny. On the road home from the butcher the Wise Man may descry in the hedge a root of dandelion and, if he is in luck, garlic . . .

Mr Campion turned over on his face. 'Oh God,' he said.

CHAPTER 8

Apron Strings

—

HE became aware that the sound which had awakened him
was the opening of his door, and that someone, whose hand
was still on the knob, was talking in the passage just outside.
It was Charlie Luke.

'. . . wasting your time on the roof,' he was saying with
an awkward gentleness. 'You'll also break your neck. It may
be nothing to do with me and if I'm speaking out of turn I
apologize, but – don't take it like that. I'm only putting you
straight.'

The tone, if not the words, put Mr Campion in the picture.
He listened for the reply, but the slender thread of sound, when
it came, was unidentifiable.

'I'm sorry.' The D.D.I. sounded out of his element. 'No, I
shan't tell anybody, of course not. What d'you think I am?
The loudspeaker on a railway station? Oh, I beg your pardon,
Miss White, I was not aware that I was shouting. Good morning!'

There was a violent movement outside and the door shuddered
open an inch or so, but was closed again as he sent a parting
shot after her.

'All I say is, keep your feet out of the wheel.'

He came in at last looking worried rather than crestfallen.

'Little toffeenose,' he said. 'Well, she can't say I didn't warn
her. Morning, sir. Renee gave me these when I said I was coming
up.' He set a tray containing two cups of tea on the dressing
table. 'It's a homely little place for a murder, isn't it?' he went
on, looking round the bedroom. 'No tea where I've been all
night. "You'd think there'd be something in all these urns," I

said to the Super, but he didn't catch on. Well, we got the old blighter up and into Sir Doberman's galley-pots.'

He carried Mr Campion's early-morning tea to his bedside and comfortably settled himself on the throne-shaped chair.

'Officially I'm interviewing Renee's lawyer nephew,' he said. 'I don't suppose that tale's going to wear but I suppose we may as well stick to it as long as we can.'

He filled the big chair and suited it. His muscles looked like stone under his coat and his diamond-shaped eyes were as bright as if he had spent the night asleep and not waiting in a cemetery.

'Miss Jessica's spotted me as a sleuth,' observed Mr Campion. 'She saw us all in the park.'

'Did she?' Luke was not surprised. 'Oh, they're not barmy, any of them. I told you that. I made that mistake in the first place. They're not, are they?'

The thin man in the bed shook his head and his eyes were thoughtful.

'No.'

Luke took a draught of cool tea.

'Renee has a crazy tale about Pa Bowels last night,' he began. 'Some story about him making a coffin on appro for Edward. "That be damned for a tale," I said.'

Campion nodded. 'Yes, I noticed a delicate odour of fish. I don't see the mechanism, though, do you? Lugg is staying over there, by the way. This should be a job for him. Not very ethical, perhaps, but they're old enemies. What's he passing? Tobacco? Or furs, perhaps?'

The D.D.I.'s face grew dark with anger.

'Old perisher!' he said. 'I hate a surprise like that right on my own manor. That won't do. Smuggling in coffins, the oldest blessed trick in the world. I'll give him Bowels. I thought I knew this street like the back of my own neck.'

'I may be wrong.' Campion was careful to avoid a soothing note. 'His passion would appear to be undertaking. His story may even be true. I shouldn't be surprised.'

Luke cocked an eye at him in approval. 'That's the difficulty with people like these old blighters round here. The silliest blessed story may be true. I don't say that Jas isn't a good tradesman but I don't know that I'd fall for the great artist stuff.'

'What will you do? Go over the piace with a toothcomb?'

'Oh yes, now we know we've got him for whatever it is. Unless you'd like him left until this other business is over, sir? A thing like that will keep, of course. We may as well get him with a packet of the stuff and let him have a real holiday.'

Mr Campion considered Mr Bowels. 'He'll expect you,' he said. 'My publicity agent would never forgive me, either, if I didn't show ordinary intelligence.'

'Lugg? I've heard of him but we've never met. They tell me he's been inside, sir?'

'Ah, that was before he lost his figure. He did one inartistic little cat-burglary. No, I fancy you'll have to go over the Bowels emporium if only as a matter of form. If you find anything, he's a negligible rogue after all this notice.'

'And if we don't he'll lie low until he thinks he's safe, and then we'll pull him in.' The D.D.I. took a handful of waste-paper from an inside pocket and picked it over carefully. Once again Campion was impressed by the graphic quality of his every movement. The scribbles became almost loudspeaker announcements as he glanced at them; this was unfortunate, that was unimportant, the other could wait, and so on, all done by fleeting lights and shadows passing over the vivid bony face.

'Hyoscine hydrobromide,' he announced suddenly. 'Now then, sir, what are the chances of Pa Wilde and the chemist having a basinful of that in his locker?'

'Small.' Campion spoke with the authority he felt was expected of him. 'My impression is that it's rarely used in medicine. There was a fashion for it some forty years ago as a depressant in cases of mania. It's the same sort of thing as atropine, but more powerful. It earned its reputation as a poison when Crippen tried it on Belle Elmore.'

Charlie Luke was not satisfied. His eyes were very narrow above his huge cheekbones.

'You must see that shop,' he said.

'I will. But I shouldn't stir him up until you must. Try the doctor.'

'Okay. Very likely.' He made a mark on the scrap with a very small pencil. 'Hyoscine hydrobromide. What is it? D'you happen to know, sir?'

'Henbane, I think.'

'Really. What, the weed?'

'I think so. It's very common.'

'I should think it is, if it's the plant I mean.' The undercurrent of force in Luke's voice was like an accompaniment of growls. 'I had a crush on the teacher when I was at school and my nature book was on the hot side, lovely lined-in drawings. "Yes, Miss, I *have* worked hard . . . thank you, Miss . . . you ain't half got a thin blouse on, Miss . . ." Henbane, yes I know, little yellow flower. Awful stink.'

'That's it.' Campion felt he was being visited by a dynamo.

'Grows everywhere.' The D.D.I. was lost in wonder. 'Damn it, you could find it in the park.'

Mr Campion was silent for some seconds.

'Yes,' he said at last, 'yes. I suppose you could.'

'But then you'd have to make the muck.' The D.D.I. shook his dark head on which the curls were as tight as a lamb's. 'I'll try the doc first, but you'll have to see Pa Wilde if it's only to widen your mind. Then I must tackle the bank manager. Have I mentioned him?'

'Oh yes, a neat little soul. I met him for a moment coming out of Miss Evadne's room. She did not introduce me.'

'If she had she'd have given him a fancy name and you'd have got no further. He's due for a visit. "The bank can give no information whatever save under subpoena", that's what he told me.'

'Meaning it nasty?'

'No.' The diamond-shaped eyes were serious. 'He's right, of course, and I'm all for it in theory. I like to feel my two half-crowns in the Post Office are a deadly secret between me and the girl behind the wire. Still, I don't see why he shouldn't tell us a bit in his private capacity, do you?'

'As a friend of the family? Yes, we'll inquire, anyway. Miss Ruth was spending too much money before she was killed; I've got that far. That may be a motive or it may not. Yeo says that money is the only respectable motive for murder.'

Charlie Luke made no direct comment. He had returned to his little pieces of paper.

'Here we are,' he said at last. 'I got all this out of Renee, not without coaxing. Mr Edward paid her three quid per week and got his washing done. Miss Evadne pays the same now. Full board, that is. Mr Lawrence pays two pound for part board. That means damn all, because she won't see anybody hungry. Miss Clytie pays twenty shillings because that's all she's got, poor kid. She doesn't get lunch. Miss Jessica pays five shillings.'

'Eh?'

'Five shillings. Fact. I said to Renee, "Don't be a ruddy fool, ducky, how do you do it?" and she said, What did I expect? The woman won't eat a thing except the boiled horse-feed she cooks up herself, and her room is right at the top of the house, and so on and so on. "You're barmy," I said. "You can't keep a dog for five bob these days," and she said Miss Jessica wasn't a dog, she was a cat. "You see yourself back in panto," I said. "The fairy godmother." That brought out the truth. "Look here, Charlie," she said, "suppose I do put it up, then what? She has to get it from the rest of the family, doesn't she? They'll all have to economize then," she says, "and who loses, you great ape? I do, don't I?" She's dead right. She could clear them all out, of course, but I think she likes them. Feels they're high class and remarkable . . . like keeping kangaroos.'

'Kangaroos?'

'Well, armadillos. Interesting and unusual. Something to tell the neighbours about. There's not much entertainment these days. You have to find it where you can.'

As usual he was talking with his hands, face and body, painting in Renee by making a curious pinching gesture with his thumb and forefinger. Why this should have exactly reproduced that lady's sharp little nose and rattling tongue Campion did not know, but he saw her vividly all the same. He felt invigorated, as if life was coming back to a long-numbed corner of his mind.

'And Miss Ruth?' he inquired, laughing. 'She just paid one-and-ninepence and left it at that, I suppose?'

'No.' The D.D.I. had been saving the best until last. 'No. For the last year before she died, Miss Ruth used to pay erratically. Sometimes it was as much as seven quid, and sometimes she brought pence, literally. Renee was supposed to keep strict account. She says she was about a fiver down at the finish.'

'That's suggestive. What was Ruth's official figure?'

'Three pounds, like the others. I tell you what, though, Renee's rich.'

'She must be. Sort of latter-day Lord Shaftesbury, on the evidence.'

'She's got money, a lot of money.' Charlie Luke sounded sad. 'I hope she's not in something with Jas Bowels. That would destroy my faith in women, that would.'

'I hardly think so. Would she have dragged me down in the middle of the night to catch him if she were?'

'That's right.' He brightened. 'Well, I'll trot along now and do some homework. Shall we go and see this bank chap? His name is Henry James. (I don't know why that name sounds familiar.) I'd like to get there round about ten.'

'What's the time now?' Campion felt guilty at being in bed. His own watch appeared to have stopped, since it said a quarter to six.

Luke glanced at a silver turnip which he brought out of his coat pocket. He thumped it vigorously.

'You're about correct. Ten to six as near as dammit. I came in soon after five, but didn't wake you before in case you'd had a late night.'

'We old men, we like our sleep,' said Campion, grinning. 'You've got a few hours' routine work now, I take it?'

'Lord yes. They don't wait for me. We're short-handed, too. This came, by the way.' He studied a cleaner scrap than the rest. 'Just a memo. The Governor of H.M.'s prison at Charlsfield reports that they have one Looky Jeffreys up on a two-year stretch for housebreaking in their infirmary. He's dying, they think. Got something nasty in his innards.' He paused. 'Poor chap,' he said seriously. 'Anyway, he's delirious, and all the time he keeps whispering "Apron Street, don't send me up Apron Street". Says it over and over, apparently. As soon as he's lucid they question him, but then, of course, he can't or won't explain. Says he's never heard of the place. There's three Apron Streets in London, so they've notified the police of each district. Probably isn't anything to do with this one. Still, makes you think.'

Mr Campion sat up, a familiar trickle, partially and shamefully pleasurable, running slowly down his spine.

'Do I understand he's frightened?' he demanded.

'Seems so. There's a note on the end: "Physician reports sweating and deep agitation. Although other words, all of a filthy character, are uttered with normal volume, the references to the street are always whispered."'

Campion pushed back the bedclothes.

'I'll get up,' he said.

CHAPTER 9

Money Talking

–

As a bank manager's office it was as dated as a Penny Black stamp. It was small, with a rich Chinese red and gold paper, a Turkey carpet, a coal fire, and a corner cupboard which might well have contained sherry and cigars. There was a desk made of mahogany and shaped like an ostentatious vault, and a green leather armchair for the client, with a high back and earpieces outlined with brass studs.

Over the fireplace hung a competent mid-Victorian oil painting of a gentleman in a fancy waistcoat and a collar whose mighty wings all but obscured the lower part of his face.

As Campion glanced round him it came into his mind for no reason at all that the word 'bankrupt' used once to be printed 'b––pt' as if it were improper.

In this setting Mr Henry James looked modern and slightly uncomfortable. He stood behind his desk considering his visitors dubiously. He was neat to the point of fussiness, and his receding light brown hair was brushed so closely to his head that it might have been varnished there. His linen was as white as icing sugar, and the small bow-tie at his throat had a pattern so discreet as to be the next best thing to invisible.

'Dear me, this is very awkward. In all my experience I don't think I've ever had anything quite like it to deal with.' The voice was as neat as the man, the vowels pure, the consonants precisely marked. 'I told you, Inspector, The Bank' – he gave it capital letters, like the Deity – 'can give no information whatever save under subpoena, and I hope to goodness it isn't going to come to that, I really do.'

In these surroundings Charlie Luke looked more like a gangster than ever. His grin was wide in every sense of the word and he glanced at his companion much as a polite dog host might offer the first bite to a guest.

The thin man in the horn-rimmed spectacles regarded their quarry with interest.

'This is social,' he said, 'almost.'

'I beg your pardon?'

'I'm sorry. I mean, could you consider forgetting the bank for a moment?'

A faint thin smile spread over the round face opposite him.

'That I can hardly do.'

It was probably an accident that both men turned and glanced at the portrait over the mantel.

'The Founder?' Campion inquired.

'The grandson of the Founder, Mr Jefferson Clough, at the age of thirty-seven.'

'Now dead?'

'Oh, dear me, yes. That was painted in eighteen-sixty-three.'

'A remarkable firm?'

'Hardly remarkable.' The tone was gently chiding. 'The best banks are, if I may say so, distinguished by a lack of that quality.'

Campion's smile was disarming.

'You know the Palinode family in a private capacity, don't you?'

The other man passed a hand over his forehead.

'Oh hell,' he said unexpectedly. 'Yes, I suppose I do. I've known them since I was a child. But they're also old clients of The Bank.'

'Then we'll avoid the subject of money. Any good?'

Henry James's face was half rueful, half genuinely amused.

'We'll have to. What do you want to know?'

The D.D.I. sighed and pulled up a chair. 'It's only routine,' he said. 'Miss Ruth Palinode was murdered . . .'

'Is that official?'

'Oh, yes, but don't publish it before the inquest is resumed and over. We're The Police, you know.'

The worried round eyes flickered with appreciation.

'You want to know how well I knew her and when I last saw her. Is that it? Well, I've known her since I was a boy and I last saw her one morning in the week she died. I've been trying to remember which and I think it was the morning before the day she was taken ill. She came in here.'

'On business?'

'Yes.'

'Then she had an account here?'

'Not at that time.'

'Then her account had been recently closed?'

'How can I answer that?' He was flushing with anger. 'I tell you it's impossible for me to say anything about the monetary affairs of my clients.'

'Gong,' put in Campion from the green leather armchair. 'Let's get back to when you were a child. Where did you live then?'

'Here.'

'In this house?'

'Oh yes. Perhaps I ought to have explained. There are living quarters over these offices. My father was the manager at that time. In due course I went into our Head Office in the City, and finally, when my father died, I came here as manager. We are not a large concern as banks go and we specialize in personal service. Most of our clients have been with us for generations.'

'Are there many other branches?'

'Five only. The Head Office is in Buttermarket.'

'I expect you remember the Palinode family in its great days?'

'Oh, I do!' The warmth of his outburst surprised them. There was tragedy in his regret. 'The mews at the back here were full of beautiful horses. Servants hurried to and fro. The tradespeople were prosperous. There were receptions, dinner parties – silver, you know, and glasses and all that . . .' He waved his hand as words deserted him.

'Candelabra?' suggested Luke helpfully.

'Exactly.' He seemed grateful. 'Professor Palinode and my father were almost friends. I remember the old man well. He had a beard, you know, and a tall hat, and eyebrows – yes, great eyebrows. He used to sit in that green chair and waste my father's time and it didn't matter. The whole district used to revolve round the Palinodes. I'm not depicting this as clearly as I should like, in fact words escape me, but it was a great time and they were very great people. The furs in church! The diamonds when Mrs Palinode went to the theatre! The Christmas parties for those of us who were lucky enough to attend! Well, when I came back and found them as they are now it was a shock, a genuine shock.'

'They're still very charming people,' Campion ventured.

'Oh yes, and one still feels a duty to them. But my dear sir, then!'

'Perhaps Edward Palinode was not the business man his father was?'

'No,' said Mr James shortly. 'No.'

There was an unproductive silence.

'Miss Jessica tells me her weekly income is measured in shillings,' Campion began.

'Miss Jessica!' He threw up his hands before a wooden expression settled on his face once more. 'I cannot discuss that,' he said.

'Of course not. But when you saw Miss Ruth last, it was the day before she died. Is that right?'

'Do you know, I really cannot be sure. She was only here for a moment. I must endeavour to fix this for you. Wait.'

He hurried out of the room, to return almost at once with a personage who might well have once been the original Mr Jefferson Clough's right-hand man. He was tall and thin and so old that the skin of his head clung with almost embarrassing tightness to his naked skull. Sparse white hairs bristled from a drooping face at unexpected places and his chief characteristic was an unpleasantly unsteady lower lip which stuck out from his jaw in a blob. His wet eyes were sharp, though, and he betrayed no astonishment at the introduction.

'It was either the afternoon of the day before she died, or the same afternoon.' His voice was harsh and didactic. 'The afternoon.'

'Do you know, I don't think so, Mr Congreve.' The manager raised his voice when speaking to him, they noticed. 'My impression is that it was the morning of the day before.'

'No.' He had the complete assurance of the old and obstinate. 'The afternoon.'

'The deceased was taken ill just before lunch and died at two in the afternoon,' said Charlie Luke mildly.

The old man stared at him blankly and Mr Henry James repeated the information in a louder tone.

'Hearsay,' said Mr Congreve with conviction. 'I know it was the afternoon because I looked at the lady and thought how fashions had changed. It was the afternoon of the day she died. She was perfectly well then.'

Mr James glanced at Campion apologetically.

'It was one morning that week, I feel certain,' he said. 'I do really.'

A superior but forbearing smile pursed the wobbling lips still tighter.

'You have your way, Mr James,' he sniggered, 'you have your way. Poor lady, she's dead now anyway. It was the afternoon. Well, if I can't help you any further, gentlemen, good-day to you.'

The D.D.I. watched him out and then rubbed his own lip vigorously.

'Yes, well, we shan't put him in the witness box,' he said. 'Anyone else in the office outside who might help, Mr James?'

The neat little man looked so uncomfortable that they might have misunderstood him.

'Unfortunately no,' he said at last. 'I've given the matter some thought, naturally, but our Miss Webb was away with influenza for some while just then and Congreve and I had to manage alone.' He coloured slightly. 'You may think us short of staff. We are, very. It's almost impossible to get the right sort of people nowadays. At one time, I assure you, it was very different. I've seen fourteen clerks at the high desk in the counting-house. This was a rather larger branch then.'

Campion had the rather uncomfortable impression that Clough's Bank was shrinking before his eyes.

'Suppose we stick to the morning of the day before she died, shall we?' he suggested. 'She was quite well then, was she?'

'On the contrary.' He was slightly indignant. 'I thought she might be very ill. She was excitable, you know, very overbearing and extravagant in her demands. In fact, when I heard next day – yes, I'm certain it was next day – that she'd had a stroke I wasn't at all surprised.'

'You accepted the diagnosis without question?'

'I did, I'm afraid, absolutely. Doctor Smith is a very conscientious man, highly thought of. As soon as I heard I said, "Well, I'm not astonished. There's one weight off the shoulders of those poor people."' As the words left his lips he started and his expression grew blank. 'I should never have seen you. I knew it. I knew it from the first.'

'I don't know,' Campion murmured. 'It was generally agreed that Miss Ruth was trying. Relatives often get on one another's nerves. Even so a family seldom takes practical action, so to speak.'

The little manager was grateful.

'Yes,' he said mendaciously. 'That was what I meant, of course. I feared for a moment that you might misunderstand me.'

Charlie Luke prepared to rise and as he did so the door opened to admit Mr Congreve again.

'There's a person to see the Inspector,' he murmured, his voice lowered to hoarseness. 'We don't want him in the front office, Mr James. I think he should come in here.' He nodded to Luke. 'I didn't send him away,' he said.

As a piece of offence tempered with magnanimity the performance was masterly. He did not wait for a reply but stood aside and made sweeping motions to someone behind him.

A plain-clothes man with a gloomy deep-lined face came quickly in. Apparently he saw no one at all save Luke.

'Could you come next door, sir?'

The D.D.I. nodded and they went out together without another word being spoken. Mr Congreve closed the door and shuffled over to the window which gave on to the street. He pinched the net curtain an inch to one side and without ceremony put an eye to the chink. Presently he began to laugh, the foolish high-pitched giggle of the very old.

'It's our right-hand neighbour, Mr Bowels,' he said. 'Now what's he been up to, eh?'

'Perhaps he's gone up Apron Street,' observed Campion stupidly. His pale eyes watched the ancient head lazily, but there was no movement. Mr Congreve remained quite still, peering out into the street. After a long time he straightened his back.

'He can't do that, sir, because this *is* Apron Street,' he said severely. 'You must be a stranger if you don't know that.'

'I'm afraid old Congreve's hearing varies.' Mr James made the observation with apology, and added as he conducted his visitor to the street door, 'He has been with us a great many years and has certain privileges, I'm afraid, or thinks he has.' He paused, sighed and blinked. 'I tell you,' he said with sudden fury, 'even Money isn't what it used to be. That's pure heresy, but sometimes I believe it. Good morning.'

CHAPTER 10

Boy with Bike

—

'IT's a pretty go,' said Jas Bowels with relish, 'and that's the only possible thing to say, a pretty go. I've screwed the gentleman down in it and that's a fact.'

He stood on the cobbles of the mews, a splendid figure in black fancy dress. His frock coat was a fraction longer than anyone else could have worn it without absurdity, but on him, his rippling white hair giving him dignity, it was superb. He stroked his good silk hat, not too shiny nor aggressively new, but strong and solid and sad-looking, with a soft hand.

'I can see your eyes on me, Mr Luke,' he said, smiling at Charlie with fatherly tolerance. 'I call these me Mourning Glory. It's a pun of a kind, I daresay. It comforts the bereaved, you know; not the joke, the garments.'

The plain-clothes man, who looked more grief-stricken than any of the small male chorus of part-time mutes who busied themselves about the solid horse hearse which they had just trundled out of its coach-house, laughed bitterly.

'You're no comfort to me,' he remarked unnecessarily. 'Go on, tell us again now the Inspector's here. Where is this here coffin you fetched out of the cellar of Portminster Lodge last night?'

'At Number Fifty-nine, Lansbury Terrace, where we're just off to now.' The triumph in his voice would not be suppressed. It crept from under the heavy commiseration like a volatile oil. 'If I'd only known you wanted to see it, Mr Luke, I'd have cut off my right hand rather than have used it. I would really.'

Charlie Luke made a face like a smile.

'Beautiful nature you've got, Bowels,' he said. 'The body is actually in it, is it? All the relatives standing round it at this very moment, I suppose?'

'Kneelin'.' There was not the faintest flicker of a smile in the innocent eyes. 'They're a deeply religious lot. Son's a lawyer,' he added as an afterthought.

The plain-clothes man's dull eyes were lifted to meet his superior officer's. There was no question in them. For the time being Jas had won.

'He happened to need it this morning. It happened to fit. He happened to have an accident with the one he had made for a customer. He happened not to know we might be interested.' He spoke drearily.

'You've put the words in me mouth, Mr Dice,' said Jas with pleased surprise. 'It's a funny thing, and I wasn't going to mention it because it isn't a nice thing to have happen, but the casket I'd made for the gentleman warped. It's the green elm. Shocking stuff we're getting nowadays. Water drips from it. "Why," I said to Rowley, "why, boy, that's out of true," I said. "There'll be a crack in the bottom of that before we get it there." "Worse nor that, Father," the boy said to me. "That might go in the church." Well, we didn't want that because for one thing it's liable to make a noise like a pistol shot. That would be a do and no mistake. "Lord, Rowley," I said, "I'd never hold up my head again." "And rightly," said he. "And rightly," I replied. "What's best to do?" "There's your masterpiece, Father," he said, "just come from over the road." "Well," I said . . .'

'Turn it up.' Charlie Luke spoke without rancour. 'Keep it for your reminiscences. We'll just take one more look round the house if it's not inconveniencing you.'

Mr Bowels drew a handsome if over-large gold watch from a pocket on his stomach.

'Now that is a pity,' he announced. 'I can't manage it, Mr Luke, not unless we go down to Lansbury Terrace at a gallop, and that might be misunderstood and cause bad feeling.

But as luck will 'ave it, I've got my brother-in-law in the kitchen. He's setting over the fire with a 'eavy 'ead. He'll be pleased to show you round and be a witness.' He paused, a knowing flicker twisting his tiny mouth. 'Not that you and me don't trust each other, but I know how you police gentlemen like a householder to come round with you in case of any word out of place later. You go in and say, "Mr Lugg, Mr Bowels sent us," and he'll show you round from crypt to belfry, as you might say. He'll be happy to,' he added with malice.

'Very well, we'll do that.' Luke made no secret of his satisfaction. 'See you after the party, Bowels.'

The silky white head shook sadly.

'You didn't ought to joke, Mr Luke, not on this subject,' he said with apparent sincerity. 'It's my trade and I take it cheerfully, but it's very serious to the gentleman concerned. He's not laughing.'

'Isn't he?' said Charlie Luke, and the bones of his skull stood out as he drew his hand over his thin face, dragging the flesh away from them.

Jas started and became entirely blank.

'I don't think that's very nice,' he said stiffly as he turned away.

They found Mr Lugg in the kitchen, but he was not alone. Mr Campion, who sat opposite him in a high-backed armchair, rose as they came in and apologized.

'I saw you chatting among the crows and so I wandered round the front and through the shop,' he explained. 'Lugg says they handed him a Mickey Finn last night.'

A pale blear-eyed bundle of resentment peered up at the newcomers from a basket chair. Mr Lugg, clad in his best suit and spats, was yet collarless and unbuttoned. He was very angry.

'A Guinness and two half bitters, I ask you. Me!' he said with venom. 'I went orf like one of me brother-in-law's customers and now I feel like one. That's typical of Jas, absolutely typ. Talk about your dead sister until you're all crying and then slip you the knock-out drops. In 'is own 'ouse, too, do you notice that? In 'is own 'ouse! A woman, a so-called 'elpless woman, wouldn't 'ave done a thing like that.'

Somewhat surprisingly, it was Sergeant Dice who responded most satisfactorily to this outburst.

'Put it there,' he said, holding out his hand. 'That's sense.'

Lugg was gratified, despite his troubles.

'Pleased to meet you,' he said, bestowing a bunch of sausage-shaped fingers upon his new champion. Mr Campion, glancing apprehensively at Charlie Luke, found him charmed with the incident. He hastened to introduce him and Lugg relaxed. 'There's nothing 'ere,' he said to Dice, 'I've staggered round the whole tuppenny-ha'penny outfit and there's not a wax flower out of place. I don't know what the old hypocrite is up to and that's a fact, but whatever it is it's something extra.'

'Extraordinary?' Campion suggested.

Lugg gave him a glance of pure reproach.

'No,' he said. 'I speak English, I 'ope. Extra, meaning something else. Something that's nothing to do with the little bit of now-its-your-turn over the road. Sit down quietly if you're Christians. I can 'ear a fly stamp this morning.'

When they had settled themselves he explained very carefully.

'Jas is up to something extra, nothing to do with worm-shovelling and nothing to do with Palinode. We knew that, I should 'ope, when we got the letter from 'im in the first place. Jas wants the excitement in the big 'ouse cleared up quick so that the rozzers – beg your pardon, Mr Dice, and you too, Mr Luke; that was common – so that the Force can go 'ome and read the congratulation telegrams and 'e can get on with 'is own lark, whatever it is. That was why 'e wrote at all, the poor silly basket.' He was about to tap the table by way of emphasis, but thought better of it just in time. 'What 'e didn't realize was that my employer 'ere would make a job of it, and 'e certainly didn't expect me to come for a brotherly stay. When I was still on the doorstep I said to 'im, as 'e was standing there looking at me and me little bag, "You'll have to tie your own jaw up, chum, if you ain't more pleased than this." Of course he pulled hisself together at once. He thinks I'm young Rowley's rich uncle. This 'ere 'arris tweed I've got on smells of the 'eather, expensive.'

He was recovering rapidly. The little black eyes were sparkling, almost, and Mr Campion, observing a certain raptness in Charlie Luke's dark face, felt deeply relieved.

'Luring us!' continued Lugg, getting into his stride. 'Luring us down 'ere, 'e 'ints 'e could tell us something. 'E could, and it's not a lot. I got it out of 'im before I'd been in the parlour to see the photos of poor Beatt's 'eadstone.'

'About the betting?' Campion put the question sharply and all three turned to look at him.

'So young Viscount Clever's found it, 'as 'e?' Mr Lugg was sufficiently nettled to forget that they were not alone. He made an acrobatic recovery. 'Don't think I was addressing you, sir,' he said, thick white lids modestly veiling his bloodshot eyes. 'I was commenting, to meself only. That was all Jas had to offer us after raising our 'opes with 'ints. Miss Ruth Palinode used to like to put a bob on an 'orse like anyone else might. Jas thought it was interesting because it was secret. Ignorant persons often make that kind of mistake.'

Luke glanced from man to master with a collector's appreciation. 'How did you get on to that, Mr Campion?'

The pale eyes behind the horn-rims looked vaguely apologetic.

'Divination,' he said modestly. 'Everyone kept telling me she had a vice, wasn't an alcoholic, and was so mathematical it suggested a system, that's all. Rowley put the cash on for her, I suppose.'

'She only staked a bob or two a day so Rowley didn't take much notice until about a month after she was dead. He's like his Ma in that; slow. He did it out of pure kindness, too. That's Beatt again. But I expect 'e twisted the poor old 'ay-bag, that's Jas.'

'Fascinating. Did she ever win?'

'Now and again. Lost in the long run, like most women do.'

'That's a fact.' Sergeant Dice spoke with quiet fervour.

'Yes, well, that explains a lot.' Charlie Luke's ace-of-diamonds eyes were snapping again. 'Money's tight. If one member of the family goes bust the burden falls on the rest. All shut up together. Nothing coming in. Silly woman chucking the stuff away. Worry.

Desperation. Someone got to do something to stop her . . .' In full flight he paused to consider. 'How's that for a motive?' he said, looking at Campion. 'Could be. No? Not good.'

'No motive for murder is exactly first-class,' said Campion diffidently. 'Some of the most ingenious practitioners seem to have done their best work for odd half-crowns. What is Jas up to, Lugg? Do you know?'

'Not yet, cock. Give us a hour.' Lugg was truculent. 'I've only bin 'ere a 'alf-hour when I've bin meself. I don't go by divvies. I 'ave to use me intelligence. Someone come in last night soon after I arrived and Jas saw 'im or 'er alone at the front door. I didn't get a glimp. 'E come back smiling with those two gravestones of 'is sticking out of 'is disgusting mouth, and said it was business, meaning another death, you see. But 'e was shook. Smiling and sweating. 'E's up to something, shifting booze perhaps.'

'What gave you that idea?' Charlie Luke was on to the suggestion like a terrier.

Lugg remained enigmatic. 'It crossed me mind, that's all,' he said. 'It's something 'eavy that 'as to be carried careful. Besides, 'e was telling me one of 'is 'appy tales. 'E sees a lot of fun in 'is job, that's 'is story. It's about the Balsamic 'otel. They don't like anythink unpleasant to appear in that place, it's far too lah-di-perishing-dah. So, should a visitor snuff it, and they don't want anyone refined to be upset by the sight of a coffin being took down the stairs, they send for Jas and Son, and down the stiff comes in the body of a grand piano.'

'I've heard of that,' said Campion. 'How does that lead us to the odd half bottle?'

' 'Otel business,' said Lugg huffily. 'I'm not telling you a fact. All I'll commit meself to saying now is that Jas is on to something private and that the knockings-off over the road are separate.'

As the final rumble of the rich voice died away the door behind them burst open and a small grimy face, working with dreadful glee, appeared on the threshold.

'You're the police, aren't you?' He was a small boy, nine at most, and peaky, with the mouth of an angel and the eyes of a Pekingese. 'Come on, you'll be the first there. They've sent up the street for a copper but I knew you was 'ere. Come on! Dead man.'

The response was immediate and gratifying. Everyone shot up, including Mr Lugg, who reeled but recovered.

'Where's this, son?' Charlie Luke appeared enormous as he looked down at the child.

The boy seized him by the skirt of his jacket and pulled. He was all but incoherent with delight and importance.

'Dahn 'ere, dahn 'ere! Dahn 'ere in the mews. Come on, be the first. Got yer badge?'

The child raced over the cobbles, dragging Charlie Luke. A knot of people hung round a battered grey door which stood open some little way down the yard. The rest of the narrow place was deserted. Bowels and Son and their attendant crows had vanished.

The crowd made way for Luke, who paused long enough to hand his guide firmly to a woman in the doorway. As he and Campion came into the dimly lit shed they thought at first that the place was empty, but a ladder in the corner led to a loft above and through the square opening came the sound of sobbing.

The crowd behind them was silent, as fascinated crowds are at critical moments. Campion was the first to reach the ladder. He came up through the dusty boards to confront an unexpected scene. A shaft of watery London light crept through a cobweb-hung window set high in the white-washed wall and fell on a splash of fair-isle pullover. Kneeling on an oil-stained raincoat by the body's side was a shabby figure with blue-black hair. Miss White was crying her heart out.

CHAPTER 11

The Time for It

—

THE black bar of dried blood looked hideous in the fair hair, and the pathetically young if slightly puggy face beneath it was a dangerous colour, but there was life there.

Campion laid a hand on Clytie's shuddering back.

'It's not going to happen,' he said quietly. 'Now then, how did you find him?'

From the other side of the sprawling body Charlie Luke, squatting on his haunches, nodded encouragement.

'The doc'll be here in a minute. He's had a spiteful cosh by an expert but he's young and he's tough. Now come on, missis.'

She did not raise her head. Her black silk hair made curtains across her cheeks.

'I didn't want anyone to know.' Her voice was weary with pain. 'I didn't want anyone to know, but I thought he was dead. I thought he was dead. I had to shout for someone. I thought he was dead.'

Her grief was childlike and abandoned. All the dignity of the youngest of the Palinodes was submerged in tears and surrender. Her working clothes, which were shapeless and unlikely rather than unsuitable, enhanced the sadness of her crumpled body.

'Oh, I thought he was dead.'

'Well, he's not.' Charlie Luke mangled the words into an inarticulate grumble. 'How did you find him? Did you know he was here?'

'No.' She raised a face, shiny and dirty as a weeping child's to Campion. 'No. I knew he'd got permission to keep the bike here. He arranged it yesterday. Last night we said good night rather late, after ten. You saw me coming in. But then this morning at the office I waited for him to ring me up.' She struggled with the words and gave it up. The tears rolled miserably down her short nose. Campion produced a handkerchief.

'Perhaps you'd had a quarrel?' he suggested.

'Oh, no!' Apparently that horror was unthinkable. 'No. He always rings me up. It's almost business. He sells us photographs – I mean his firm does. He didn't ring. He didn't ring this morning. Miss Ferraby – she's in the downstairs office as well as me – was due in at any moment. I get there first and so . . . and so . . .'

'And so you rang him, of course.' Campion was peering at her through his round glasses with complete sympathy.

'He wasn't there,' she said. 'Mr Cooling, who works near him, said he hadn't been in and if he wasn't ill it would be just too bad.'

Charlie Luke put a hand over his eyes by way of comment. Mr Campion continued to look intelligent.

'So then you telephoned his home,' he said coaxingly.

'No, he hasn't got a home. I rang his landlady. She – she – she – oh I can't!'

' "No I won't, Miss, 'ooever you are!" ' Charlie Luke produced a shrill insulting sound which was also, somehow, telephonic. ' "No! And while I've got you there I may as well say you ought to be ashamed. Out all hours of the night . . . wasting good money . . . good-for-nothing . . . poor woman . . . got to live myself . . . not a charity if some people think so . . ." What had the old tank-trap done? Turned him out?'

For the first time she looked at him directly, tragedy, bereavement, even love forgotten in her amazement.

'How do you know?'

The D.D.I. was still a young man and even a handsome one in his own peculiar way. At the moment both attributes were apparent.

'It's occurred before,' he said, adding with an exquisite gentleness unexpected in him, 'come on, kitty, open your eyes. It's a shocking experience but you've got to do it some time.

Ma Lemon was waiting up for him and slung him out with his other shirt and his mother's portrait, did she?'

Miss White sniffed deeply.

'You guessed he'd be somewhere near the bike. That right?'

'Well, it was all he had, except me.'

The D.D.I. met Mr Campion's eyes and looked away.

'Of course you're not grey yet,' murmured Campion to him.

'Ah, but my wind isn't what it used to be.' Luke spoke absently and he bent down to take another look at the wound in the fair head. 'Hair's very thick,' he pronounced. 'It may have saved him. Very expert coshing, though. Very nasty. Someone meant business.' He returned to Clytie. 'Do I understand you just walked out of the office and came down here to find him or traces of him? Was the door unlocked?'

'Yes. Mr Bowels was going to put a lock on today. We only hired it yesterday.'

'The place belongs to the Bowels, does it?'

'It belongs to the old Mr Bowels, but the young one let it to us. I don't think his father was going to know at first.'

'I see. You just ran out of the office and came down here and looked in the shed. Why did you come upstairs?'

Miss White considered. There was nothing that was not frank about her hesitance.

'I had nowhere else to look,' she said at last. 'If he wasn't here he . . . well, he was gone. I was frightened, I suppose. Oh, don't you know how you feel if someone's lost?'

'Oh yes.' Campion was matter-of-fact. 'Naturally. You just went on looking, saw a ladder, and – er – went up it. As I recall, that's in order, Inspector.'

Charlie Luke grunted. 'Recall is the word. And then what?'

Clytie's face, which had lost its fiery colour, was now very white and tight-skinned.

'Then I saw him,' she said, 'and I thought he was dead.' She turned her head away as the sound of feet in the shed below signalled the arrival of reinforcements.

'Just one thing, Luke.' Campion sounded diffident. 'Who is he?'

'Howard Edgar Wyndham Dunning, or was when we last asked to see his driving licence.' Luke kept irritation out of his voice by the hair of its tail.

Miss White won. 'I call him Mike,' she said.

Sergeant Dice was the first up the stairs and he turned to assist the doctor, who was inclined to resent it. That this was Doctor Smith, Campion had no doubt whatever. In fact, it was with surprise that he realized that they had not met and that his recognition was based solely on D.D.I.'s description.

'Morning, Luke, what have you got here? More trouble? Eh? Yes, yes. Oh dear.' He had a clipped accent and a small quiet voice, and he approached the patient with a certainty with which a man approaches his own particular property. 'Your man couldn't find the police surgeon so he brought me,' he went on, kneeling beside the body. 'Move out of the light, young woman. Oh it's you, Clytie. What are you doing here? Never mind, move right back. Now. Ah!'

There was a long silence and Campion, who stood next to Miss White, could feel her shaking. Luke stood just behind the doctor, his hands in his pockets, his huge shoulders hunched until he looked like a bludgeon himself.

'Yes, yes. Well, he's not dead, and that's a minor miracle. He must have a skull of iron.' The precise words sounded cold. 'This is a beastly blow, Luke, utterly brutal. Someone meant to kill him. He's very young. Ring up St Bede's. Tell them I said it's urgent.'

As Dice disappeared down the stairs Luke touched the doctor on the shoulder.

'What's it done with? Can you tell?'

'Not unless you show me the weapon. I'm not a magician. Something designed for just such a purpose, I should say.'

'What? You mean a real cosh, not a tyre-lever?'

'I don't think so. Not unless, of course, you can produce one covered with blood and hair. The assailant may have had a superhuman strength.'

'But if he hadn't?'

'Then I think he must have had help from his weapon. That's all now, Luke. I must get him to bed. He's cold. Is this filthy raincoat all there is to cover him?'

Clytie pulled off her Raglan, which was both too long and too wide, and handed it to the doctor without speaking. He put his hand up to take it, hesitated, glanced at her face, and changed his mind about protesting. He took the boy's pulse again and nodded non-committally as he replaced his watch.

'When did it happen, doc?' Luke inquired.

'I was wondering. He's very cold. I don't think I can give you any sort of definite answer to that question. Late last night . . . or early this morning. Now we must get on.'

Campion took Miss White by the elbow.

'He'll be all right now,' he said. 'If I were you I'd come home and get another coat.'

'No.' Her arm was as unresponsive as stone. 'No, I shall go with him.' She was perfectly calm now and slightly alarming in her composure. There was a trace of Miss Evadne's assurance in her quiet obstinacy.

The doctor glanced at Campion. 'It's useless,' he murmured. 'Cause less trouble if you don't argue. She can wait in the hospital. He's a sick boy.'

'Doctor Smith?' Clytie's voice was precariously balanced.

'Yes?'

'I shall rely on you not to mention this to my aunts, or – or to Uncle Lawrence.'

'I expect you will.' He spoke absently. 'No, my dear, I shan't rush round telling tales. How long has this been going on?'

'Seven months.'

He got up stiffly from the dirty boards and dusted his trousers.

'Well, you're eighteen and a half, aren't you?' he said, his small head swaying out at her and his bothered eyes searching her face. 'It's the time for it. A fool isn't damned until he's older than that. It's human, too. That's a change in your family, if you'll permit me to say so. Were you with him when this happened?'

'Oh no, I found him just now. I can't think what – how – who did it. I thought he was dead.'

He considered her, to see if she was lying, no doubt, and turned to Campion, who was effacing himself with his usual success.

'It's another mystery, is it?'

'It would appear so.' The slightly high voice was misleadingly foolish. 'Unless of course it's the same one.'

'Good heavens!' His eyes widened and his rounded back was more hunched than ever. 'This is dreadful. The worry! The possibilities involved . . . The doubts which naturally arise in one's mind . . .'

Clytie interrupted with a cry of protest.

'Oh, don't!' she said, her voice breaking. 'Don't bother about that. Don't bother about anything unimportant. Will he get better?'

'My dear,' there was apology and gentleness in him suddenly, 'I shouldn't be surprised. No, I shouldn't be surprised at all.' As the words left his lips he raised his head to listen and they heard the ambulance bell, its shrill frightened voice sounding high above the deep snore of the distant traffic.

Charlie Luke stood in the shed, frowning, his fingers playing with the loose coins in his pocket.

'I want to talk to you, doc,' he said. 'I've got the report from the P.A.'

'Oh.' The old man drooped as though a further burden had been placed on his bent back.

Campion made haste to excuse himself. He walked quickly out of Apron Street and the maze of little roads to the north swallowed him.

It took him some time to find Lansbury Terrace and when he came upon it at last it proved to be a wide road not far from the canal where the original Regency houses had made way for smaller, modern residences with mock-Tudor windows and gabled roofs.

Number Fifty-nine was as pleasantly anonymous as the rest. The dull red door was shut, the net curtains demurely unrevealing.

Campion hurried up the wide stone steps and touched the bell. To his intense relief it was opened by a middle-aged woman. He confronted her with disarming embarrassment.

'I'm afraid I'm late,' he said.

'You are, sir. They've been gone over half an hour.'

He stood wavering, a lean column of open indecision guaranteed to arouse the executive instinct in any practical woman.

'Which way? I mean it's down there, isn't it?' He pointed vaguely behind him.

'Well, sir, it's quite a distance. You'd better take a taxi.'

'Yes, yes, I will. I shall know it, shall I? I mean . . . these big cemeteries . . . two or three at a time . . . confusing. Awkward to arrive wrong – er – wrong function. Dear me, how stupid of me! I *am* late. Tell me, they're limousines, are they?'

It was a princely dither and she took pity on him.

'Why, you can't miss it,' she said. 'It's horse carriages. Very nice and old-fashioned. There's a lot of flowers and a lot of people. You'll see Mr John, too.'

'Yes, yes, indeed yes.' Campion looked back and down the steps. 'I must hurry, I see that. I shall know it. A great many flowers on a perfectly black coffin.'

'No, sir, on an oak coffin. Rather light. You'll know it, sir, of course you will.'

She stared at him a little oddly, as well she might, but he had raised his hat nervously and was hurrying off in the wrong direction.

'I shall take a taxi,' he said over his shoulder. 'Thank you very much. I shall take a taxi.'

She went back to the house thinking that he hardly seemed to know to whose funeral he was going, and meanwhile Mr Campion sought a telephone booth. His tread was lighter, his back straighter, and his pale eyes more vacant at every step.

He found a little red temple at the corner of the dusty road and spent some time consulting the directory chained inside.

Knapp, Thos, Conf. Wireless Parts.

The words stared at him from the page. The number was a Dulwich one and he dialled it, hardly daring to hope.

''Ullo.' The voice was reedy and suspicious. His heart leaped. 'Thos?'

''Oo's that?'

Mr Campion's smile broadened.

'A voice from the past,' he said. 'The name is Bertie, or used to be, I recall with some distaste.'

'Gawd!'

'You exaggerate.'

''Ere' – the voice rose and wavered – 'you go on talking for a bit.'

'You're getting cautious in your old age, Thos. Not a bad idea, of course, but it seems odd in you. Let me see, seventeen years ago – or say once upon a time – a fine upstanding lad with a perpetual sniff lived with his lady mother in Pedigree Place. He had a charming hobby connected, almost literally, with telephones, and his name was Thos T. Knapp, the "T" standing as I remember for "tick".'

'Got yer!' said the telephone. 'Where yer speaking from? 'Ell? I made sure you was dead. 'Ow are yer?'

'Mustn't grumble,' said Campion, keeping in the picture. 'What are you doing? You've gone into trade, I see.'

'Well –' The voice was affable. 'In a way yes, and in a way, no. Muwer's gora, you know.'

'No, I didn't.' Campion hastened to express his regret as a recollection of that rag-bag of a giantess appeared vividly in his mind.

'Cut it out.' Mr Knapp was averse to sentiment. 'She 'ad a pension, didn't she? Went out like a light when 'er time came, bottle in 'er 'and. Comin' down for a chin-wag? S'pose you couldn't do with a hundred thousand electric light bulbs and no questions asked?'

'Not at the moment, but thank you kindly and I'll keep it in mind. I'm busy. Thos, ever heard of Apron Street?'

There was a long silence, during which he had time to envisage that little ferret face and long prehensile nose. The conviction that there must be by now a moustache below it filled him with dismay.

'Well?' he murmured.

'No.' Mr Knapp was only partially convincing, a fact he appeared to appreciate for he went on almost at once: 'I tell you what, Bert, old chum, as one pal to another, keep orf it, see?'

'Not very clearly.'

'It's unlucky.'

'What is? The place?'

'I don't know about the street, but you don't want to go up it, not from what I 'ear.'

Campion stood frowning into the receiver.

'I'm in the dark,' he said at last.

'So am I.' The irritation in the thin voice was convincing. 'I'm out of the know these days. It's a fact. I've got a missis on the up and up. But I 'ear a bit of news occasionally as one does, and that's a slice of the latest. Don't go up Apron Street, that's what they tell me.'

'Care to look about you?'

'Don't mind if I do.' There was a flicker of the old enthusiasm in the acceptance.

'It's worth about five bar.'

'I'll do it for love if it costs me nothing,' said Mr Knapp generously. 'Okeydoke. Same address?'

CHAPTER 12

Poppy Tea

—

'I see 'er,' said Mr Lugg with firmness. 'I see 'er with me own eyes and she comes back to me.'

'Touching,' said Mr Campion brightly. He had just entered Mrs Chubb's room overhanging the round bar of the Platelayers Arms, to find his old friend and knave in possession and no sign of the D.D.I. Lugg was better. He was not quite so angry, either. There was a hint of excitement in the lift of his many chins and his expression was deeply inquisitive.

'You will allow it was a funny thing,' he said. 'It's a rum shop, too, and the old corp be'ind the counter 'e's not ordinary.'

'What are you talking about?' Campion sat down on the other side of the table.

'That's right, be'ave like an official. Don't listen and then ask.' Lugg was contemptuous. 'They missed something on that there island you was going to govern. "Kindly write down three times and then tear up" – quite the professional. I see Bella Musgrave, that's what I'm sayin'.'

'Bella Musgrave.' Mr Campion repeated the name blankly but as recollection came to him his eyes widened. 'Oh yes . . .' he said. 'That hideous little police court . . . Oh, lord yes, I remember her. Neat little woman with the face of a child.'

'Now it's two children,' said Lugg succinctly. 'But it's 'er all right. Same black veil, same clean bit of airy-fairy under it, same gentle eyes full of 'ypocrisy. D'you remember what 'er speciality was?'

His employer regarded him steadily for some moments.

'As I recall it – Death,' he said at last.

'That's right. In a commercial way.' Lugg's black eyes were beady with interest. 'She was the woman who used to go round with the cheap bibles. She'd look up the deaths in the papers and then trot round to the 'ouses. "Wot, not dead?"' He imitated female mock-commiseration rather horribly. '"Oo I'm ever so sorry. Such a loss to me too. The Departed bought one of these 'ere and put down a small deposit. Only fifteen bob to pay." The sorrowers forked out to get rid of 'er, of course, and took in a bible worth nine-pence 'olesale. You remember, cock. Not at all the article.'

'Yes, I do. There was something else too. Wasn't she the heartbroken widow in the Streatham insurance swindle? Single-minded gal.'

'That's 'er and now you've placed 'er per'aps you'll pay attention to this little lot. She's about again and in Apron Street. I've just seen 'er. She gave me an old-fashioned look but she didn't know me.'

'Where was this?'

'In the perishing chemist's. I keep telling you.' He was near exasperation. 'I went in for a pick-up after my un'appy accident last night and as I was talking to old Paregoric in she comes. 'E give 'er a look and she give 'im one and she went in the back.'

'Really? That's very extraordinary.'

'Well, wot am I telling you?' The fat man wriggled in his chair with petulance. 'What are you doing, dreaming of a White Christmas? Sorry, cock, that was beneath me, but it's a funny thing, isn't it?'

'Extraordinary. By the way, I've been talking to an old friend of yours. Remember Thos?'

The great white face expanded with astonishment.

'Lumme, that's putting the clock back,' he said at last. ' 'Ow was the old dreg? Not 'ung yet?'

'On the contrary, he's married and respectable. He's doing a little job for us.'

'Oh, a hemployee. That's all right,' he said magnificently. 'Quite a useful feller if kep' in 'is place.'

Mr Campion looked at him with distaste. 'You're a horrible chap, Lugg, considered dispassionately.'

The fat man chose to be affronted. 'I'm too old for that, and don't bring sex in, it's common. What about this 'ere chemist? Bella may be 'is auntie, of course. Come to think of it, she might be. 'E's the kind of chap to 'ave that kind of relation. But on the other 'and it's funny. I mean to say, if she's a death fancier this is right up 'er apron, isn't it?'

'Talking about relations, there is Jas,' observed Mr Campion unpardonably. 'Mr Luke is still with him, I suppose?'

'I 'magine so. He come out to me as I come into the shop. Not a nice idea a coffin shop, is it? 'E asked me very polite if I might come down 'ere and tell you 'e might be delayed. 'E looked as if 'e'd bin active.'

'How was your brother-in-law?'

Lugg sniffed. 'I didn't 'ear no groans,' he said. 'That chap'll go far, won't 'e, that Charlie Luke?'

'Oh? Why do you think so?'

'Well, 'e can't leave it alone, can 'e?' The black eyes were sardonically amused. 'No five-day week for 'im. 'E'd 'ave apoplexy waitin' for Monday mornin'. 'Ullo!'

Swift light steps were racing up the wooden stairs from the street. The door shuddered open and the D.D.I. appeared. The room shrank a little as his personality pervaded it.

'Sorry, sir, I couldn't leave the old blighter,' he said, grinning at Campion. 'He and his son are like a couple of provincial comics. If we weren't up to our eyes I'd have them along here and make them go through it again for your entertainment. Come to that, we could put them on at the next police concert. "That shed was let without my knowledge," says Jas. "Boy!"' As usual, Charlie Luke was transforming himself into the visual object clearest in his mind, in this case Mr Bowels's well-frilled frock coat. The fascinated Campion could all but see its silky creases. '"I done it, Father, and I know I done wrong. I arsk your pardon,"' he continued, bringing the thinner Rowley vividly before them. '"I done it out of charity, Father, same as you always taught me. The young fellow went on his hands and knees and begged and prayed . . ." and so on and so on.'

Luke settled himself at the table and thumped the bell for Mrs Chubb.

'I could have listened all day,' he said seriously. 'He's very angry, Jas is, angry with Rowley and livid with someone else Maybe young Dunning, but I don't think so.'

'You don't think either of them is the owner of the cosh?'

'It could be.' He frowned. 'I wish I knew what their lark was. I've put a man on to that, of course. Earnest young chap with a good heart but not quite enough upstairs. He's the best I've got at the moment. We're under strength anyway, and then there's this general call-out for the Greek-Street gunman, to make more work.'

Mr Lugg looked down his nose.

'There's too much of that break a jooler's winder, fire at a copper, and 'it a bloomin' civilian,' he said virtuously. 'They get away with it too.'

'We're short-handed, that's all. Still, we'll get old Jas. I can't see him as a poisoner, though, can you, Mr Campion?'

The arrival of their hostess with a tray of beer and sandwiches silenced any opinion the lean man might have had to offer. He got up lazily and wandered to the little window which overlooked the bar. For some minutes he stood there, idly watching the swaying wedges of crowd below. But suddenly he was on the alert, his head poking forward, his eyes puzzled behind his glasses.

'Look at that,' he said to Luke.

Two men had just come into the saloon section of the bar and were pushing their way to the counter. They were obviously together and appeared to be in confidential mood. One was the unmistakable Mr Congreve from the bank and the other, gallant if shabby in an impossibly long-waisted blue overcoat, was Clarrie Grace. They were talking with the ease and intimacy of friends.

'I've seen that before.' Charlie Luke was thoughtful. 'It's been going on for about a week. Maybe it's just the usual pub acquaintanceship but now I see it with your eyes, so to speak.' He made horn-rims for himself with his vast expressive hands. 'Yes, it's unlikely, isn't it? I've never actually spoken to the old boy before today. Yes, I see they are a rum couple. I'll look into that.'

'Int'resting neighbourhood you've got 'ere,' put in Lugg in his better-class voice. 'There's the chemist's auntie, for instance, what about 'er?'

Luke's response was gratifying. He swung round, his eyes sharp and excited.

'Pa Wilde's got a new woman, has he?'

'She's female.' Mr Lugg didn't seem prepared to go further. 'Does 'e often 'ave lady visitors?'

'Now and again.' Luke was grinning. 'It's a local joke. Sometimes, very seldom, a woman comes for a night or so. She's never the same and always utterly respectable, to look at anyway. Besides, have you seen him, Mr Campion?'

'No. Fun to come. He's not the type perhaps, is that it?'

'Who is?' The D.D.I. was both worldly and sad. 'That's the one subject on which there's no rules. He just likes a certain miserable ladylike funereal type and he only likes 'em for about ten minutes. It's peculiar, but then people *are* peculiar in that respect. Come to that, he's a staggering old peculiar himself.'

'Pardon me.' Mr Lugg had risen and his accent was a *tour-de-force*. 'Did you say "funereal"?'

'Yes.' The D.D.I. seemed taken aback by the elaboration of vowel and consonant. 'At least, they're always dressed in black and they usually look a bit tearful, if you know what I mean. I haven't seen this one.'

'I 'ave. She's Bella Musgrave.'

Charlie Luke remained unenlightened and a satisfied smile passed over Lugg's moon-face.

'O' course you're only young,' he murmured, smugness oozing from him. 'Now me and my employer 'ere . . .'

'Who is twenty years younger,' interrupted Mr Campion brutally, 'are bursting to tell you that she may or may not be a small-time crook whom we once saw sent down for eighteen months in the year of the Great Exhibition or thereabouts. How did the doctor take your analyst's report?'

'Oh, resigned, you know.' Luke spoke with sympathy. 'It wasn't his fault, as I've told him. He told me one thing. You know the younger Miss Palinode, Miss Jessica, the gal from the park? He says she's been giving the old man at the dairy cups of poppy tea. He's a patient of the doc's and suffers from sinus trouble. The doc says he found him pretty well doped and yet he said he'd had nothing but this muck which the old girl gave him for his pain, which it had stopped. The doc says if she'd used the right poppies at the right time of the year the old lad would have had a basinful of raw opium which would have put him out like a light.'

He hesitated, his dark face troubled.

'There's enough suspicion there to detain her, but I don't like it. It sounds so barmy, doesn't it?'

'I've been thinking about her.' Mr Campion sounded as if he were making an admission. 'But I don't believe she could have made hyoscine from henbane she gathered in the park.'

'No,' said Luke. 'I'll have to follow it up, of course, but it doesn't sound likely to me. She's a strange old woman; makes me think of fairy tales, I don't know why. She . . .' He broke off and stood listening, and they followed his glance towards the door. It began to open very slowly and cautiously, an inch at a time.

Miss Jessica in walking-out costume was an unlikely sight in any circumstances, but this opportune arrival was actively disconcerting. As she caught sight of Campion on the other side of the table a smile which was partly shy appeared on her small pointed face.

'So there you are,' she said. 'I wanted to get hold of you before I went for my walk. There's just time. Come along.'

Charlie Luke was regarding her with open disbelief.

'How did you get here, ma'am?'

She looked at him directly for the first time.

'Oh, I observe, you know,' she said. 'You were not drinking downstairs and I felt you must be here, so I searched until I found you.' She returned to Campion. 'Are you ready?'

'Perfectly,' he said, crossing over to her. 'Where are we going?' He was so much taller than she was that he enhanced her wispy oddity. Her motoring veil was tied a thought more carefully than usual and had been pinned in front to hide the cardboard. But her multitudinous skirts were still arranged in irregular tiers above her battered shoes and corrugated stockings. Today she carried a bag. It was made of a piece of an old waterproof tacked together inexpertly by someone who understood nothing about sewing save the principle. It appeared to contain papers and kitchen waste in equal quantities, since both made attempts to escape from every dubious seam.

She handed it to Campion before she spoke. It was a charming gesture, feminine and confiding.

'To our solicitor, of course,' she said. 'You can't have forgotten you told me we should help the police and I agreed with you.'

It came back to Campion that he had said something of the sort before leaving her downstairs in the back kitchen.

'And so you've decided to?' he said. 'That's going to be a great help.'

'Oh, but *I* always intended to. I've now seen my brother and my sister and they both agree that the person to give you any information you may require is our solicitor, Mr Drudge.'

The unusual name passed Luke by, Mr Campion noticed, so he took it that the firm was not unknown to him. The D.D.I. looked both respectful and relieved.

'That's all we need, confidence, ma'am,' he was beginning. 'We're not out to –'

'My confidence is here,' cut in Miss Jessica, smiling at Campion, but there was no archness in her manner. She remained both a lady and a mind.

Campion gripped the bag. 'Splendid,' he said. 'We'll go, shall we, or will you have some lunch first?'

'No thank you, I've eaten. I do want to fit this visit in before my afternoon stroll – into the park, you know.'

She stood aside and let him precede her to the street.

'That unfortunate boy,' she said, as they went up the cul-de-sac of Edwardes Place together, causing a stir among the more observant of the passers-by. 'I heard from the cobbler that he'd had an accident. With his machine, I suppose? They are dangerous. And yet, you know, I've always felt I'd like to try one.'

'A motor-cycle?'

'Yes. I should look strange, of course, but I know that. There's a great deal of difference in ignorance and indifference.' She smoothed the uppermost of her garments, which was a thin summer frock of a fashion long forgotten, and which served as an overall, or perhaps a dust cover, above something thick and knitted.

'All the difference in the world,' he assured her with complete sincerity. 'But I'd advise against the motor-bike on other than aesthetic grounds.'

'Yes,' said Miss Jessica, exhibiting an unexpected squeamishness in view of her performance of the night before. 'I know. They smell.'

It was the first illogicality he had noticed in her and he found it comforting.

'Where is this office?' he inquired. 'Shall I get a cab?'

'Oh no, it's just round the corner in the Barrow Road. My father believed in employing local people. They may not be the best, he said, but they are one's own. Why are you smiling?'

'Was I? I suppose I was thinking it was rather a large town to be parochial in.'

'I don't think so. London is made up of many villages. We Palinodes have carried one kind of squirearchy to its ridiculous conclusion, that's all. I shall forgive you anything as long as you never find us sad.'

'I think I find you frightening,' he said.

'That's very much better,' said the youngest Miss Palinode.

CHAPTER 13

Legal Angle

—

THE elderly clerk who greeted them could not help explaining the grudging deference with which he treated Miss Palinode by mentioning that he remembered her father.

As they followed him through a vast outer office, which now housed only himself and two girls, Campion prepared himself to deal with a formal patriarch as full of prejudice as a very old gardener. Therefore, when at last they found him, Mr Drudge was a surprise. He sprang up from behind a desk which if not an antique was at least a curio. At first glance it seemed unlikely that he was anywhere near thirty. His camel-cloth waistcoat was gay, and his suede shoes had once been wonderfully conceived. His youthful face displayed frank apple blossom and innocence, qualities enhanced to absurdity by a tremendous sink-brush moustache.

'Oh, hullo, Miss Palinode. Nice of you to blow in. Things a bit umpty at home, I rather suspect. Take a chair. Don't think I know you, sir,' he added.

The hearty voice rang out happily.

'No flap on here,' he said. 'Pretty damned quiet. Anything I can do?'

Miss Jessica performed the introductions. It startled Campion to find that she knew exactly who he was himself and what he was doing in the affair. The preciseness and accuracy of her information suggested that a textbook had been her informant. She was watching him, too, and the curl of her lips suggested that she was amused.

'This Mr Drudge is of course the grandson of the Mr Drudge who attended to my father's affairs,' she continued placidly. 'His father died at the end of the war and this Mr Drudge inherited the practice. You may be interested to know that he has a D.F.C. and bar as well as the necessary legal qualifications.'

'Oh, I say, come, come!' The protest was uttered in a single howl.

'And that his name is Oliver,' went on Miss Jessica as if there had been no interruption. 'Or,' she added devastatingly, 'Clot.'

Both men looked at her with some embarrassment and she showed her small teeth in a brief smile.

'A flying term,' she said. 'Now you must read these letters, Mr Drudge; one from Evadne and one from Lawrence. Then you can give Mr Campion all the information he may require.' She placed two chits in his hands. Both had been written on the smallest possible piece of paper and Mr Drudge's large fingers had some difficulty in negotiating them.

'I say, this is pretty comprehensive, don't you know,' he announced at last, peering at her with enormous baby-grey eyes. 'No offence to you, sir, but these instruct me to bare the soul, so to speak. Not that there's anything to hide.'

'Exactly.' Miss Jessica spoke with great satisfaction. 'I've been talking to my brother and sister and we decided to trust Mr Campion implicitly.'

'Don't know if that's wise or civil. The poor type has his own loyalties.' He smiled at Campion disarmingly. 'However, there's not a lot to divulge, is there?'

'No, but he may as well know all there is,' Miss Jessica smoothed her muslin skirt. 'You see,' she said to Campion, 'we are not fools. We are self-centred and we live out of the world . . .'

'Pretty ingenious, if you can do it,' interposed her legal adviser with apparent envy.

'Quite. But, as I said, we are not utterly unpractical. While my sister Ruth's death was merely the subject of vulgar suspicion we thought it best to ignore the whole thing. You would be surprised to know how much unnecessary worry a simple policy of polite disinterest can save one. However, since we now see that the matter is more serious than we had hoped, we have decided to protect ourselves as best we can from any mistake the police may make, and the best way to do that is obviously to give them every facility, as indeed Mr Campion has pointed out.'

She made the little speech with dignity and Clot Drudge, after eyeing her with surprising shrewdness for a moment or so, sighed with relief.

'I care for that,' he said seriously. 'Definitely I care for that. Press on, sir, won't you?'

Mr Campion sat down.

'I don't want to intrude into anything which may not be actively helpful,' he was beginning, when Miss Palinode intervened.

'Of course you don't. But you would like to see if anyone had a money motive, and I expect you'd like to know if there are other motives still at large. You can look up my sister Ruth's will at Somerset House, but you don't know the provisions of mine, or Lawrence's, or Evadne's, do you?'

'Oh, I say, hold it,' Clot Drudge interposed. 'I don't think you ought to go as far as that.'

'I disagree. If we don't give the police the details they may imagine the wrong ones. For charity's sake, I think we should begin with Edward.'

'Edward rather began things,' Mr Drudge conceded, caressing his moustache as though to keep it quiet. 'Wait a moment. I'll get the griff.'

He went out and she bent forward confidentially.

'I fancy he may be going to consult his partner.'

'Oh, there's a partner, is there?' Campion sounded relieved.

'Yes. Mr Wheeler. Our Mr Drudge only has a few clients as yet, I'm afraid, but he's highly intelligent. Don't be misled by his vocabulary. After all, it's not more extraordinary than the one lawyers customarily use, is it?'

'I suppose not,' he said, laughing. 'You get a lot of fun, don't you?'

'I try to be rational. Now about Edward. Not to put too fine a point upon it, he was a gambler. He had vision and he had courage, but not judgement.'

'An unfortunate combination.'

'I suppose so. But,' she added with an unexpected flash in her intelligent eyes, 'you've no idea how exciting it was. *Consolidated Resins*, for instance: one day we were worth hundreds of thousands. Lawrence was going to endow a library. And the next day, just when we'd got used to it, we were almost penniless. Old Mr Drudge used to get so angry. I'm not at all sure that the strain didn't bring on the trouble which killed him. But Edward was magnificent. He put his faith in *Dengies*, and then there was always the *Filippino Fashions*.'

'Crikey!' said Mr Campion with a sort of awe. 'Did he touch *Bulimias*?'

'Now that's a name I remember,' she admitted. 'And something *Sports*. And *Gold Gold Gold United*; that was such an interesting name. And then there was the *Brownie Mine Company*. What's the matter? You look quite pale.'

'Passing faintness,' said Mr Campion, pulling himself together. 'Your brother sounds to me to have had a gift. He went by the prospectuses, I suppose?'

'Oh no. He was very informed. He worked very hard. He just chose the wrong shares. Evadne and Lawrence lost faith in him and they kept seven thousand pounds each. I went on longer. Edward died worth seventy-five pounds in cash and one hundred thousand pounds in various shares.'

'Nominal value?'

'Yes.'

'Where are they?'

'Oh, he left them to various people. None of them are saleable at the moment, I am afraid.'

The lean man in the horn-rims sat looking at her for a moment or so.

'Well, it was a performance,' he said at last. 'Did he keep faith in these ventures? Did he hope they'd recover?'

'I don't know,' she said softly. 'I used to wonder if he knew they were valueless, or if he still thought of them as money. He was used to being rich, you see. There's a great deal in being used to a thing. I'm afraid he died just in time.' There was a moment's silence before she said suddenly: 'To the uninformed Edward's will might look as if he'd died wealthy. All our wills suggest that we have money. That is why I wanted you to come here and learn the facts.'

'I see,' he said. 'You've all made little presents of a thousand or so *Gold Gold Gold United* to kind old friends everywhere, have you?'

'We've shown that we would have looked after our people if we had been able,' she said stiffly.

'Dear me. And is there any hope at all of any of these securities gaining value?'

Miss Jessica looked a little hurt. 'Not all the companies are in liquidation yet,' she said. 'Mr Drudge watches them for us, but he says Edward was very thorough. That's a joke, of course.'

Campion thought it wisest not to comment. Mr Edward Palinode appeared to have had a genius for finance in reverse.

The office clock on the wall struck the half-hour and Miss Jessica rose.

'I don't want to miss my walk,' she said blandly. 'I like to be on my seat by the path just after three. I'll leave you to the documents if you don't mind.'

He crossed the room to open the door for her, and as he handed her her bag a spray of wilted leaves sprouting out of it reminded him of something.

'Don't,' he said gently, 'don't doctor the locals. No more poppy tea.'

She did not look at him and the hand which took the bag trembled.

'Oh, I *have* been wondering about that . . .' she said. 'But I haven't broken my rule. I always taste everything first.' She glanced up, her eyes earnest and imploring. 'You don't believe I killed him, do you, not even by mistake?'

'No,' he said stoutly. 'No, I don't.'

'Nor do I,' she said and sounded unexpectedly relieved.

A few moments later Mr Drudge returned with a folder. He was making a not unpleasant whirring sound under his breath, a fact of which he appeared happily unaware.

'Here we are,' he said. 'Oh, she's faded, has she? Not a bad idea. Lets one loosen up a bit. Well, I've been chinning with the old Skip and he says, "Bang on, jolly good show, first ray of light they've shown." Here's the essential gen. Miss Evadne and Lawrence have both got two hundred and ten per a. from gilt-edged three per C's. Poor little Jess in the trimmings has forty-eight quid. Forty-eight, mind you, in the same stock; not a hell of a lot of ackers. When Miss Ruth died her net negotiable assets were seventeen shillings and ninepence, a Breeches bible, and a garnet necklace, which we hocked to pay for her funeral. No one's killing them off for the money in it. That's what you want to know, isn't it?'

'Partly. The rest of the stock is genuinely worthless, is it?'

'Absolutely plugholed. My dear old owl – sorry, I feel I'm getting to know you – it's utterly in the mire.'

In his new expansiveness Mr Drudge was developing a slight stammer.

'Do – oh – n't think we hadn't thought of that. The Skip was on to it like a sto – oh – at. Even I thought of it. We've gone over the scrip with eagle eyes, absolutely eagle. It's amazing. The old boy never bought a sausage that didn't pong like a go – oh – at. No wonder my old man had heart failure.'

'How did it happen?'

'He wouldn't see reason. He was obstinate and no one could hold him. Kept on pranging. Never learnt.'

'Do I understand that all this worthless stuff is distributed among the family?'

'No such luck. It's spread round the landscape.' Mr Drudge's round grey eyes were serious. 'Give your mind to this, sir. My old man, who had handled the family's affairs since the Flood, got written off just before Edward Palinode blew up and went down in flames.'

Campion nodded to indicate partial comprehension.

'Face it,' said Clot. 'My partner, the Skip, knew nothing of any will Edward had made until the tax harpies vultured down for death duties. He showed them the light pretty damned quick and during the engagement he got a bellyful of Palinode. At this point I blew in and he shot me the whole basketful. I got cracking and one of the things I did was to make old Ruth, who wasn't an utterly unsporting number, understand that she'd be doing more for her loved ones if she left them a fiver each instead of the odd ten thousand in *Bulimias* or *Filippino Fashions*, and she re-wrote her homework. However, by the time she died, not long after, the silly kite had spent even the fivers.'

'I see.' Mr Campion had begun to feel deeply sympathetic. 'Could you give me a list of the people who were going to get shares and then had or didn't have cash?'

'Definitely. The whole briefing is here. We've been going over it ourselves. Take it home and use it as you think fit. Miss Ruth's trouble was that she loved everybody. She put them all in her will, the jolly old grocer, the chemist, the doctor, the bank manager, the landlady, the undertaker's son – even her own brother and sisters. The whole family is round the bend, you know, definitely.'

Campion took the folder of carbons and hesitated.

'Miss Jessica was saying something just now about the Brownie Mine Company,' he ventured. 'Wasn't there a faint rumour of possible life there a few months or so ago?'

'Whizzo!' Mr Drudge was admiring. 'You types know your stuff. There was, just after she died. She held a fairly hefty parcel of the stuff and I felt I was clot by name and clot by nature because I convinced her that the scrip was toilet paper pure and unmedicated. In fact I laid it on so thick that she insisted on leaving it all to an old boy who had pinched her room. One of the lodgers. His name's in there. Beaton, is it?'

'Seton.'

'That's right. She did it to annoy him. I got the wind up when the rumour eased out, but there you are, it was nothing.'

'A brutal joke of hers,' Campion said slowly.

'God, yes!' The grey eyes bulged. 'I told her. I tell 'em all but they don't hitch on. I tell you what about the Palinodes. I know that breed. Met it in the war. They think everything, think what they feel. You don't feel so fierce if you only think it. Deep, this, but jolly true. They know what they'd *think* if anyone played such a stinker on 'em, but they don't know what the poor clot would *feel* because they don't. Got that?'

'Yes, I think so.' Campion was looking at him curiously. 'What did you and your partner make of the Brownie Mine incident? Did you consider it at all?'

'We gave it our best.' He was very solemn. 'Lord, yes, we're reasonably alert. We rather cared for the idea of the old lodger writing her off as the hope of fortune hove in sight, but then we thought perhaps not. Type would have had to know about the legacy, and there's no proof that he did. That's one thing. And then the tip about Brownies was never even a likely starter. Finally, too, the Skip feels that a lad in that position would have hit the besom over the head with a bottle and not fiddled about with beverages. How do you feel?'

Campion considered Captain Seton and the more he thought of him the less he liked the theory.

'I don't know,' he said. 'I'll let you know when I've read this lot.'

'Jolly good show. Don't hesitate to call on us. We feel our clients are screwy but not bloodstained. Besides, we take a dim view of their massacre. If anyone writes 'em off it ought to be us; that's our view.'

He was still chatting affably as he conducted his visitor through the outer office to the head of the stairs. Mr Campion remained thoughtful.

'You haven't a young man called Dunning on your books, have you?' he said as they shook hands.

'Fear not. Why?'

'No reason at all, except that he *has* just got himself banged over the head with a bottle or something like it.'

'Good lord! Same wrap-up?'

'It would appear so.'

Mr Drudge held on to his moustache. 'I'm blistered if I see how that fits in,' he pronounced.

'So am I,' said Mr Campion truthfully and they parted.

Out in the Barrow Road it was raining in that curious secret way which is a London speciality. Hurrying passers-by looked as if they had damp sweat patches on every prominent area. Yet there were no visible drops in the air.

Campion walked up Barrow Road. It was the first break he had had in which to give his mind to the various brightly coloured threads which made up the puzzle. He walked for a long time, considering each strand in the tangle, following each loose end as far as it would take him. He was still a long way from the solution when he turned aside to plunge into the web of small roads which must take him back to Portminster Lodge. As he stepped out from the pavement to cross over a narrow side street, a ramshackle truck with a wobbling black hood was advancing towards him down the otherwise deserted way and he paused in the centre of the road to allow it to pass.

Its sudden murderous swerve towards him astounded him, even as his instinctive leap saved his life. The lorry's swing was completely reckless and impulsive and appeared to be intentional. Campion was as amazed as if the ancient vehicle had snapped at him. The driver made no attempt to stop. After his single abortive dart he scuttled on, the bunched tarpaulin curtains at the back swinging out like pigtails.

In the second before the lurching shape disappeared, Campion caught a fleeting glimpse of its interior. A single packing-case, very long and unusually narrow, lay across the jolting boards, and from the darkness just above it a woman's plump face peered out at him.

It was Bella Musgrave. She was sitting on the packing case, her podgy body swaying as the truck staggered round the bend and vanished.

The sight of her squatting there, round and sinister, shook him much more than his own narrow escape. In view of her various professions her driver should have been a death's-head, he reflected grimly, and it occurred to him suddenly that it was probably Rowley who had yielded to the sudden temptation to try and run him down.

He was so certain of this that when he ran into the Bowels, father and son, walking demurely down Apron Street together he was astounded. He was also deeply interested, for whoever the driver had been he had certainly recognized him, which argued that he was an old enemy. This in turn made him a professional practitioner. So far, the professional crook element had been conspicuously absent from Apron Street. Campion was relieved to find a trace of it at last.

CHAPTER 14

The Two Chairs

—

A little over an hour later, when it was very nearly dark and the lights of Apron Street were fairylike among the glistening blue curtains of the wet evening, Mr Campion pocketed the careful letter he had been writing to Superintendent Yeo and let himself quietly out of his bedroom into the chill gloom of Portminster Lodge.

Long experience had taught him the value of the written word when definite information was being requested, and he was now in search of Lugg, who was to be his messenger.

He tiptoed across the hall and succeeded in getting out of the house without being waylaid by Renee. The iron gate was wet to his touch and the fine rain was well on its way to soaking him by the time he reached the pavement. He was just approaching the chastely decorated window of Jas Bowels's establishment when he happened to glance back across the road to Apron Street's gayer side.

The chemist's doorway was an opal arch in a multi-coloured frame, through which, as he glanced at it, a familiar mountain appeared. Lugg stepped into the road, looked both ways, and hurried back again.

Campion darted across the greasy road after him and stepped out of the street into a small clear space set in the midst of an unbelievable jumble of cartons, bottles, boxes and jars which reached the ceiling on all four sides.

There was a counter, but the effect was no more than a hole in the debris. On his right a recess suggested a dispensary, and beside this a tunnel led to mysterious regions beyond.

There was no sign of Lugg, nor indeed of anyone else, but as his step sounded on the worn linoleum Charlie Luke's harassed face appeared in the opening above the barricade of merchandise protecting the dispensary. He was hatless and his short wiry black hair was tousled as if he had run his hands through it.

'This has torn it,' he said. 'Where's the circus, sir?'

Mr Campion sniffed the air. Above the thousand odours which filled the shop there was one which was urgent and alarming and which caught at his throat.

'No connexion with any other firm. I just dropped in,' he said. 'What have you done? Upset the almond essence?'

Luke straightened himself. He was rattled and his eyes were wretched. 'I've done it this time. I ought to be shot, strung up and shot. 'Strewth, I could do it myself! Look at this little lot.'

Campion peered down into the well of the alcove. He could just see two feet drawn up horribly into the cuffs of striped trousers.

'The chemist?'

'Pa Wilde.' The D.D.I.'s voice was husky. 'I wasn't even questioning him, not as you'd say questioning. I'd hardly begun. He was still behind the counter. He gave me a funny little look . . .' He made his eyes bulge and turned them slightly upwards, producing a startling picture of helpless underhand terror. '. . . Then he nipped round here. He was always very quick on his feet, like a spadger. "Just a minute, Mr Luke," he said, squeaking as he always did, "just a minute, Mr Luke," and as I turned towards him, not angrily, not even suspiciously, he pushed something into his mouth and then . . . oh lord!'

'Hydrocyanic acid.' Campion stood back. 'I should come out of it if I were you. It's powerful stuff and there's no air in there. Don't hang over it, for God's sake. Were you alone?'

'Not quite, thank God. I had a witness.' Luke came round through the tunnel into the body of the shop. He was pale and his shoulders were hunched as he played noisily with the coins in his trousers pockets. 'Your chap Lugg is about here somewhere. We came in together. I met him on the corner, as arranged. I had to go down to the inquest on Edward after you left the Platelayers. Pure formality. Adjourned for twenty-one days. But I had to be there.'

'Bella Musgrave left here in a van about an hour and a half ago, I should say,' Campion remarked.

'You've seen Lugg, then?'

'No. I saw her.'

'Oh.' Luke looked at him curiously. 'So did he. I left him to keep an eye on the place. Like a ruddy fool I decided I'd attend to Pa Wilde myself. Lugg was to wait for me outside the Thespis. Just after four he saw the van drive up and take a packing-case on board. It was heavy and Pa gave the men a hand.'

'Men?'

'Yes, there were two of them, both sitting in front. Nothing out of the way about that. Chemists have empties, same as brewers.'

'Did Lugg see them?'

'I don't think close enough to recognize. He didn't say. He didn't suspect them at first, but as soon as the case was loaded the old woman hopped out of the shop and into the van after it. Lugg steamed up, hoping to have a chat, but they were away in double-quick time. He got the number, but a fat lot of good that'll be.'

Mr Campion nodded. 'That's what I thought. I jotted it down but it's bound to be faked. Did he tell you anything about the shape of this packing-case?'

'Not that I remember.' Luke had other worries. 'I've sent for the police surgeon this time. I wouldn't have had this happen, not for a thirty-thousand win in the pools.'

Campion produced a cigarette case. 'My dear chap, he could hardly have "talked" with more force,' he said. 'It's very suggestive. D'you remember what you said to him exactly?'

'Yes, it wasn't much. I came in with Lugg behind me.' He sketched in a balloon absently with his hand. 'I said,

"Hallo, Pa, what about this girl-friend of yours? D'you know who she is at all?" He said, "Girl-friend, Mr Luke? I've not had a girlfriend for thirty years. A man of my age, in this profession, gets a very depressed view of women after a time and that's a fact." ' The D.D.I. sniffed. 'He always said "and that's a fact". Kind of signature-tune, poor old basket. I said, "Come, come, Pa, what about Bella, the human teardrop?" He stopped what he was doing, which was mucking about with the little light he used to melt sealing-wax, and looked at me over his nose-nippers. "I don't follow you," he said. "That's one mercy," said I, "or we should look a couple of daisies. I'm talking about the mourning Musgrave. Don't be a mug, Pa, she's just left here with her box." "Her box, Mr Luke?" he said. "Pa," said I, "this is coyness. What's she done? Left you for Jas Bowels?" '

He was acting the scene as he recalled it and his ferocious good humour was vivid and rather dreadful.

'I saw him begin to shake,' he went on, 'and I thought he was unexpectedly windy, but it didn't register on me as it ought to have done.' He pushed a hand over his face and through his hair as if he were trying to rub the whole thing off his head. His voice was doleful.

'I told him, "Don't deny the girl, chum. We've seen her and her little black handbag." God knows why I put that bit in. Lugg had just mentioned it to me as we came up the road, I suppose. Anyway, it was that which did it. After I said that he gave me the little look I've told you about and said, "Just a minute, Mr Luke," and came over here. I could see his head through all these corn-cures. I actually saw him put the stuff in his mouth, and even then I didn't catch on. There was no reason for it, you see. Then he made a noise like a pheasant and went down among the bottles, while I stood here like a perishing pillar-box with my mouth wide open.'

'Unnerving,' Campion agreed. 'What was the gallant Lugg doing?'

'Standin' like a gasometer, with me mouth *shut*,' said a thick voice from the tunnel. 'What did you expect us to be?

Mind readers? There was no reason for it, cock. He must 'ave 'ad a conscience like a salmon tin in a dust bucket. The gentleman 'ere hadn't even raised his eyebrows, let alone 'is little finger.'

Luke swung round on Campion.

'I can't believe it was necessary,' he said. 'I mean I can't believe he'd done anything very serious. He hadn't the guts. The hyoscine may have come from here.' He waved a hand at the farrago around them. 'But I never suspected him of administering it.' He walked round into the dispensary again and beckoned to Campion to follow him.

As they stood looking down at the hideous body, which in contorted death seemed so much smaller than it could reasonably have been expected to be in life, he shrugged with sudden impatience.

'It's no good,' he said. 'I can't show you what I mean. He was a silly, vain old chap, not the size for anything big. That's no more like the poor beast than a heap of old clothes. See that little dyed moustache? That was the pride of his life.' He bent over the undistinguished face which was now a deep and bluish red. 'Looks like a piece of fluff picked up on a bus.'

Campion was thoughtful. 'Perhaps it wasn't so much what he'd done as what he knew,' he suggested. 'Did you recognize the men who drove off with Bella, Lugg?'

'I don't know.' The fat man spoke softly. 'I was some way down the street, you see. The chap who first 'opped out and came in 'ere was a puffick stranger, that I do know. But the second chap, 'oo must 'ave bin driving – the truck faced up the street, away from me – did remind me of someone. Peter George Jelf, that was the name that came into me 'ead. Reunion, that's what this case is, cock.'

'Dear me.' Mr Campion spoke mildly. 'As you say, how the old faces gather. Yes indeed.'

He returned to Luke, his eyes narrowed.

'The Fuller gang was just before your time, I fancy,' he murmured. 'Peter George Jelf was third in command until he went down for seven years on a robbery-with-violence charge. He was never a first-class mind, as they say in some circles, but he was very thorough and not without courage.'

''Ired malefactor,' put in Lugg with relish. 'The judge said that, not me. This chap today 'ad 'is way of walking. It might not 'ave been 'im but I think it was.'

The D.D.I. made a note on the tattered packet he had drawn from his pocket.

'That's another little question for the back room, if H.Q. is answering any more questions for me. A poor view is going to be taken of this lot and I don't blame them. I'd sack myself . . . if I had a good man to take over.'

'Have you got a mite of bicarb?'

The question, uttered from just inside the doorway, startled them both. Mr Congreve stood teetering on the mat, his lips wobbling and his wet eyes bright and shrewd.

Campion had closed the door after him when he had first come in but had not fastened the old-fashioned bolts. The man had edged in so softly that they had not heard him.

'Where's the chemist?' The harsh yet hollow voice was unpleasant in the silent shop. He took a step forward inquisitively.

Charlie Luke thrust out a long arm and picked up a squat bottle of white tablets from the front of the counter. The only visible words at that distance were 'Triple Strength'. He glanced at it absently and held it up.

'There you are, Pa,' he said. 'Cascara. Better for you. Pay next time.'

Mr Congreve made no attempt to take the offering. He had ceased to advance, but his thin neck was outstretched and his eyes were moving.

'I'd like to see the chemist,' he said with a confiding leer. 'He understands me.' The odour in the shop caught his attention and he sniffed deeply and with curiosity. 'Where is he?'

'Gone downstairs,' the D.D.I. spoke without ulterior thought. 'Call later.' He strode across the room, placed the bottle firmly in the old man's hand, and turned him round. 'Mind the step,' he said.

Mr Congreve reached the pavement just as a group of solid hurrying men bore down upon the doorway from a police car. The last they saw of him was his eyes glinting with excitement and his blob of a lower lip quivering as he mumbled to himself.

Mr Campion touched Lugg's sleeve and they stepped back out of the way of the newcomers and drifted quietly down the tunnel of cartons to a half-glass door in the gloom. Lugg kicked it gently open.

'This is where 'e lived,' he said. 'What a life, eh? Never got away from 'is work.' He waved a plump hand at a scene which resembled an alchemist's shop devised by some enthusiastic stock company. A small bed in one corner was the only sign of domesticity. The rest was an untidy mass of bottles, cooking pans and kettles, carelessly piled on some sticks of Victorian furniture.

'No wonder the lady friends didn't stay,' Mr Lugg observed virtuously. 'This lot must have bin something to cry over even for Bella. No need to go through there, that's the kitchen and it's the same story. There's only one spot of interest and that's on the next floor. I don't know 'ow long we've got before the busies come trampin' in.'

'How true,' Mr Campion agreed and he turned across the tiny room to a doorway through which he had caught a glimpse of a dark staircase.

'I've bin over the 'ole place and most of it 'asn't bin opened for years.' Lugg was panting, but cheerful. 'The top floor 'asn't got a stick in it and the front room on this landin', which is furnished as a bedroom, is nothink but a moth-farm. The only place worth seein' is this little outfit 'ere.'

He led the way across a passage and threw open a door on the left. It was pitch-dark inside but he found a light switch and an unexpectedly vivid glare shone from the single bulb in the centre of the ceiling. Campion stepped into a narrow room whose only window had been boarded over very carefully. It was almost empty. The floor was uncarpeted and a long narrow table stood against the farther wall. By its side sprawled an old-fashioned basket-chair filled with shabby cushions, and there was nothing else at all save two wooden upright chairs. They were arranged in the centre of the floor, facing each other a few feet apart.

Mr Campion looked about him.

'How very suggestive,' he said.

'What is it? A board room?' Lugg was mildly sarcastic but he was puzzled. 'Two gals sits playin' cats' cradles and a bloke sits watchin' them from the armchair?' he offered.

'I should hardly think so. Is there any packing material anywhere in the house? Rock-wool and so on?'

'There's a back place full o' shavings, just be'ind the kitchen, but there's none up 'ere, cock, not a trace.'

Campion said nothing. He wandered round the room eyeing the boards, which were comparatively clean. Lugg's face was glistening.

'Tell you one thing,' he said. 'Jas 'as bin 'ere, I'll lay to that.'

Campion turned to him eagerly. 'How do you know?'

The vast white cheeks had the grace to colour. 'It ain't evidence, exactly. At any rate it's not a finger-print. But you look at them cushions in the chair. That chemist feller was a little chap. Someone with a base of substance 'as sat there, my lad.'

'It's a thought.' Campion's thin mouth widened. 'You ought to do a monograph on it. As a science it's young. Needs a lot of data. Put it up to Yeo and see what he says. It would be informative to hear him, anyway. Any other ideas?'

''E's bin 'ere.' Lugg was obstinate. ''E smokes them little whiffs. I smelt them when I first come in. It's gorn orf now. Don't you think 'e's bin 'ere?'

Mr Campion paused, a tall figure between the two chairs so curiously placed.

'Oh, yes, he's been here,' he said. 'Quite a habit with him, I should think. The question is, what does he put in it.'

'Put in what?'

'In the box,' said Mr Campion, and he described the shape with his hand. It was long and narrow, and one end of it rested on either chair.

CHAPTER 15

Two Days Later

–

IT was a very small ward. Mike Dunning was still very ill. Waves of nausea, followed by vivid terrors which he dimly recognized as unreasonable, overcame him every so often, so that he hesitated and smiled secretly as if he were drunk.

Sergeant Dice, who hovered in the doorway, and Luke and Mr Campion, who sat one on either side of the white iron bed, were little more than shapes in the gloom. But the young nurse, who in daylight looked like an advertisement for holidays in Devon, was tall and steady at his feet. Her white coif was comforting and sometimes he forgot and told his story to her.

'Clytie,' he said again. 'It's Clytie I've got to think about. She doesn't know a thing. It's the way they've brought her up. You wouldn't understand.' He would have shaken his head but the pain warned him just in time. 'She's a kid. She's so sweet, but she didn't know a thing when I found her. She frightened me. She wasn't safe out. Why did you send her away?'

'She'll come back,' said the nurse. 'Tell these gentlemen how you came to get hurt.'

'Don't hold out on a chap, ducks.' His dark eyes, fringed with coarse fair lashes, were anxious. 'You don't know those Palinodes. They'll get hold of her again and shut her up until she grows like them. That's why I took her in hand. I had to.' He swayed a little and a secret smile, apologetic and foolish, passed over his soft boy's mouth. 'I'm responsible for her,' he said, opening his eyes wide. 'She hasn't got anybody but me.'

'Who hit you?' repeated Charlie Luke for the fifth time.

Mike considered the question. 'I don't know,' he said. 'Funny thing, I don't know at all.'

'After you left your landlady you decided to sleep with your bike,' Campion began softly.

'That's right.' He seemed surprised. 'The old bath-tap turned me out. I was jolly annoyed. It was after midnight.' He was silent for a while. 'I must have walked,' he said.

'From right out there?' murmured Luke in the dusk. 'How long did it take you?'

'I don't know. A couple of hours . . . no, not as much as that. I heard two strike when I was watching them.'

'Watching who?' Luke's question was a little too eager, a little too loud. The patient closed his eyes.

'I forget,' he said. 'Where's Clytie now?'

'On the third seat on the left of the corridor, just outside the door,' said Campion promptly. 'She's all right. Was it still raining when you stood watching?'

His eyes, half hidden by the ugly lashes, became thoughtful again.

'No, it had stopped by then. It was dark, you know. I thought I'd better get to the bike because there wasn't a lock on the door and I was worried about it. I hadn't anywhere else to go, either, nowhere I could afford.'

He paused, but this time there was no prompting, and presently his exhausted voice continued.

'I turned into Apron street and pushed on to the mews. There was enough light from the sky to see one's way, but I went quietly because I didn't feel like explaining to any darned bobby.' He blinked. 'I was right on top of the coffin shop when the door opened and they came out, old man Bowels and the son, who let me the shed. They were the last people I wanted to meet just then, so I side-stepped promptly. The only cover was the shop window itself, which juts out from the wall about a foot. I thought they were bound to see me, but it was pretty dark and I held my breath. They would not get on with it. There was a hell of a lot of mucking about in the porch, locking the door, I suppose. Presently they went over the road together. I could see them because the light was grey, like a neg, and old Bowels had a sheet over his arm.'

'A what?' Charlie Luke forgot his caution as the macabre highlight slid into the boy's dark picture.

'A sheet,' the patient persisted. 'It must have been. Nothing else looks like a sheet, does it, except a tablecloth? He had it neatly folded over his arm. It gave me the willies. They went over to the chemist's and stood there for a bit and I thought they must have rung the bell because I heard a window open upstairs, and somebody spoke, although I couldn't hear what was said. And then after a while I couldn't see the gleam of the sheet any more, so I took it they'd gone in.'

'Sure it was the chemist's?'

'Quite. I know Apron Street pretty well now by any light.'

Any ungracious comment from the D.D.I. was forestalled by Mr Campion.

'That was when you heard the clock strike two, was it?' he inquired, reflecting that his own interview with the undertakers, from the window of Renee's drawing-room, must have taken place some time after three.

Mike Dunning hesitated. The scene was returning to him slowly and it surprised him all over again.

'No,' he said finally. 'No. That was when I saw the Captain and Lawrence.'

'Were they there too?'

'Not at the chemist's. After the bone-snatchers had gone, I went over the road to the Palinode house.'

'What for?' Charlie Luke demanded.

'To look at it.' He was so tired that he spoke without even truculence, yet nobody in the room, not even Sergeant Dice, pretended that the reason was unapparent. 'There was no light in Clytie's window – her room's in the front, you know – and I don't think I should have risked chucking a stone at it if there had been one. I just made sure she was asleep. I was turning away when I saw Lawrence Palinode – that's her uncle and the worst of the lot of them – come sneaking out of the front door and down the steps.' His smile grew mischievous, like an urchin's. 'I thought he was after me,' he said. 'X-ray eyes and all that. But then I realized I wasn't in it. There is one street lamp on that corner which is kept alight all night and it happened to shine on him as he stepped off the path. I heard him shoving quietly through the bushes until he came up against that row of stucco urns they call a wall. I wasn't very far from him, as it happened, but I was in complete shadow from the house. I could just see about half his face when he leaned over out of the laurels.'

'Where was the Captain? With him?'

'No. He was across Barrow Avenue on the corner of the terrace, by the postbox. Lawrence was watching him and I was watching Lawrence. It was all damned silly but I daren't move. I couldn't think what everybody was doing beetling about in the dark. That was when I heard the clock on the R.C. church in Barrow Road strike two.'

'How could you see Captain Seton at that distance?'

'Oh, I couldn't.' Mr Dunning's naturally cheerful disposition was reasserting itself. 'I couldn't see him at all for a long time. Old Lawrence was watching something over there and I watched too. Then I saw someone step out of a doorway, pass in front of the pillarbox, and look up the Avenue towards the Barrow Road. He was only there a minute and then nipped back again. Presently the whole thing happened again, and something about the shape of the chap – the way his hat went, I think – struck me as familiar.'

'Was there enough light for you to see all this?' The D.D.I. was fascinated.

'Yes, I told you it was like a neg. Black shadows and everything else a sort of chilly grey. I kept getting different silhouettes of the chap every time he appeared, and every time I got more certain it was the old boy. He's all right; Clytie likes him. Then the woman turned up.'

Campion saw the whites of Charlie Luke's eyes, or thought he did. The D.D.I. was splendidly silent.

'She came wruffling up the pavement,' the husky voice continued, 'and I never saw her face, of course, but I guessed she was oldish from the way she walked, and I could see she was fat although she was all bundled up. The Captain stepped out and spoke to her as if he knew her, and they stood there talking for about ten minutes. I thought they were arguing. The old boy was wagging his hands about. Lawrence was half over the wall. That neck of his stuck out like a stalk. He was trying to hear what they were saying, I think, which was absurd even if they'd shouted. At last the woman turned away and came straight for us, or I thought she was going to. Actually she crossed to the other side of Apron Street and went into the mews. The Captain came into the house and Lawrence went in himself. I know, because I had to stay where I was until he'd gone.'

Charlie Luke scratched his head. 'Sounds as if it *must* have been the Captain and he *was* waiting for her. Pity you didn't see her. Are you sure she went into the mews?'

'Absolutely. I watched. There's a way through into Barrow Road.'

'You're sure the Bowelses didn't come back into the mews?'

'No. How could they? There's no back way to the chemist's shop and I wasn't ten yards from the front window.'

'Then what happened?'

Mike leant back farther in his pillows and the nurse seemed to be about to declare the interview at an end. He rallied, however, and went on eagerly.

'I went into the mews and found the bike,' he said. 'That's right. There was a light under Bowels's back door and I remembered the son had told me they'd got a relation staying with them. I sidled down to the shed, afraid that the chap might hear me. The bike was there all right. I shut the door before I lit a match to see. I hadn't a torch.'

'Did you notice anybody?'

'No, there was no one downstairs. I thought I heard someone in the loft and I spoke, I think. I can't remember. Anyway there was no more noise and I thought I must have heard one of the horses next door. There was nothing to sit on and the bricks were pretty well running with damp, and so I thought I'd be better off upstairs. I was tired as hell and I'd got to think. I'd only got a pound in the world until payday.' His forehead wrinkled under his bandage. 'That's another problem,' he said, and grinned disarmingly. 'We'll give that our attention later. Well, I lit a match and held it down to keep it alight, and tottered up the ladder. That's absolutely all I remember. Somebody socked me, I suppose. Who was it?'

'Hardly the Captain's girl-friend,' said Campion foolishly.

As they got up Dunning put out a hand to him.

'Send her in, there's a good scout,' he muttered. 'I've got to talk to her. You don't know what sort of mess she'll get into without me.'

'Of course, that's when it's serious,' remarked Campion to the D.D.I. as they walked down the concrete steps of the hospital together after the errand had been completed.

'Poor ruddy little kids!' exploded Charlie Luke unexpectedly. 'No one's looking after either of 'em so they're taking care of each other.' He paused. 'Like a couple of drunks,' he said. 'Well, it wasn't Lugg's relations after all.'

'No, it would appear not.' Campion was puzzled. 'I think I should like a chat with Jas.'

'He's all yours. I've got to go down and see Sir Doberman now. There was a message from him just before this call came through from the hospital about Dunning. I don't know what the old boy's dogged up now.'

They had reached the gates and he stood for a moment, restless and unhappy. His eyes were worried and deep in his head.

'Do you know where this blasted case is getting to, sir?' he said. 'I know I'm short-handed, what with H.Q. pinching half the chaps, and I know it's a difficult assignment, the Palinodes being such unusual people, but do you see any light in it at all? Perhaps I'm just losing my grip.'

Campion, who despite his height looked slighter and smaller than the other man, took off his spectacles to regard him mildly.

'Oh, it's coming, Charles,' he said. 'It's teasing out, don't you know. As I see it, the point to keep in mind now is that there are clearly two different coloured threads in the – er – coil. The question is, are they tied at the end? I feel they ought to be, but I don't know. What do you think?'

'I sometimes wonder if I can,' said Charlie Luke.

CHAPTER 16

Undertaker's Parlour

—

THE glass door of the Bowelses' establishment was fastened but there was still light within when Mr Campion pressed the bell and stood waiting. Considered dispassionately, the window was not without interest. It contained one black marble urn, which could only have been an embarrassment anywhere else and two wax wreaths under glass.

The only other item was a miniature easel bearing a black-edged card which announced 'Reliable Interments. Taste, Efficiency, Economy, Respect,' in small but florid type.

He was reflecting that an unreliable interment hardly bore imagining when he caught sight of Mr Bowels, snr, rising up from the stair-well which was just visible through the door. He appeared to be eating and was struggling with his jacket, but he moved with gratifying speed and presently pressed his face against the glass.

'Mr Campion!' he said with delight. 'Well, this is a treat, this is.' He allowed his smile to give place to cautious concern. 'Excuse me for being so personal, but nothing professional, I hope, sir?'

Mr Campion was affable. 'That depends on which of us you have in mind. Perhaps we could go down to your kitchen for a moment, could we?'

The broad face became expressionless for less than a second and Campion had hardly time to recognize the fact before the man was beaming again, light on his feet and deferential.

'Now I should regard that as an honour, Mr Campion. This way. You'll forgive me going first, I'm sure.' He bowed his way round the visitor and his voice filled the building like a gong.

Campion followed him down the stairs to a narrow passage which smelled stuffy and warm after the refined emptiness of the shop. He bobbed along, taking very short steps, and talking all the time.

'It's humble but comfortable,' he was saying. 'We see enough of magnificence, me and the boy, and it hasn't got happy associations, so in private life we like to be homely. But I'm forgetting; you did us the honour the other day when Magers had indulged, poor fellow.'

He stopped, his hand on the latch of a narrow door. He was smiling, his large front teeth all but hiding his small lower lip.

'After me, if you'll permit,' he said, and went in.

He became happier at once. 'We're alone, I see,' he said as he backed into the dimly lit and cluttered apartment and set a chair for his visitor at the supper table. 'I thought the boy was here but he's gone back to his work. A beautiful craftsman – just sit here, sir; then you'll be on my right side and I can hear you, if you please.'

As Campion sat down Jas walked round to his own seat at the head of the table. His white curls shone in the comfortable gloom and there was dignity in the set of his wide shoulders. Here he achieved a new authority, for all his mock subservience. He sat there, an impressive anachronism, unlikely and nearly as decorative as a coach-and-four.

'Magers is away,' he remarked, his small blue eyes shrewd and curious. 'As soon as there was that tragedy over the road he came hurrying in, said good-bye, and we haven't heard of him since. I expect you knew that, sir?'

Campion nodded but offered no explanation. Jas bowed. No other description could fit that graceful, acquiescing inclination.

He took another line. 'A very shockin' thing, poor Wilde. He wasn't a friend of ours, exactly, but we were very close nodding acquaintances, as one might put it. We'd both been tradesmen in this road for quite a time. I didn't go to the inquest, but I sent Rowley out of respect. "Suicide when the balance of mind was disturbed," they brought in; that's always the kindest way.'

He folded his hands on the checkered tablecloth and dropped his inquisitive eyes.

'We're putting him down tomorrow morning. I don't suppose there'll be a penny to come, but we shall do him with as much luxury as if we were waiting on you yourself. That's partly out of kindness, Mr Campion, and partly out of business. Sad as it may seem to you, who'd hardly suspect it, a tragedy is our best advertisement. Sightseers come in hundreds and it's the procession they remember, so we always do our best for the sake of trade.'

The new note of formality which his host was displaying puzzled Campion. He thought he observed a tea-party atmosphere about the interview, as if they were somehow in company. At the risk of shattering it completely he produced his first squib.

'What were you carrying over your arm when you went down to see your close nodding acquaintance at two in the morning the day before yesterday?'

The old man made no sign of surprise but favoured his visitor with an expression of disapproval and reproach.

'That's the kind of question I should have expected to hear from the police, Mr Campion,' he said sternly, 'and if you pardon my saying so, it would have come much more delicate from them. Let every tradesman do his own dirty work, that's what I feel.'

'Very proper,' said Campion sententiously, 'and that brings us to two o'clock in the morning of the day before yesterday.'

Jas laughed. His amused, half roguish, half deprecatory grin was disarming.

'How 'uman 'uman nature is, ain't it?' He gathered up his own peccadillos and dropped them into the mighty pool of the world's sin. 'That Mr Corkerdale, on duty in the garden of the lodge, happened to notice us, I suppose?'

The lean man allowed the question to pass and the undertaker's rueful smile broadened.

'I shouldn't have said it was quite as late as that,' he went on, 'but it may have been. Magers was with us, the first time for thirty years. We'd been talking of the dear departed and Magers had dropped off into a sleep which was practically a stupor, poor fellow.' He paused, and his small eyes searched the other man's face for signs of progress. Finding nothing, he went on again gallantly.

'You'll remember me telling you, Mr Campion, when we met over at the house, that I was in a bit of a muddle about a casket at the time?'

'Did you? I thought you tried to sell it to me.'

'No, Mr Campion, that was my fun. We had to get hold of a casket in a hurry for the funeral at Lansbury Terrace. Rowley had recollected the one in my lock-up over the way. "But before we do that," I said to 'im, "before we do that, son, there's just time to go down to Mr Wilde to take 'im what I promised 'im."'

There was another fruitless pause, during which Mr Campion remained blank and attentive. Jas became more confidential.

'You're a man of the world like myself, Mr Campion. You'll understand, I know. Poor Wilde was a very neat person. Untidiness upset him. He had a front room over the shop right on the street. The curtains were a disgrace and I chipped 'im about them. Well . . .' he lowered his voice, 'we use a little cotton stuff in the trade – it's very nice to look at – and the long and the short of it is that I promised him a yard or two just for the look of the shop. After all, it helps us if the street don't go down. I took it over by night for fear of jealousy among the neighbours, and as he hadn't used it when I fetched his body to the mortuary I took it back, and I can show it to you in the workshop this minute. That's all we were doing.' He finished the lie with a flourish and sat back well pleased with himself.

'Yes,' said Campion, and the word was neither acceptance nor rejection. 'And the other thing I wanted to ask you was why you bothered to send for me in the first place?'

Mr Bowels froze. Alarm spread over him like a tide. The wide face lost its pink and became pallid, and the small mouth became circular in protest. It was the first time he had shown any sign of open discomposure since Campion had met him.

'I, sir? I send for you?' He was shrill in protest. 'You're making a big mistake there. I did no such thing. Not but what me and

142

the boy's not very glad to know you. Very proud, I might say. But *send* for you, sir? Oh, dear me no! Why, it wouldn't be my place, would it, sir? – even supposing I had any reason.' He was silent, and the solid hand on the red and white tablecloth trembled. 'I may 'ave wrote a friendly letter to my relation after finding myself in the papers,' he went on, 'but if 'e read anything special into that, well, 'e was more of a fool than I took 'im for. I'm *glad* to see you here, Mr Campion, because I want to see the whole thing cleared up, and that's a fact, but no, sir, I didn't send for you, sir.'

Mr Campion was more puzzled than ever. He could understand Mr Bowels being anxious to repudiate any responsibility, but not why he should be so frightened about it.

'I can see that a police inquiry would not be very good for your trade,' he began cautiously. 'The publicity can't be helpful and I realize that you knew that Miss Ruth Palinode was in the habit of putting an occasional shilling or two on a horse, but I don't think that point was strong enough to make you send for me.'

Mr Bowels blew his nose on a large white handkerchief, apparently to gain time.

'I didn't send for you,' he said, 'but trade is trade and the police are the first to forget it. In my business it's discretion, discretion, discretion all the time. Who wants an undertaker with a long nose and a gabby tongue, even if he's doing no more than his duty? However, you and me being friendly, and me trusting you to see I never get anywhere really detrimental like a witness-box, there is a little something that perhaps I ought to mention. I only saw one thing which was really curious when Miss Ruth Palinode died. It was a very small thing and may not have had any significance, but it made me think. I saw Mr Lawrence Palinode washing up.'

A mental picture of that gangling, near-sighted man with the sweet smile and incomprehensible conversation presented itself to Campion.

'Where was this?' he inquired.

Mr Bowels was still pale but some of his old knowingness had returned.

'Not in the kitchen,' he said darkly. 'She died early in the afternoon, a very unusual time. You may not know it, but early in the afternoon is a most uncommon time for what you might call mortality.'

'How soon did you get there?'

Tea-time. Nearly five. Miss Roper sent Mr Grace over. The family didn't stir hand nor foot, and that wasn't unnaturalness, mind you. They're human but helpless, the Palinodes, made worse because they don't think it's quite the right thing to be practical.'

He was getting over his fright and reasserting himself. The difference between this story and the last was subtle but inescapable. There was now none of the carefree ease of improvisation. Campion felt he was probably telling some sort of version of the truth.

'I was just settling down to my meal when Mr Grace knocked, and as I knew the family I got up at once, put on my black coat, took my measure and went over,' he continued. 'Mr Grace said he'd rather not come upstairs, but there was nothing surprising in that. Often people won't take you up, even when it's someone they know well. On the other hand, some enjoy it. It's temperament. Anyhow I wasn't surprised when he left me on the stairs. "Leave it to me, sir," I said. "I'm not likely to make any serious mistake of identity." That was my little joke but 'e didn't see it. Anyway, I went up alone, all quiet and respectful, for we tread as light as we can. I hesitated in the doorway, just to make sure, and there he was – washing up.'

'Mr Lawrence Palinode?'

'Yes.'

'In Miss Ruth's bedroom?'

'Yes. There was the dead lady covered with a sheet, and there was her brother – cool, but nervous, if I make myself plain – with every mortal cup or glass or spoon the room contained out on the old-fashioned wash-stand. He was dipping the last one into the jug as I came in and he swung round like a shop-lifter when he heard the door. The next moment he was very polite and kindly, but of course I'd seen him. As soon as I was alone I took a look at what he'd been up to. Quite clean, they were, spread out all along the marble. It was quite open.'

He sounded mildly indignant.

'Is that all?'

'The whole truth, sir. I thought it was significant.'

'Have you told anybody else?'

'No one. That's a lesson I learnt at my father's knee. "Undertakers don't talk no more than their clients"; that was 'is motto. Of course when the ex'umation order came along I thought to myself, but I didn't speak. It's some time ago, and it's only my word against his, isn't it?'

This was very true. Campion was digesting the information and its probable worth when Jas rose.

'Could I offer you a glass of anything? Mr Luke says I drink embalming mixture, but that's only 'is idea of fun.'

'No, thank you. I'm just going.' Campion got up a little too quickly. His sudden movement startled the old man and he glanced sharply across the room to the corner immediately behind his guest.

Campion was too old a bird to look at once, but as he resettled his chair tidily under the table before following his unprotesting host towards the door he glanced casually at his side and received the shock of the day.

There was a grandfather clock in the alcove beside the range and next it, flattened between it and the wall, not four feet behind his chair a man was standing. He was completely motionless and deep in the shadow, and must have been there throughout the entire interview.

Campion went on out of the door which the undertaker was holding open for him. His step was light and brisk, his face misleadingly blank. His host felt fairly certain that he had noticed nothing unusual.

However, as he hurried across the road, nodding to the dapper figure of Mr James, the bank manager, who saluted him graciously with a furled umbrella, he turned up his collar and prepared to push through the small crowd of sightseers which had begun to collect outside the front gate of Portminster Lodge. He was particularly thoughtful.

That polished skull and wobbling blob of a lower lip had been distinctive, and he gave his full attention to the hitherto neglected ubiquity of Mr Congreve.

CHAPTER 17

High Wind in the Area

—

'ALL right. Don't say another word. I'm going. I've had it. You've taken me wrong and I've had it.'

Mr Campion paused in the doorway from the area just in time to catch the full force of the words. Clarrie Grace was standing half-way across the kitchen in an attitude unconsciously theatrical. He was dressed for travel.

Renee faced him from the stove. She was red and trembling, but even in the height of rage her full eyes were troubled and kindly still.

'Oh, for goodness' sake, Clarrie,' she exclaimed, 'put a sock in it, do! Go if you want to, but don't say I threw you out and don't tell the street about it. There's a crowd outside, I hope you know.'

Clarrie shut his mouth and opened it again. He glanced at Campion and found in him a heaven-sent audience.

'Love,' he said to Renee, 'love. Dear, dear, sweet old girl. Have a lick, just a lick of common. I'm only trying to help you. I don't want to see you make a fool of yourself. If you like to think I've interfered, I'm sorry.' And then, at the top of his voice: 'I think you're damned well barmy, that's all!'

'That'll do.' She was very crisp and commanding. 'Don't open your mouth again. You've said quite enough. I shan't forget it, Clarrie. He's making all this fuss, Albert, simply because I told the child I shall ask her boy here. Poor kid! he's got to go somewhere, hasn't he? He's got no home and no money, and they won't keep him in hospital indefinitely.

Isn't that just the way to make a girl do a silly thing, to turn your back and leave her with the responsibility like that? Go on, Albert, answer me.'

Mr Campion saw any hope he may have had of remaining discreet and neutral vanishing abruptly.

'I've not quite gathered what it's all about,' he said cautiously. 'It's Clytie and Mike Dunning, is it?'

'Well, of course, dear. Don't be a fool.' Her asperity stung round his ears like a carriage-whip. 'I'm not proposing to run an orphan asylum.'

'I thought you were,' muttered Clarrie infuriatingly, so that she turned on him.

'You make me tired, you do, all you men. Here's a nice motherly girl – don't you laugh, Clarrie; I know – all young and upset, and very much smitten, worrying what to do for a poor sick boy. If I have him here I can have a look at him, can't I? If he's not suitable, and no one knows that until they've met him, then we can put her off him in a proper Christian way . . .'

Clarrie made a noise like a skittish horse.

'So you're proposing to nag the poor kids, are you? This is new. You didn't tell me this.'

'Rubbish! I'm only trying to look after her as if she were my own.'

He sat down at the table, folded his arms, and laid his head, hat and all, upon them.

'Why?'

'Why?'

'Yes, why! Isn't that what the whole blessed barney is about? Look here, Campion, you be judge. I've been trying to tell this silly old duck – whom I love like a ruddy mother, mind you – that she can't look after the perishing world. That's fair, isn't it? Isn't that fair?'

Renee's reaction was unexpectedly violent.

'Piggy!' She screwed up her eyes in an attempt, apparently, to convey the image visually. 'Pure Piggy! Oh, it's not your fault. Your mother was all right, she was a pal of mine, and a more generous girl never breathed. But your dad! . . . I can see him in you this minute, the rat.'

Mr Grace made no attempt to defend his father, but he looked crestfallen and aggrieved. Campion received the impression that the blow was below the belt. It was evident that Renee thought so, for she became, if not apologetic, at least anxious to justify herself.

'Well, it's not nice to keep watching what others are getting. What if I do give the family upstairs a little more than they can pay for? I can afford it and it's my business. Sneaking round and trying to pump old Congreve at the bank about my account isn't gentlemanly.'

'That's a lie, of course.' Clarrie spoke without conviction. 'Besides, Congreve doesn't give much away. He's trying to pump me half the time. He scraped acquaintance with me and I told you about it, and you said – stop me, if I'm wrong – that banks always were nosey.'

'You're an eel, nothing but an eel.' She gave Campion a faint uneasy smile. 'I know what I'm doing,' she said.

'If you do, that's all right.' Clarrie sounded weary. 'I only tried to protect you, you silly old fool. I just see half-a-dozen elderly number eight hats taking more out than they put in. I don't want to know why you let them, mind you – although that would seem queer to some people – I only wondered if you could do it. Since you say you can, and you assure me you're not setting fair for the poor-box, I'll say no more. Keep the lovebirds, sweetheart, and half the street besides if you like, I don't care.'

Miss Roper kissed him. 'That's an apology,' she said. 'Now don't spoil it. Do take your hat off in the house, love. Look, Albert does.'

'Sorry, I'm bloody sure!' said Mr Grace, and, snatching off the offending felt, he threw it at the stove, where it rolled among the cooking pots and began to smell at once. Miss Roper's dying passion flared. Quick as a lizard, she hooked the poker into the cooking ring and thrust the hat into the flames. The iron ring sat down on it, blotting it out for ever. Then, without turning, she busied herself, moving pots and kettles with busy importance.

Perfectly white, and with tears of fury in his flat blue eyes, Clarrie rose to his feet and opened his mouth.

Mr Campion, seeing no good purpose he could possibly serve, left the old friends together, finding touch, so to speak, just outside the door to the back stairs. There he all but fell over Mrs Love, who was kneeling by a pail at the foot of them.

''As 'e gorn, I say 'as 'e gorn?' she demanded, hopping up and seizing him by the coat sleeve. 'I can't 'ear everything, I say I can't hear everything.'

She was shouting and Mr Campion, who had formed the impression that she could not hear *anything*, bellowed, 'I hope not.'

'So do I,' she said in a surprisingly normal murmur, adding unexpectedly, 'it's a funny thing, though, I say it's a funny thing.'

As he edged his way round her he realized that the repeated statement indicated that some sort of reply was not only expected but demanded.

'Is it?' he ventured non-committally, gaining the stairs.

'Well, of course it is.' She thrust her rosy ancient face very close to his own. 'Why should she *give* them so much free? They're only lodgers, aren't they? You would think she owed 'em something, I say you'd think she owed 'em something.'

The shrill words, which were so uncomfortably shrewd, echoed his own thoughts and brought him to a pause.

'Going up to yer room now?' she inquired, and suddenly grovelled. 'There!' she said. 'There! I never told you. It went out of me mind, see? It's all the 'appenings put it out of me mind. There's a gentleman in your room come to see you about arf an hower ago. Seemed very respectable, I say very respectable, so I put 'im up there.'

'Did you, though?' said Mr Campion, who expected no caller. He moved towards the staircase. Her voice followed him cheerfully.

'I wouldn't let no ordin'ry person in there, because you never know what you're going to miss, I say you never know what you're going to miss.'

She must, he thought, be quite audible all over the house. He paused before the door of his own bedroom in surprise.

There was a conversation going on inside. No words were distinguishable, but the sounds which reached him suggested a polite social gathering. His eyebrows rising, he pushed open the door and went in.

Miss Evadne was sitting on the nordic throne before the dressing-table, with her back to the mirror. She was still wearing the long Paisley garment in which he had first seen her, but now there was a lace fichu draped over her shoulders, and a diamond ring in an old-fashioned gold setting shone on her large well-shaped hand. At her feet, wrestling with the plug of the electric kettle, which he was attempting to mend with a nail-file, knelt a rotund grey-haired man in formal black coat and striped trousers.

As he raised his head Campion recognized him as Sir William Glossop, the financial expert and adviser to the Treasury, whom he knew but slightly.

CHAPTER 18

Thread from Threadneedle Street

–

WHEN Campion entered, the amateur electrician would have risen gratefully had not Miss Palinode's gesture kept him on his knees.

'Do please go on. You're managing very nicely.' Her gracious cultured voice was packed with authority. 'I think that little screw goes there, doesn't it? No, perhaps not. You're out a great deal,' she added, presumably to Campion.

It was very gentle chiding.

'I am trying to get quite ready for my little conversazione tomorrow, and I noticed that this difficult thing had come apart. So annoying of it! I am not very clever with my hands, I am afraid.'

Her laugh, which was delightful, conveyed that a notion so absurd was amusing and yet somehow flattering to them.

'So I came along to find you. I know you theatrical people are so resourceful. You weren't here, you see, but your colleague came to my rescue.'

Sir William favoured Campion with a glance from under his lashes. His small sophisticated mouth was pursed with irritation. Anyone less like any actor he had yet met Campion could not imagine. He held out his hands.

'I'll have a go, shall I?' he suggested.

'I really wish you would.' The announcement was heartfelt and the older man rose, to take a more congenial position on the hearthrug.

Miss Evadne smiled at him.

'"You do look, my son, in a moved sort,"' she quoted '"as if you were dismayed. Be cheerful, sir: our revels now are ended."'

She watched his face with an amused tolerance which he found disconcerting.

'I'm afraid these gadgets are beyond me,' he said uneasily. He was not a man who believed in the smile as a social lubricant. Miss Evadne found him shy.

'You're not a Shakespearian, I see,' she said kindly. 'I took it that you were. Now why was that?' Her glance, falling on his Falstaffian girth, reminded her and her eyes twinkled. 'Never mind. You must both come in tomorrow, of course. I don't know that there will be anyone particularly influential there this week. However, it should be amusing, I think.'

She glanced down at Campion, who was making headway.

'I always ask a few of my good friends from the neighbourhood, tradesmen and so on, for I do feel my nice Thespis people should meet their audience, don't you?'

Campion got up, his task completed. 'Salutary all round, I should think,' he said cheerfully and met a surprised but gratified gleam in her smile.

'That's what I think,' she said. 'Now, is that mended? Splendid! Good evening to you both. I shall see you tomorrow just after six, then. Don't be very late. I get too tired to talk rather soon.'

She took the kettle, nodded to Campion to open the door for her, and made an exit which would have graced a royal drawing-room. On the threshold she paused to glance back at Glossop.

'Thank you for making such a gallant attempt,' she said. 'We're neither of us quite so clever as this kind man, are we?'

Campion was aware that she realized that she was being very naughty and that it was an olive branch of a sort. He closed the door, grinning, and turned back into the room.

Sir William, who looked as out of place as a seal among the Morris and motifs, regarded him gloomily.

'I was waiting for you when that woman walked in,' he said. 'She seemed to think she knew me. Who does she think I am, a policeman?'

Mr Campion met the wise sad eyes, which seem so often to go with a profound understanding of money, with a certain embarrassment.

'Well, no. I'm afraid she's pretending to believe that we are both on the stage.'

'An actor!' He glanced casually at himself in the large heart-shaped mirror at his side, and came as near smiling as at any time during the interview. 'Good lord!' he said briefly, but he did not seem unpleased. Another thought occurred to him. 'Is she your murderess?'

'A runner-up,' said Campion cheerfully. 'This is all very unexpected, Sir William. Anything I can do?'

The other man regarded him thoughtfully.

'Yes,' he said at last. 'That's why I'm here, of course.' He seated himself on the bench Miss Evadne had vacated and produced a small and shining pipe, which he filled and lit.

'I've been talking to Stanislaus Oates, or rather Oates has been talking to me,' he began at last. 'You put a query in a letter to Superintendent Yeo. Do you know what I'm talking about?'

'It does not leap to mind.'

'Good.' He seemed relieved. 'Your letter was a personal one to the Superintendent. He went to Oates. Oates mercifully mentioned it to me direct, since we happen to be working together at the moment on another matter. That means four reliable people; that's all right, I think. Now, Campion, what exactly do you know about Brownie Mines?'

The pale eyes behind the horn-rims grew momentarily blank and Campion sighed. It had been a hunch of the wildest kind. With some of the old thrill he saw the card turning up.

'Almost nothing,' he said. 'A woman who has been murdered held a number of shares. They are thought to be worthless. Some months ago there was a rumour about them, that's all I know.'

'Really? Oh, well then, that's better than I thought. Just keep absolutely silent about the whole business, if you will.'

'If I can,' corrected Mr Campion mildly.

Sir William shook his head. 'That's not good enough, my dear boy. There must be absolutely no suggestion. Do you understand me? There must be absolutely no suggestion in the press or anywhere else. No suggestion, I say. Need I put it any plainer?'

'Nice for the murderer,' suggested Mr Campion.

'I beg your pardon? Oh, I see. Good lord, are you suggesting that this wretched woman may have been poisoned because she owned . . . ?'

'I'm not suggesting so much as inquiring.' Mr Campion looked like a thin owl. 'I have known perfectly genuine murders undertaken by enthusiasts for as little as three pound ten. My – er – my client possessed, as far as I remember, something over eight thousand negotiable whatnots in this charmingly titled concern. You must see that it makes a difference to me and the police generally if there is an outside chance of these ever having meant money. It's our duty to find out, isn't it? She certainly had nothing else of which the value is even problematical.'

Sir William rose. 'I see what you mean,' he said slowly. 'You can see the importance *I* place on it, or I shouldn't be here. I made certain that you were on to very much more than this, although of course I realized that you were unaware of its seriousness since you merely queried it. My one thought was to get down here myself and shut you up as soon as I could.'

'Look here.' Mr Campion produced his little bargain modestly. 'Neither Chief Inspector Luke nor I wish to put our little paws in high finance. We have caught a clue and all we want to know is if it is of value to *us*. Its importance to you and His Majesty's Government is not our affair. In fact, you tell us how dangerous your Brownie is and we'll keep his fair name out of it.'

'What Brownie? Oh I see, a figure of speech. Well, I'm not going to commit myself, because quite frankly the fewer people who know anything about the matter the better, but

I'll tell you this much. There are three derelict gold mines – I won't say where, of course – which are suspected of yielding a certain metal.'

'Nameless,' said Campion.

'Exactly. A certain metal of great scarcity, which is in demand for the manufacture of certain items vital for this country's defence.' He paused and Campion lowered his eyes. Sir William grunted. 'It's now being investigated,' he said. 'Secrecy is absolutely vital. My dear chap, think where they are!'

Campion, who had no idea if Brownie had sunk his mines in Chelsea or Peru, was content to look intelligent, while a second thought occurred to Sir William.

'If some fellow has killed an old woman to get hold of that scrip, I tell you what, Campion, he's a crook. The secret has been kept like the grave. He's a dangerous criminal and there's a serious leakage. You must get hold of him and the sooner the better.'

'A thoughtless chap all round,' said Mr Campion gently. 'Very well. We know nothing here save the one cogent thing, which is that there's a motive in the stuff.'

Sir William's wise eyes became introspective.

'An excellent one,' he said. 'I'll leave you to it. Keep me posted. I'm relying on your discretion, of course I needn't mention that.' The question in his voice and face belied the words.

Mr Campion had no time to look injured. An idea had presented itself.

'Was it dark when you came in?' he demanded.

'Not quite, I'm afraid.' Sir William looked guilty. 'I know what's in your mind. You think I may have been recognized. It occurred to me when I saw the house surrounded. I had not thought that there might be sightseers. Incredible morbidity!' He hesitated, considering. 'It's a strange decayed sort of neighbourhood. I see this is the Apron Street which possesses a branch of Clough's. There's a fantastic anomaly in a modern world!'

'I gathered it was an old-fashioned concern.'

'Archaic. Perfectly sound financially, but living in the past There are two or three little branches left; one at Leamington, one at Tonbridge, one at Bath. It used to cater for a fashionable class now practically extinct. They pay out less in salary than any house of the kind, but get good service.' He sighed. 'Extraordinary world! Well, I'm sorry if I shouldn't have come here, Campion. Annoying, too. I was so anxious that we shouldn't be seen together that I took the trouble to come and find you instead of fixing a meeting at the club or the office. I don't think I was recognized. Besides, if there is no mention of the matter we've been discussing, there's no spark for the tinder. Who could put two and two together except yourself, eh?'

Mr Campion helped him into his greatcoat. As usual, when he was worried he looked affably blank.

'Myself and one other, and he's the lad who matters most, don't you think?' he ventured.

The visitor stared at him.

'The murderer?' he demanded. 'Good heavens, you're not suggesting the chap is hanging about outside the house, are you?'

Mr Campion's gentle smile grew positively foolish.

'Well, of course, it's warmer indoors,' he murmured.

Ten minutes later, when his guest was safely smuggled off the premises with as much discretion as it was feasible to arrange, he sat still without smoking for some minutes.

His thought, meandering amid the undergrowth, came upon something self-evident. Since Miss Evadne was not quite the unworldly person she was pretending to be, she was not, surely, a woman to insist upon entertaining at such a moment for the sweet sake of obstinacy alone? Yet she was determined to give her party. Why?

No solution occurred to him and he passed on to her brother, Lawrence, and the curious little tale which Jas Bowels had told about him. The undertaker had missed the obvious there, he was open to bet.

The abrupt opening of the door cut into his reflections. Charlie Luke swept in without apology and pulled two quart bottles out of his raincoat pockets.

'Only beer,' he said.

Campion looked up with interest. 'Good news?' he inquired.

'Nothing to get the bunting out for.' The D.D.I. was pulling off his coat as if it were attempting to resist him. His hat sailed on to the chest of drawers and he made a long arm for the tooth-glass. 'You drink pretty and I'll have the bottle,' he said, filling it up. The room was full of him. 'Sir Doberman isn't hopeful. He wanted to see me to ask me if I'd dug up the right chap. Poor old boy! He's as disappointed as a kid with an empty parcel.'

He took another swig from the bottle and sighed over the satisfaction it gave him.

'There's the usual inquiry from H.Q. about "the delay in effecting an arrest",' he continued briskly, 'but it's on the half-hearted side today. They're feeling low. Greener has been reported in France. He's the active partner of the two Greek Street gun-boys there's been such a hooey about. Paul, the other one, has vanished into thin air.'

Campion looked serious. 'That's a bad thing,' he said.

'Exactly.' Luke was ferociously cheerful. 'After ten days with the lid off. After every port has been watched like the last bun at a school-treat. Little Apron Street has had about half the man-hours on it it deserves. However, as they say in the high-class books, however . . .' He set the bottle down carefully between his feet. 'It's an ill wind. At last I've got a couple of chaps working on Pa Wilde's stock, and the call has gone out for bier-tending Bella, but nothing of interest has turned up to date except that the old bloke hadn't made much money out of whatever he was up to.' He sighed deeply and sincerely. 'Poor old pill-grinder! I wouldn't have had that happen for a pound of my pension. I got something for you, though.'

He ferreted in an inside pocket.

'The doc's had another anonymous letter. Same writing, same postmark, same paper. The dirt isn't quite up to standard.' He held his large nose absent-mindedly. 'But the same lively soul is cunningly expressed. She hopes we burn.'

He produced a sheet of paper which might, Mr Campion reflected, have been expressly manufactured for the purpose of remaining untraceable. It was thin, it was common, it was off-white and it had no water-mark. It was obtainable in quantity in almost every shop in the metropolis. Even the handwriting was familiar in its unformed, back-sloping illiteracy.

Upon examination it was not without interest. After a string of unprintable words, somewhat carelessly arranged but chosen with a certain unpleasant relish, the writer became more more explicit.

> *Well you old blank you have got away so far because all drs are cowards but you have not got much out of the dead have you and why I will tell you now and this is straighter than you could ever be you blank.*
>
> *The brother who is a blank grasping and mean is the one who is being so clever as He thinks and has got what she left the blank of a Poor so called Captain who is nothing but a poor fool am watching you who are to blame for all trouble and Misery god know amen glass tells all dont forget persons like you are all blanks and the ones to make others sufer though pretending always pretending to bring kindness and do good the police are worse always a ready hand for cash and double cross. They will burn in hell on earth as i hope you do. You are the worst you blank blank blank blank blank blank.*

'Nice old girl, ain't she?' Charlie Luke glanced over his shoulder. 'She can do better than this, though. There's not so much repetition when she's on form. See anything which takes your fancy?'

Campion spread the paper on the bedside table and punctuated the letter lightly in pencil. When he had finished he underlined certain words so that a simple message emerged.

'*The brother is the one who is being clever. He has got what she left to the captain, who is a poor fool.*'

'It's fascinating if it's true,' he murmured.

'How come?' Luke's head was on one side.

'Because Miss Ruth's legacy to the Captain, whom she disliked, was eight thousand first preference negotiable shares in a deadly secret.' His smile was broad. 'Sit down,' he invited, 'and listen to me break a confidence.'

Before he spoke again, though, his pencil wandered on down the unpleasant little missive and underlined yet five more words in the unsavoury harangue.

CHAPTER 19

The Snarl

—

THE large room immediately on the left of the front door at Portminster Lodge had been designed in those days when thought, time, and, above all, space were devoted to fine eating.

Lawrence Palinode's father, whose somewhat hand-painted portrait hung over the fireplace, had entertained the wit and scholarship of Victorian Europe in this small banqueting hall, but now his son worked at one end of it and slept at the other.

His camp-bedstead was wedged between two rather fine Georgian mahogany pedestals complete with brass-mounted urns, and it was evident that he kept his clothes neatly folded in and about a sideboard now too large for any private household.

The general effect was, curiously, not at all uncomfortable. The tapestry-covered armchair on the hearth was bag-seated but very tidy and well brushed, and the solid table with rounded ends, which ran the whole length of the worn carpet, was neatly divided into three sections, the first a desk, the second a filing department, and the third a fairly well-fitted sandwich bar. The rest was books, not one of them dusty or dog-eared. They filled walls and side tables and the tops of cabinets, overflowing into heaps in corners and on chairs.

Yet it was the tidiest living-room in Charlie Luke's wide experience. He remarked upon it as he stood looking round with Campion at his side.

They had entered without invitation and were giving it what Luke had called 'the old once-over' while they waited for the owner. On one side of the desk end of the table a butler's tray on a stand had been arranged. It was packed solid with books in use, all neatly stacked, spines uppermost.

Campion bent over them. The first title he read was *Forensic Medicine* by Sidney Smith, and the second *Toxicology* by Buchanan. As his eye ran along the line his expression grew more and more blank. The inevitable *Gross* was there, and a *Materia Medica*, Lucas on *Forensic Chemistry*, and a very old *Quaine*. He began to look for other friends and was interested to see *Glaister, Keith Simpson*, and the engaging *H. T. F. Rhodes*, as well as a large section of supplementaries including *Streker and Ebaugh*, and *Mental Abnormality and Crime* in the 'English Studies in Criminal Science' series.

It was a small but comprehensive working library of criminology.

He took up the *Materia Medica* and glanced at the flyleaf, sighed with comprehension, and was continuing his investigations with the other books when Luke interrupted him.

'Chase me!'

The old-fashioned Cockney expletive had the force of the unusual. Campion looked up to find his circumflex-accented eyes wide with astonishment. He was holding out a sheet of paper which he had just taken from the mantelshelf.

'Foul-mouthed Freda again,' he said. 'Look.' Campion went over and together they read the fellow to the note to the doctor. As he read, Campion felt the chill which always assailed him whenever he met the abnormal. This was madness, cold and festering. The message, when taken out of the mass of decay, was simple.

'*You . . . have robbed a . . . fool.*'

The envelope, which still lay on the shelf, was correctly addressed to Lawrence Palinode and the local postmark was clear.

'Posted yesterday morning.' Luke put the letter back where he had found it. 'I don't know if this is the first note he's had. If it isn't, why the hell hasn't he reported it? Looks damn funny to me.'

He walked on down the room, his fingers playing noisily with the coins in his pockets. As he followed him, Campion could almost hear his mind working.

'Well, we'll have another talk with him,' he went on as they reached the second half of the double room. 'I may as well admit I didn't understand a quarter of what he said last time. Maybe it's my lack of education.' He spread out his hands to convey emptiness. 'We'll have another go.'

Campion touched his arm. 'At this very moment.'

From the hall outside excited voices reached them clearly, Lawrence's goose-tones sounding high above the others. The door rattled and there was a moment of hesitation as they heard him say, 'Come in, come in. I insist.'

Luke and Campion, who were standing in the shelter of the folded dividing doors, remained where they were. In the darkness of the corner they were, if not invisible, at least not instantly obvious.

Lawrence came in with a rush. His hand brushed the light switch and in his extreme preoccupation he did not notice that the room was already lit. His tall, heavy-boned figure was clumsier than ever and he was trembling so violently that the door he held shook noticeably and a book from a pile on the chair behind it slid to the ground.

In stooping for this he knocked over the others, made a movement to recover them, changed his mind and stood up again with a gesture of resignation.

'Come in,' he repeated, the notes of his voice jarring the piano wires. 'Come in at once.'

Clytie White stepped slowly into the room. She was colourless, her dark eyes looking enormous. The blue-black helmet of her hair was dishevelled and her ugly old-fashioned clothes stood away from her thin body as if she had shrunk within them.

'The Captain has gone on upstairs,' she said so softly that they could hardly hear her.

'Never mind about that.' He closed the door and leant his back against it, lying in a crucified attitude which was certainly unnatural but not consciously affected. His mouth, which in the normal way was pale and inclined to be prim, was now bright and imperfectly controlled. His eyes, which were naked and blind-looking without his thick pebble-glasses, seemed to be very near tears. The ugly honking voice, so much louder than was necessary, came at last.

'Miserable girl!' he said distinctly.

It was pure barnstorming melodrama, absurd in the extreme, and yet disconcerting because of his appalling sincerity. His pain was a living thing in the room.

'You look like my sister when I saw her first.' He was accenting alternate syllables without realizing it, and the halting verse and the hideous voice in conjunction stepped up the reproach to the point of savagery. 'She was pale like you, and pure. Pure like white paper. But she was lying. She was creeping out, slyly to make love in the streets like a drab.'

He was no actor and no Adonis, yet he was terrible rather than ridiculous. Campion sighed. Charlie Luke stirred uneasily.

Clytie stood stiffly in front of her accuser. Her dark eyes were watchful and intelligent, like an experienced child's. She suggested wariness rather than alarm.

'She married my father,' she said unexpectedly. 'Don't you think you may all have made her deceitful, as you have me? I don't *like* making love in the park.'

'Or in the public corridor of a hospital?' His contempt was agonized. 'You do it because you can't help it, I suppose? The itch is in you, is it? Hot hands over the pavement in the yeasty dark, and the shuffle of the curious rustling by. Do you know, you make me retch? God! You disgust me! You disgust me! Do you hear?'

The girl was shaken. She grew paler and her fastidious nose came down over her mouth. The resignation of long-misunderstood youth appeared in the droop of her body.

'Well?'

She met his gaze and a faint irrepressible smile of sheer naughtiness ran across her lips.

'It isn't like that at all,' she said. 'D'you know, I don't believe you know anything about it except what you've read.'

He winced as if she had struck him in the face, and Mr Campion, who had recognized something in his outburst, felt his own eyes growing blank behind his spectacles.

Lawrence was now naturally more angry. He flung himself across the room towards the fireplace.

'And I have read a great deal.' He whipped the envelope off the mantelshelf and thrust it at her. 'Do you deny you wrote this?'

The readiness with which she took it made her astonishment convincing. She glanced at the address in bewilderment.

'Of course I didn't. That's not my handwriting, I hope.'

'Isn't it?' He was leaning towards her in dreadful self-inflicted agony. 'Isn't it? Aren't you responsible for all the unsigned letters which have brought your family this horrible notoriety? Isn't it you who is flinging this stinking mud all over us? Isn't it?'

'No.' As she comprehended the accusation the blood had poured into her face. She was openly frightened of him this time and her eyes were wide and black. 'That's a filthy thing to say.'

'Filthy? My God! My girl, do you know what you write? My God! From what incredible subconscious do you drag such sludge? Read it and then for heaven's sake admit it.'

She stood hesitating, the envelope still in her hand. She was frowning, the queries about his sanity as obvious as if she had spoken them aloud. At last she pulled out the dirty fold of paper and held it unopened.

'Honestly and truly I never saw this before,' she began cheerfully, but as if she knew she had no hope of convincing him. 'I'm telling the literal truth, Uncle Lawrence. I've never seen this before, and really I'm not the sort of person to write anonymous letters. All that stuff about adolescence you've been looking up – can't you see it really doesn't apply to me?'

'Read it, Clytie.' His voice was breaking. 'You've done this thing and you must be made to realize how terrible it is. That is your only chance. You've got to be made to realize.'

She opened the note, glanced at it, and flung it out at arm's length.

'I don't think I want to.' There was more than a touch of Miss Evadne in her dignified disgust. 'Can't you see that you're making a rather beastly mistake? You've absolutely no business to treat me like this. I won't have it. Take this disgusting thing at once or I'll chuck it in the fire.'

'Read it. Read it aloud to me.'

'I won't.'

'Read it.'

Charlie Luke strode swiftly down the room and snapped up the letter from between them. He was thoroughly shocked.

'That'll be quite enough.' He involved a thousand-volt charge into his primness and succeeded in looking like the Angel of the Lord from a modern morality play.

It was typical of Lawrence Palinode that he did not notice that he had not come through the door.

'I did not hear you knock,' he said with dignity. It was, probably, the one remark which could have disconcerted Luke at that particular moment. His mouth opened and closed again without words, but his stare remained piercing and packed with disapproval.

He stood looking at Lawrence for perhaps fifteen seconds before he transferred his attention to Clytie. She was far more startled than her uncle and was inclined to be defiant. Luke's opening gambit took her completely by surprise.

'You've got some walking-out clobber,' he announced, 'togs you've been wearing on the quiet.'

She nodded guiltily.

'Go and put 'em on. It's time you grew out of all this, don't you think?' The wave of his hand embraced family authority and all Lawrence Palinode's literary researches into the mental states attendant on puberty in one comprehensive gesture. 'In my district there are girls of seventeen who've been damned good wives and mothers for eighteen months or more,' he added by way of explanation. There was a gentle reasonableness about him which was always noticeable when he was talking to Clytie. It was as though he understood her so well that their acquaintance was timeless.

She comprehended him perfectly. There was not even gratitude in her grin of relief.

'Oh, you're right, aren't you?' she said. 'Yes, that's what I'll do.'

'Where are you going? Where are you going?' Lawrence started after her, his hand on her shoulder.

She released herself gently, almost kindly.

'To be my age, my dear,' she said. 'I shan't be long.'

He stood looking blankly at the closed door for a moment and then swung round to see Campion in the room for the first time.

CHAPTER 20

Monkey Talk

—

'I'M not at all pleased by this intrusion, you know, not at all pleased.' Lawrence Palinode made a petulant movement with his entire body, counteracted any effect it might have had with his sweet shy smile, and sat down at the desk end of the long table, knocking over a small pot of ink which stood there. He mopped up the mess with a special wedge of blotting paper which he appeared to keep for such emergencies, and continued, the volume of his voice flaring and dying like a faulty loudspeaker.

'I was having a very important talk with a member of my family. Don't exceed your office. You really mustn't do that.' His long red neck swung out at them like a wand with a weight on it. 'You have a letter of mine, Inspector. Hand it back if you please.'

Charlie Luke regarded the sheet of profanity in his hand.

'Do you mean you wrote it?' he inquired bluntly.

The near-sighted eyes widened with interest.

'I? In moments of aberration, I suppose? It's an interesting theory but hardly tenable. No. Give it to me, please. I regard it as a ra-ather important document at this juncture.'

'So do I, sir.' Charlie Luke put the paper in his inside pocket.

Lawrence Palinode's lantern cheeks became patched with colour.

'That's hardly fair,' he protested. 'You have all the others.'

'How do you know?'

'My dear man, this is not quite a *fantoccini*. People do talk to each other and some of them even read the newspapers.'

Luke was sulky and dogged.

'Why did you think this letter came from the same writer if you hadn't seen the others?'

'Oh, but I had. At least I saw the first one and made a note of it. The doctor showed it to me when it arrived. When this one appeared in the post this morning I recognized Madame Pernelle again.'

'Why bring her into it? I thought you were accusing Miss White five minutes ago?'

A shadow of tragedy, irreproachably genuine, passed over his bald face with the underhung jaw, but he had himself well in hand. He emitted a crow, apparently at self-discovery.

'Ah, the Bowl of the Sister!' he exclaimed. 'It's a woman, you see. Probably you don't find that as shattering as I do.' After a pause he shook his head. 'You may be right. Perhaps all I know of her is that she is Madame Pernelle.'

As a statement for police purposes it was hardly satisfactory. The D.D.I.'s heavy brows came down like a thundercloud. He was utterly puzzled and newly irked by remembered frustration.

Mr Campion felt it was time to intervene.

'I don't think we need coax the anima into this,' he murmured, adding outrageously, 'the police are too Jung for it. You don't really know Madame Pernelle either, do you, Chief?'

'Know her? Of course I do!' Luke was furious. 'She keeps a supper bar in Suffolk Street, next door to the church. Poor old duck! She's as big as a barrel and as good as the beer. She can hardly speak English, much less write it. Mr Palinode has made this accusation before and we've been right into it.'

Lawrence sighed and shrugged his ungainly shoulders. Campion sat down and produced cigarettes.

'As I remember, la Pernelle is also a particularly virulent and abusive scold somewhere in Molière,' he remarked presently.

'*La Tartuffe*. A matter of ordinary education.' Lawrence sounded weary. He looked at the D.D.I. with mild exasperation. 'It's very difficult to talk to you.'

'’Strewth!' said Luke under his breath.

'What made you think your niece might have written these letters?' Campion took off his spectacles and became conversational.

'I would rather not answer that.'

Despite Luke's snort of protest, Campion nodded towards the butler's tray.

'Are all those library books?'

'Most of them, unfortunately. My resources don't permit me to buy as many books as I should wish.'

'How long have you had those out?'

'Oh, I see what you mean. Since I read the first anonymous letter. Naturally one wishes to read up a subject before one ventures to attempt anything practical.'

'Naturally.' Campion was grave. 'Forgive me, but have you concentrated entirely on the anonymous letters?'

'Of course.'

'Why?'

The last male Palinode favoured him with another of his delightful smiles.

'Because, as far as I am concerned, that is the only mystery,' he said blithely.

Luke eyed his colleague. Campion seemed perfectly at home.

'I gathered that,' he chatted on affably. 'You washed up *every* glass and cup, you see. Had you concentrated on one we might have been forgiven for arriving at a different conclusion. What put it into your head that your sister had committed suicide?'

Lawrence considered the question with detachment.

'I had not contemplated giving an opinion,' he said at last, 'but it saves a great deal of trouble, you being so well informed. The undertaker saw me, I suppose? Well, Ruth was extravagant and had mortgaged her little income. My sister Evadne and I broke our rule of non-interference and taxed her with it. She went to bed very upset and died the following day. She was quite incapable of controlling her expenditure.'

'Do you mean she liked to gamble?'

He raised his eyebrows. 'You know so much I don't see why you've not seen the perfectly obvious before.'

'Where did she get the poison?'

He lay back in his chair, striking an attitude so casual as to be unsafe.

'That really is something for you to find out. I know nothing of any details.'

'Why did you wash up the glasses and cups in her room?'

He hesitated. 'I don't know,' he said at last. 'Frankly I went up because the good woman who looks after us here seemed to expect it. I stood looking at Ruth and reflecting that it was unfortunate that she had inherited the strangely faulty mathematical streak which there is in our family. And at that moment it occurred to me that she must have poisoned herself. I rinsed the vessels in her room, because, I suppose, I didn't want anyone else to pick up anything dangerous by mistake.'

'That be hanged for a tale!' Luke's credulity snapped with a bang. 'Are you saying you thought your sister poisoned herself and you didn't do anything about it, yet as soon as the doctor came in with an anonymous letter you went up like a heath-fire?'

Lawrence ignored him. 'It was the first document of the kind I had seen,' he remarked to Campion. 'The extraordinary hatred in it had a psychological effect upon me. Extraordinarily interesting! I was fascinated, in a literal sense. I don't know if you've ever experienced that?'

Campion did understand him perfectly and there was a hint of apology in his next question.

'Am I to believe that the result of your investigations so far is that your niece wrote these things?'

Lawrence turned his head away.

'If you overheard my conversation with her you must know,' he said.

'Have you any evidence at all?'

He turned back at once, his face flushing.

'My dear sir, my inquiries are my own affair. You can hardly expect me to give you the benefit of them, especially if they concern my own family.'

Campion was silent for some moments.

'I wonder if I might point out that the process of elimination has its dangers?' he ventured at last.

Lawrence lost his anger like a surprised child recovering from tears.

'You think so, do you?' he demanded with interest,

Campion remained serious. 'The young are always mysterious,' he remarked. 'Even when one feels that one can be reasonably sure of everyone else, they alone remain an enigma.'

Luke could bear it no longer.

'What has that got to do with it?'

Lawrence answered him.

'In words of one syllable, when I had made sure in my own mind that no one else in the house *could* have written the letters, I turned to the one person I did not really know. I observed that she had a secret of some sort.' His face became rigid with disgust. 'I did not know then what it was.'

'Who unravelled that ghastly mystery for you?' Luke's amusement was ferocious. 'The Captain came out with it, I suppose?'

'Yes. I was speaking to him on another matter and he told me. He put it very crudely. I didn't believe him and I made him take me to the hospital where this wretched boy is lying, and there we – we found Clytie.'

He looked as though the memory was going to make him physically sick, and once more Mr Campion took charge.

'I don't see why you confine your suspicions to the house.'

'Oh, but that was obvious.' Lawrence rose, upsetting papers and books as his heavy, loose-jointed fingers unfolded. 'I've gone *over* and *over* this,' he declared, his peculiar voice blaring on the emphasized words. 'It's the *internal* evidence one can't get away from.' He shambled over to the chest in the bay of the window.

'I've got a copy of the original letter here somewhere.' He jerked the drawer out much too far and spilled assorted papers out over the parquet.

'Forget it.' Luke was showing signs of strain. 'I know it by heart.'

'Do you?' Lawrence was weaving helplessly above the unholy muddle on the floor.

'I could recite it this minute,' the D.D.I. assured him with feeling. 'The first piece, anyway. I don't remember any internal evidence.'

'It was that remark about the flowers.' Lawrence took a nervous step towards him. 'Do you remember? After a stream of calumny against the doctor for his "blindness to murder foul and dirty" it went on, "even the lilies cart-wheeled and should have told any but a fool".'

The intensity of disgust which he infused into the quotation betrayed the shocked excitement which the letters had for him. This sin against the precious written word had in his cosmos an evil all its own.

Luke was deeply interested. 'I remember it,' he agreed. 'When did the cut flowers cart-wheel?'

'Just before the funeral, and no one was in the hall then but the household. No stranger. Even the undertakers hadn't arrived.'

'They were in a wreath, perhaps?' suggested Campion, who felt that the story needed a midwife.

'Of course they were.' He seemed anxious to explain. 'You see, someone bought a wreath – not a member of the family. We are not demonstrative. The actor Grace, who spends much of his time with our pleasant Miss Roper, sent it, I believe. I understand it was left leaning against the wall at the head of the stairs. In the morning most of the household happened to be in the hall. We were waiting for the undertakers to begin the funeral. I was not going myself; I had some work to finish. But my sisters felt they should put in an appearance. We were all present, even the aged nymph who chars for Miss Roper, when suddenly something dislodged the obsolete panache and it slid over the edge of the top stair. It was supported by the wall and it came rolling down over and over, scattering petals. It was a ridiculous incident, but I remember the charwoman's scream. Miss Roper ran forward and caught it and straightened it out as best she could.'

'What did she do with it then?' Charlie Luke had been listening to the recital with that mixture of suspicion and anticipation usually reserved for the improper story.

'Oh, put it on a chair, I think. Certainly, a little tousled, it rested on the coffin when they set out.' He shrugged his shoulders. 'It was quite unimportant and yet it is clearly referred to in the letter. It was that which so horrified me. These obscene communications came from amongst us. The hidden lunacy is here.' He shuddered unaffectedly and his eyes were shocked and vulnerable. 'It is a very terrible thing. You must be able to see that.'

Luke remained unimpressed. 'I don't think you've any proof against Miss White,' he said. 'That's just the sort of rum little tale people repeat. Someone who was there told it to someone who wasn't; that's all that means.'

Lawrence's expression grew slowly appalled. His face became crimson with shame and revulsion.

'You mean they wrote them together – Clytie and that depraved young man?'

'No, sir, I do not. Can't you leave your niece out of it? You haven't a shred of evidence against her. Anybody who saw the wreath roll down the stairs could have told absolutely anybody else. The char may have an auntie who goes in for fancy correspondence. Miss Roper may have chatted in the meat queue.'

'That I should never believe. Miss Roper is a most superior person.'

Charlie Luke drew a deep breath but decided not to defend himself or Renee. Instead he said abruptly:

'Why were you watching Captain Seton in the street out here at two o'clock in the morning of the day before yesterday?'

If he hoped to surprise he was unlucky.

'That was quite infuriating.' The goose-voice was placid. 'I heard someone creep past this door and I assumed it was Clytie. She was on my mind because I had had words with her before, that evening. I did not realize she had come into the house, and when at my sister's suggestion I Cawnthroped I found she was. She resented my interference.'

'By "Cawnthroped" you mean "looked", do you?' Campion suggested hastily as Luke's dark face showed promise of becoming black.

'Oh yes. Foolish of me. A family reference you could hardly have been expected to know, although it appears in *Elegant Extracts* in the third edition.' He went over to a bookcase and returned with a volume. 'Mornington Cawnthrope was a kinsman of my mother's father. Here is the reference.'

' "Archdeacon Cawnthrope, on losing his spectacles, was requested by his wife to look in a mirror and see them. 'Ah, that I cannot do,' quoth the Archdeacon, 'for if I *look* I shall not *see*.' 'Yet if you do not look,' replied the lady, 'I declare you will not *descry* them, for they are on your nose all the time.' " '

He closed the book.

'We always thought that very amusing,' he said.

Mr Campion cast a sly glance at Luke and was glad he had come. The policeman was looking at Lawrence earnestly and the expression in his eyes was unfathomable.

'You say you thought you heard Miss White creep past this door very early that morning,' he said at last.

'Oh yes, I did.' Lawrence put down the book with regret. 'I followed her and I stood watching her as best I could, but it was very unsatisfactory.' He smiled with charming self-depreciation. 'You see, I'm practically blind in the dark. I was made to look foolish when she returned at last and it was merely Captain Seton who had gone to post a letter.'

Luke sighed. 'Did you see if he met anyone on the road by the postbox?'

Lawrence smiled again. 'I couldn't see anything at all,' he said.

'Did he tell you he'd gone to post a letter?'

'No, I assumed it. All he told me on that occasion when I reached him in the hall was that his name was not Clytie.'

'When did you obtain from him the legacy left him by Miss Ruth Palinode?'

The words were spoken quietly enough but their effect was remarkable. Lawrence Palinode shambled backwards, treading on his own feet and all but over-balancing.

'Who gave you that information?' he demanded in tremendous excitement. 'Oh, I see. You guessed it from that letter. Yes, it was in there. That was why I tackled Seton this afternoon. I thought he must have told Clytie – if she was writing the dreadful things, I mean.'

He was incoherent and his hands were shaking.

'That letter accuses me of robbing him, which is ridiculous. I gave him five pounds, a lot of money, for something "not Peru".'

'South American stock, was it?' Luke was still doing his best.

Lawrence looked at him as if he thought he had gone mad.

'I don't think so. All I remember is that they were shares in somebody's mine, and were, as I told you, perfectly worthless. Our solicitor told my sister so. She left them to Seton to annoy him, since he is notoriously short of money. That was her form of humour, not very enlightened. I bought them from him some weeks ago as soon as he received them. He's not one of the family and I felt it my duty to see he was not victimized. It is all very well to joke at the right moment, but I thought that tasteless of Ruth.'

He made his explanation with spirit but not frankness. Luke remained dubious.

'Where are they now?'

'I have them safe.'

'Would you sell them again for a fiver?'

'Certainly not.' He was uneasy and was taking refuge in a display of irritation. 'They were part of the family inheritance.'

Mr Campion, who had been sitting quietly for some moments, looked up.

'Perhaps you have already sold them?'

'I have not sold them.' There was an unexpected quality of obstinacy in his denial. 'They are still in my possession. I shall always refuse to sell them. Have you finished your interrogation, Inspector?'

Luke touched Campion's shoulder. 'Okay,' he said briskly. 'You'll remain in the house, won't you, Mr Palinode? Meanwhile we'll go up, shall we, sir?'

Lawrence pitched himself untidily into his chair before the desk and upset yet another inkpot.

'Close the door behind you if you please,' he said over his shoulder, as he mopped up for the second time. 'You're going up to plague Seton now, I suppose. May one ask what for?'

Charlie Luke winked at Campion.

'We're going to take a butcher's hook at him,' he said happily.

CHAPTER 21

Homework

—

CHARLIE Luke poured the last of the water over the Captain's grey and nodding head.

'Hopeless,' he said succinctly and sat back on his heels. 'The old nitwhisker's had it. Must have drunk the bottle without counting. He'll have to sleep that lot off before we get a peep out of him.'

He nodded to the young detective who had been assisting him and together they lifted the old man on to his narrow bed. Mr Campion surveyed an unregenerate scene. Ever since he and Luke had come in, to find the Captain lying in his armchair, a corkscrew and an almost empty whisky bottle at his feet, a glass clutched to his military bosom, and the noise of trumpets issuing from his open mouth, the process of disarrangement had continued.

The young detective, arriving providentially with a message for Luke, had responded to the emergency with experience and enthusiasm. Luke, too, had his private methods of reviving the alcoholic, but the old Captain had defeated them.

Faced with the embarrassing, he had taken refuge in his secret bottle, hoarded carefully in the old leather hatbox, and it had not let him down. At the moment he was away somewhere, temporarily safe from the sordid present.

Charlie Luke stood at the end of the bed, his chin thrust out and his dark face gloomy.

'Silly old basket,' he said without animosity. 'He gave me the cold horribles when I saw him. I thought he'd done a Pa Wilde on me. I don't entirely care for everybody's grandpa taking knock-out drops the moment I put my nose in.'

It occurred to Campion that he needed reassurance.

'I feel it may be Renee that he's frightened of, don't you?'

'Renee?' Luke glanced round the dismantled room. 'Lumme! I shall be the enemy there. Clean up a bit while you keep an eye on him, Pollit, will you? We'll be just across the landing.'

He led the way to Campion's room.

'There's a letter for you from the Super,' Luke said, throwing it across, 'and a couple of memos for me from Porky at the station. Now what? Di-dah, di-dah, di-dah – huh!'

He read, as he did everything else, with a great deal of action. The type-written sheets of blue paper vibrated like live things in his hands, and when they flapped over were as wild as washing on a line.

Campion opened his own envelope and he was still engrossed when the D.D.I. rose and moved the blind an inch or so.

'There's still a crowd,' he said. He came back at last to sit by Campion again. 'I don't like this situation,' he said. 'No one's making any money out of it. Not real money. I'm talking about Jas's lark. That's not right.'

He spread out his memorandum sheets again.

'Pa Wilde was in debt all round; owed the wholesalers, the gas company, and the bank. We've been over everything, and if he was paid for whatever he was doing he certainly didn't hoard it, pay his bills with it, or, as far as we can see, even eat with it. The doctor's report here says "undernourished". Poor old blighter! I liked him because he was so bloody, if you see what I mean.'

'Blackmail?' Campion suggested.

'Seems so.' Charlie Luke shook his head. 'May have done anything in his time. He was a chemist, wasn't he?' He tipped the contents of an imaginary bottle into the ghost of a glass. 'May once have slipped somebody the wrong dope or tried to get a girl out of trouble. Either of those would have given someone a hold over him. I've been to his shop for a chat dozens of times in the past year, but that was the first occasion when he wrote himself off because of it.'

Campion coughed discreetly.

'One can't help feeling he was involved in something reasonably serious, don't you think?' he suggested.

'Maybe.' The subject appeared to rankle with Luke.

'Then there's that couple of worm-shovellers over the road,' he went on more hopefully. 'We're taking them to pieces now. I beg your pardon, perhaps you've got something there?'

He looked so wistfully at Campion's letter that its owner was sorry to disappoint him.

'Nothing constructive at all, I'm afraid,' he said truthfully. 'I asked a few questions and in almost every case the answer is, vaguely, no. Looky Jeffreys died in the prison infirmary before disclosing anything more about Apron Street save that he did not want to go up it. He was arrested while committing a singularly inefficient burglary, which he is thought to have undertaken alone.'

'That's ruddy helpful.'

'I inquired about Bella Musgrave. She and her two old sisters keep a little dyeing and cleaning agency in Stepney. At the moment she is away from home. Her sisters do not know where she is and they expect her back at any moment. Then there's this.' Campion took three closely-typed sheets from the rest. 'I asked if the chemistry boys could tell us if hyoscine could be obtained from henbane by an amateur. This is their report. Yeo seems to have translated it for us on the bottom here.'

Luke screwed up his eyes to see the pencilled note.

'"*This would appear to mean no,*"' he read aloud and sniffed. 'Everybody's helping and nothing's moving, as the donkey said to the barn door.'

Luke closed his eyes. 'That chap Lawrence is behaving peculiarly and he certainly can't talk straight. But do you know what I think about him?' He opened them again and stared seriously at Campion. 'I don't believe he could kill pussy,' he said. 'Come in – oh, it's you, George. Mr Campion, this is Sergeant Picot. He's been over at Bowels's. Any luck, George?'

The newcomer exuded reliability and respect for the law and the rights of the citizen as some men exude just the opposite.

'Evening, sir; evening, sir.' He got the greetings over with bird-swiftness. 'Well, we've seen them both. We've been over the premises again and we've taken a thorough look at the books. I can't find anything wrong.' He looked the Chief Inspector severely in the eye. 'It seems a very nicely run business.'

Luke nodded. In dejection he was as picturesque as at the height of exuberance. His shoulders were hunched and some of the life seemed to have vanished even from his hair.

'Mr Campion wondered if he had imported a body lately, collected it for relatives for burial here.'

'They've done nothing of the kind since nineteen-thirty. Undertaking isn't the ideal business for hanky-panky. There are so many checks, registrars' certificates and so on. Frankly, I don't see why he should be employed to smuggle anything. Whatever the stuff was, once it was here I should have thought a lorry would have served the purpose better. No one notices goods delivered by a lorry, but everyone takes a bit of a look at a coffin.' He shook his head. 'I don't see the point of it.'

'Don't you, George?' Luke was grinning savagely to himself. 'You didn't see the casket with the gold whatnots?'

'No, sir.' Picot folded back his notebook as he spoke. 'I inspected four ornamented caskets all in light wood. Mr Bowels, snr, admitted to removing a coffin from a cellar he rented in this house, but says he used it for a job in Lansbury Terrace. We can get a description from witnesses, but for proof we'll have to apply for an exhumation order. I didn't think you'd feel like doing that, sir, especially as nothing seems to turn on it.'

Luke grimaced at Campion.

'What about this hotel work of Bowels's?'

'The grand piano top, sir?' Picot frowned. 'He was very frank about it. It happened over a year ago. The piano top belonged to the Balsamic Hotel, not to him, and he boxed the corpse very decently as soon as he got it to his place. He has one shed done out as a sort of private mortuary. It's all above board, known to the authorities and so on.'

'What did he carry it in? Has he got a truck?' Campion put the question curiously.

'No, sir. These are his vehicles.' Picot's notebook was in use again. 'There's two hearses, one better than the other, both horse-drawn. It's not a wealthy district, you see, and the locals take their dying seriously. They're conservative about horses at funerals. For weddings they like a car. Then there's two mourning coaches; if they need more they have to hire limousines. And there's the coffin brake. That's the lot. They have four horses, all black. Three are well past their best, but the fourth is a young one.'

'Have you seen all this?'

'Yes, sir. Patted the horses.'

'What's a coffin brake? That rather sinister affair that looks rather like an ebony cigar box on wheels? I haven't seen one of those since I was a child.'

'Haven't you, sir?' Picot conveyed that it was the eminent visitor's loss. 'People round here like the coffin delivered in one of those. Seems to make it more respectful not to have the hearse call twice. The Bowelses have a very good one, old but in fine repair. Nice high box-seat for the driver. It looks very decent coming along. There is one other point I feel I should mention: all the time we spent with Mr Bowels, snr, the old gentleman was sweating like a pig. He was open in his answers and we could not find a thing out of place. He was helpful, took us everywhere without a murmur, and he was polite to a fault, but he did sweat.'

'And what do you deduce from that? That he'd got a cold?' Charlie Luke was more tired than a man could be.

'No, sir.' Picot was reproachful. 'I gathered that he was frightened stiff. I don't know why. I shall mention it in my report, of course. Good night, sir.'

The D.D.I. reached for his hat.

'I tink I go home,' he said. 'Miss Ruth has been poisoned, Clytie's boy friend has been slugged, Pa Wilde has done himself in, the Captain has put himself out, Jas is innocent but sweating, and we're just exactly where we always were. Cawdblimiah! We don't even know who wrote the poison-pen letters.'

'Oh,' said Mr Campion, 'that reminds me, I didn't give you back that last letter the doctor received. I had a little thought about that.' He took the wretched sheet from his coat pocket and spread it out on the coverlet beside him. The second passage which had interested him was near the end. He read it aloud.

' ". . . Am watching you who are to blame for all trouble and misery god know amen *glass tells all don't forget* . . ." '

His lazy eyes met Luke's own. 'I've come across that before, once,' he said. 'That communicative glass sometimes means a crystal. Got any practising clairvoyants in the district?'

Luke sat down abruptly, his hat hanging from one bony wrist.

'I was thinking about the Captain and the woman he was waiting for by the pillarbox,' Campion went on slowly. 'That old boy wears a small emerald in a comparatively new ring. It is a peculiar stone for a consciously masculine lad of his period, but Renee tells me his birthday is in May, and my Girl Guide's diary says that to be lucky those born in May should wear green, preferably emeralds. He's a self-centred man, a poor man, and a man with a lot of time.' He eyed Luke, who was staring at him. 'No one gets to hear so much from her clients as a clairvoyant. I can imagine a silly, very slightly sexy association between a chap like that and some crazy half-vicious woman between fifty and sixty whom he visits, and to whom he blabs his own and everybody else's business. When the balloon went up arid the letters were generally discussed, he must have suspected her. There may have been a quarrel.

She may have threatened to post one under his own window. I don't know. When Lawrence tackled him about the letter he certainly lost his head.'

Luke sat perfectly still. He looked as if he were genuinely petrified. When he spoke it was very softly.

'I ought to resign on this. You might have known her.'

'Do you?'

'Slightly.' He rose, still regarding the other man with a sort of shocked respect. 'I even knew that he visited her once. One of my chaps mentioned that he'd seen him coming out of her house. That was in the very beginning of the case. I didn't think another thing about it. You've got it from cold and I had all the aids and missed it.'

'Perhaps I'm wrong.' Mr Campion seemed taken aback by the violence of his success. 'It has been known.'

'Not on your life!' Charlie Luke had come alive again. In minutes he had become twice as forceful and ten years younger. 'That's the gal all right. Calls herself Pharaoh's Daughter. She gives readings for a tanner a time and we never bothered her under the Act because she seemed so harmless.'

He was concentrating, dragging the picture from the depths of his remarkable memory.

'Oh, yes!' he said with tremendous conviction. 'Yes! That's her. Her real name is – let me think – Miss – Miss – Godalmighty!' His eyes widened. 'D'you know who she is, Campion? Yes! She's his sister, dammit! Must be. His sister! She's Miss Congreve, Old Bloblip's sister at the bank. Oh God! don't let me die before I get down there!'

He was so excited that he had not heard the persistent tapping at the door. It was suddenly opened and a delighted, if inopportune, Clytie White appeared on the threshold. Unaware that she had arrived at a moment of crisis, she stood looking in at Luke, half anxious, half ecstatic. She was in all her glory. A skin-tight bodice revealed the charm of her young bosom. A mighty skirt spread out in exaggerated folds. A spotted scarf tied in a doubtful bow made her look like a dressed-up kitten, and a modern boater sat squarely and fashionably on her newly dressed hair.

'Well?' she demanded, and her voice was breathless.

Charlie Luke paused in his flight to duty. Campion had never respected him more. He stood surveying her earnestly, his eyes narrowed, the whole force of his pile-driver personality concentrated on her problem.

'I tell you what,' he said at last. 'Take off the scarf and I'll take you to the pictures Sunday.'

CHAPTER 22

Slip-knots

—

WHEN Charlie Luke finally returned it was morning on the day of Miss Evadne's revel. Campion was still in bed, but not asleep.

He had awakened with a query. It had been thrown, complete and vital, by his subconscious mind in sleep, and the more he considered it the more obvious and elementary it became.

He saw by his watch that it was close on a quarter to seven. At the same time he became aware that the house was not only stirring, but that some upheaval was taking place. He slid into a dressing-gown and opened his door, to meet an offensive of strange odours which suggested that Miss Jessica had been cooking again. He paid little attention to it, for on the other side of the landing Miss Roper was smacking Charlie Luke's face. She was as angry as a disturbed sitting hen.

Charlie Luke, grey with weariness but still remarkably good-tempered, picked her up by the elbows and held her kicking a foot or so from the floor.

'Come on, Auntie,' he said, 'be a good girl or I'll have to send a real policeman with a helmet to you.'

Miss Roper let herself grow limp and he set her down, but she still barred his way.

'One of your young men has been with him all night, and Clarrie and I have had a dreadful morning with him. Now he's asleep and you're not to wake him; he's an ill man.'

'I bet he is, but I've got to see him.'

Renee caught sight of Campion, whom she hailed as a deliverer.

'Oh, ducky,' she said, 'make this stupid boy see a little reason. The Captain's had an accident. He doesn't often do it, but when he does it's enough to kill him. Charlie's got a crazy idea he's been writing anonymous letters, which is one thing he wouldn't do, that I will say for him – though I could wring his wicked old neck for him this minute. I've got him to sleep and he won't be fit to speak to for hours. Do make him leave him alone. He can't stand, much less run away.'

A dismal sound from the room behind her confirmed her diagnosis and her small brown body fluttered like a bird's.

'Oh, run along do!' she said to Luke. 'If he's been up to anything you shall make him answer for it as soon as he's half-way to being himself. I know him. He'd admit to anything now just to get a minute of peace.'

Luke hesitated and she pushed him before her.

'Oh, I have got a day,' she said bitterly. 'There's all this to clean up, the boy's coming from hospital at noon and has to go straight to bed, and then there's this damn silly party. Evadne's asked half London by all accounts. Take Mr Luke into your room, Albert, and I'll send you both up a bit of breakfast.'

Another and more violent groan from the stricken warrior made the D.D.I.'s mind up for him.

'I'll give him half an hour,' he said, and then, catching Campion's eye, raised both thumbs in an expressive gesture. 'Right on the target,' he said as he closed the bedroom door after them and turned his head away resolutely from the one comfortable chair. 'I hand it to you.'

Mr Campion seemed pleased. 'Is the lady in the bag?'

'In the cells, crying all over the floor.' Luke shook himself expressively. 'We've had her on the carpet most of the night and now the whole station's wet. Funny thing, she was explicit enough on paper but we couldn't get a word out of her except, "Oh, my God!" for close on three hours.' He yielded to the chair's invitation as he spoke and propped his lids open.

'Did she admit it?'

'Yes. We found the paper, the ink and the envelopes, as well as a sample of the disguised handwriting on a bit of blotting paper. But she wouldn't come across until dawn. Just sat there like a bull frog.' He blew out his cheeks, lowered his brows, and made himself a high-corseted bust with his hands. Then she broke like an egg. We heard all about the dear Captain. He was so helpless and put upon. He touched her heart and moved her to do what she knew she didn't ought, having been brought up very different. How do these old boys do it? Pull out their empty pockets and cry?'

He wriggled himself more deeply into the cushions and made an attempt to keep his eyes at least half open.

'To do him justice, she's misleading. I don't suppose he had the faintest idea what he was stirring up under that mumbo-jumbo-I-see-all exterior. He probably just rambled on, trying to make himself interesting.'

'Ah,' said Mr Campion, 'and how did you get on with her brother?'

Luke frowned. 'We slipped up over Bloblip,' he admitted. 'As she opened the front door to us he slid out of the back. We shall collect him in the end, of course, but meanwhile it's annoying.'

'Was her letter-writing his idea?'

The red-rimmed eyes flickered wide at the new suggestion.

'I – shouldn't – think so. There was no hint of it. No, I think Psychic Phoeb was just letting out her own stays. That's what's so peeving. Usually in these affairs, once you do get a genuine lead the whole thing comes unravelling out like Auntie's jumper. But this just takes us to an evil-minded old blossom with a schoolgirl crush on the Captain and a grievance against the doc. He snubbed her, by the way. That sticks out a mile, although all she'll say is that she used to go to him for her stomach, but stopped. He *is* a bit short with hysterical patients, I've heard that before. The whole thing's practically a dead end, isn't it?'

'I wonder. It's extraordinary she should have been right. She accused the doctor of overlooking a murder and he had. That's pretty good going for mere spite.'

Luke was not satisfied. 'She got it from the Captain. That's why I want to talk to him myself. He may have said more than he knew. You know how it is when a chap comes pouring out his troubles twice a week. He forgets what he said last time; you don't. She got the idea out of him. What would Bloblip know about what went on over here?'

Mr Campion did not argue but began to dress.

'When does Miss Congreve come up before the Magistrate? Do you want to be there?'

'Ten. And Porky can see to her. She'll get bail. Anything I can do for you?'

Campion grinned. 'If I might advise it, I should take an hour or two's sleep in my bed. By the time you wake, the Captain may be almost intelligent if not affable. Meanwhile I should like to follow up a night-thought of my own. Where shall I find the local coroner's office?'

The final question cut short Luke's protest. He was too well trained to ask a direct question, but he sat up at once, alert and curious.

'Twenty-five, Barrow Road,' he said promptly. 'I've got several chaps released for duty now, though. No need to do your own homework.'

Campion's tousled head appeared through his shirt.

'Don't give it another thought,' he said. 'I may so easily be wrong.'

He had breakfasted by a few minutes before nine and he came hurrying down the front steps to find only Mrs Love and her pail barring his way. She wore a sky-blue coif and a white overall for morning, and was gaily arch as usual.

'Company today,' she shouted, winking a rheumy eye at him and adding in a whisper, which was like a fall of sand, 'there's a lot coming because of the crime. I say there's a lot coming because of the crime.' She laughed like an evil child, light-hearted mischief in her rosy face. 'Don't fergit the party. Come back in time. I say come back in time.'

'Oh, I'll be in long before that,' he assured her, and plunged out into the misty sunshine.

Yet he was mistaken. His call took him far into the morning and its consequence was a series of further visits. These were delicate encounters, demanding all the tact in his not inconsiderable store. Relatives were tracked and questioned, next-of-kin located but not confirmed; but, by the time the setting sun had achieved a blood-red Apron Street, he came striding down it with new excitement in his step.

His first impression on catching sight of the house was that it must be on fire. The crowd had grown. Corkerdale, reinforced by two uniformed men, was holding the gate and garden walls, while the front door at the top of the steps stood wide and tantalizing. Miss Evadne's conversazione had begun.

Inside, the atmosphere was tremendous. An air of hospitality had been achieved by the simple method of leaving all the doors open. Someone – Campion suspected Clarrie – had fixed an old brass four-pronged candlestick on the flat top of the newel-post. The candles guttered in the draught and there was rather a lot of tallow about, one way and another. But the general effect was not ungay.

No sooner had his foot touched the mat than Renee bobbed out at him from the drawing-room. She was unexpectedly magnificent in solid black, save for a small white silk afternoon tea apron adorned with rosebuds. He thought at first that her histrionic instinct had prompted her to dress up as a stage housekeeper, but her first words corrected him.

'Oh, it's you, dear,' she said, catching his arm. 'Thank God for someone with a mite of respectability. I'm the only one in the house who's remembered to put on a speck of mourning. It's not that they're heartless, but they're so busy thinking they don't have time to think, if you see what I mean.'

'Perfectly. It suits you. You look lovely.'

She laughed at him, the sun coming out in her worried eyes.

'You wicked boy!' she said. 'There's no time for that kind of talk now. I wish there were. I say, Albert' – she lowered her voice and peered down the hall – 'is all this true about the police now knowing who they want and flinging out a net and closing in on them?'

'I hadn't heard it,' he said curiously.

'Well, you've been out all day, haven't you? I think you'll find it's right. Clarrie told me not to tell a soul, and I shan't, of course, but there's dozens more police about, just watching, waiting for the word.'

'What a pity no one gives it.'

'It's nothing to laugh at, dear. They've got to have proof, haven't they? Oh, I shall be glad when it's all over, however horrible the shock is, and I've had a few. Look at my old Captain! – sneaking out to have his fortune told and play handy-pandy with a – well, I won't demean myself, Albert, but really! – an old haybag. She'd make fifteen of me. She put the fear of God into him by writing the letters. He must have known. He swears he didn't, the old liar, but as I told him, I may have kept my figure, but I wasn't born yesterday.'

She was very militant and utterly feminine. Her eyes were flashing like an angry girl's.

'Of course he's sick and sorry now,' she said, 'and one can't help forgiving him, but when he took his dying oath that he didn't even guess it was her until she admitted it, and had the cheek to threaten to post one to Lawrence in the box outside the house, well, I could have given him a fourpenny one! When he found Lawrence was right on the track, he sneaked up the stairs in a blue funk and put himself clean out with a bottle I didn't even know he had. I could kill him, I could really.'

Campion laughed. 'What are you doing now?' he inquired. 'Watching to see he doesn't get out?'

'Ducky, he can't stand!' Her chuckle was barely malicious. 'He's very penitent, tucked up waiting to be waited on. No, I'm just standing here catching old pals as they go upstairs. It's just to tell them that Clarrie's got a bit of a bar going down in the kitchen. There's a little gin and plenty of beer. You go up and talk for a bit, but don't drink anything, especially that yellow stuff they're serving in the glasses. She makes it with groundsel and it has a funny effect. When you've had enough uplift come down to the basement. I can't have friends treated to nothing when they come to the house.'

He thanked her and smiled down at her with genuine affection. The evening light was streaming through the doorway directly on to her face, picking out the contours of the delicate bones under her wrinkled skin. As he turned to go upstairs his glance travelled through the open doorway of Lawrence's room to the chimney-piece. He stared at it for a moment and then looked at her again, a startled expression on his pale face.

Another knot in the tangle pulled smoothly out as he watched it and her hitherto incomprehensible place in the household was suddenly explained and made rational. He took a chance.

'Renee, I believe I know why you do all this.'

The moment he had spoken he knew it was a mistake. Her face grew bleak and her eyes secretive.

'Do you, dear?' There was a warning in the edge of her tone. 'Don't be too clever, will you? See you in the kitchen.'

'As you like,' he murmured, and hurried on, well aware that as she looked after him she was not smiling.

CHAPTER 23

Vive la Bagatelle!

—

HALF-WAY across the wide landing Mr Lugg paused, tray in hand.

'Care for a baked meat?' he inquired, displaying five water-biscuits on a fine china plate, and turned to jerk his head towards Miss Evadne's room. 'Old Poisoners' Association beano in there. What 'o! Coffins at eight!'

Mr Campion considered him with interest.

'What are you doing, exactly?'

' 'Elping, cock. I come round looking for you and the old girl with the voice like a beak persuaded me to 'and round. She see at once that I could do it. It's very funny muck I'm pushing out, but I've took a fancy to 'er.'

'Who's this? Miss Evadne?'

'The elder Miss P. We ain't on Christian-name terms yet. "You're dirt and can't 'ardly understand what I am a-sayin' of, but I 'appens to like you." That's the sort she is.'

He appeared a little shamefaced.

'Appealin',' he said, 'especially when you know you could buy 'er at one end of the street and sell 'er at the other. They call it charm.'

'Do they? Did you get anything from Thos?'

'Not a lot. Come in 'ere a minute. This is your room, ain't it? I thought I reckernized your old 'alf comb on the fancy dressin' table.' He closed the door safely behind them. 'I only got a few pickin's,' he went on, lowering his voice discreetly. 'Thos isn't reelly in the business now. He's almost respectable. Nearly works.'

'I know. It's the curse of the age. Did you find out about going up Apron Street?'

'I picked up one little thing. Goin' up Apron Street used to be a bit of a joke until about a year ago and then suddenly it wasn't any more.'

'Wasn't it mentioned after that?'

'Not exackly.' Lugg spoke with unwonted seriousness and his small black eyes were puzzled. 'Since then they've bin afraid of it. The London boys are proper lily on it if you arst me. I did what you said and tried for a name, but the only bloke I could 'ear of 'oo actually said 'e was goin' up Apron Street was a finger called Ed Geddy, one 'o the West Street mob. Thos says 'e was stewed at the time and in trouble anyway, and 'e shot orf 'is mouth in the Garter in Paul's Lane. 'E was chaffed about it and cleared out in a bit of a temper and 'asn't bin seen since. I don't know if you know it, cock, but the West Street mob specializes in smokes. Remember that job the police fell down on, dead girl in kiosk? (she won't say "no" again). They were in that. Mean anythin' to you?'

'Not a lot,' Campion admitted, but he was still thoughtful. 'The kiosk hold-up and murder was about a year ago, but I don't quite see Apron Street as the tobacco road. Anything else?'

'I looked up Peter George Jelf an' 'is little lorry. 'E's got a two-man business in Fletchers Town. Calls 'imself a 'aulage contractor and 'is new name is P. Jack. It was 'im at the chemist's the other day all right. 'E seems to be doin' quietly but nicely, and all sweet and respectable as kiss your 'and. It's not a lot, I admit, but there's 'is address and the police can take him apart at their perishin' leisure. That's about the lot, I think, excep' for the piece of resistance I've bin keepin' to last . . . The coffin's back.'

'What!'

'Startled yer?' demanded Mr Lugg with intense satisfaction. 'It did me. When I first found you wasn't 'ere this afternoon I dropped in on brother-in-law Jas. Bein' one of the family I didn't knock, but come in through the back and nosed round the 'ouse lookin' for 'im. The carpenter's shop is in a little yard. Used to be a gardin for the dustbins. Very private. There's a winder in the shed, and as I could see the door was shut I took the liberty of lookin' in. They was both there, bendin' over the thing. Seemed to be unpackin' of it. Couldn't miss it. Black as a pianner. Got as much gold on it as a commissionaire's trousers. But I tell you one thing, it was packed flat.'

'Really!' Mr Campion was gratifyingly amazed. 'Are you sure?'

'Take me davy on it. It was folded up like one of them screens in drorin' rooms. I come quietly away.'

'D'you mean it had hinges?'

'Might 'er 'ad. Didn't see. There was sackin' round it, and a narrer packin' case I reckon it come outer stood beside it. I didn't take mor'n a look. When you're dealin' with Jas you want a warrant and an eel-'ook. I thought I'd do more 'arm than good. Besides, I'm a bit late, aren't I? All right, don't cough up if you don't want to.' The husky voice betrayed deep resentment. 'I've bin give to understand that this 'ere problem is about to pack up.'

'Oh?'

'It's news to you, is it?' Lugg said, brightening. 'Oh, it came to me all cut and dried. Our noble bluebottles, 'oo are certainly spread all over the district like relations at a weddin', are casting a net. They know 'oo they want and are just about to make their well-known pounce – fallin' flat on their kissers if the bloke sidesteps.'

'Who says so?'

'Every blinkin' person I've spoke to except the police theirselves. Little clever's still in a black-out, is 'e? That's a nice change for yer. Well, let's go back to the blow-out. You may pick up somethin' there. You don't want to miss it, cock,' he added seriously. 'Somethink from another world, this is. Make up yer mind what you're goin' ter 'ave, cup o' yerba mat or a small nettle hot. There's a ration of somethink else as well, smells as if it come out o' the flowers in the 'all. There's not a lot of call for that.'

He paused, a hand on the door. He was only partially amused.

'Get an eyeful of my old girl,' he said. 'She's worf it. She's got one stockin' 'arf down, nothin' in her cupboard but an empty sherry bottle. 'Er sis 'as bin done in and most of the visitors 'ave only come to 'ear more about it. And she's offerin' filth-and-cheese-biscuits to people 'oo've got their minds well on poisonin' to start with. Yet if 'Is Grace and Lady Godiva come in instead of me she wouldn't be surprised, much less took aback. It's what is called poise. Very taking to them as appreciates it. Would you care to be announced, or will you come in on your tod?'

Mr Campion said he would not trouble him.

Miss Evadne's party was a formal affair. Although the room was crammed and the refreshment peculiar, some of the elegance which had distinguished entertaining in Portminster Lodge in the nineties still hovered restrainingly over the sly-eyed ill-assorted gathering.

The guests stood about very close together among the bulky furniture and talked resolutely in subdued tones. It was evident that there were many more people present than on earlier occasions of the same kind, and the theatrical element was hardly dominant.

For instance, one of the first faces Campion recognized belonged to Harold Lines, chief crime reporter on the *Sunday Utterance*. His mournful eyes regarded the lean man ruminatively above the first completely full glass ever to have been seen in his hand.

The hostess stood on the hearth close to her high-backed chair. She was still wearing the red Paisley dress which echoed her complexion so unfortunately, but the Honiton fichu and gold-set diamonds of the evening before lightened the sombre effect. She was hardly handsome but her presence was commanding, and she towered over both Mr Henry James, the bank manager, and the small Latinate young man who could only be the lead from the Thespis.

Before Campion could hope to reach her he had a considerable crowd to negotiate, many of whom glanced at him inquisitively. Almost at once he found himself stomach-to-stomach with the owner of a moustache he remembered.

Clot Drudge greeted him with friendliness from behind the fuzz.

'Hullo, sir! Made it? Jolly good show.' It became clear at once that he was a little unhappy. 'Not quite the time, what?' he said, and would have waved towards their hostess had there been room. 'Pretty blush-making and all that. Worse because it's so innocent.' Surprisingly he was perfectly clear. His grandfather himself could not have slipped in a word of discreet disclaimer with neater effect. 'Apples,' he said.

The final reference was obscure, but from his new position Campion could see that on her right arm Miss Evadne was carrying a small, distinctive shopping carrier, made of wire and green string. It was still half full of bright but sour-looking apples, although many of the guests were carrying one a little self-consciously in their gloved hands. Inspiration came to him.

'Was that Miss Ruth's bag?'

'The old trout carried it everywhere.' Clot seemed astonished that he did not know. He gave up trying to speak softly and relied on the straight whisper. 'She was never without it. Used to hand out apples to everyone she met when she could get hold of any. She used to say "keep the doctor away" and pop one in your hand. Evadne must have known everyone would remember, hence this crashing binge, I suppose – Hamlet and the play, sort of. Jolly bad show.'

This simple if depressing answer to the question which had defeated him silenced Campion for the time being as he reproached himself for not realizing that Miss Evadne was just the person to insist on playing detective in her own way and alone. Her idea, presumably, was to provoke some obviously guilty reaction. The theatre, it would appear, was in her blood.

Clot's next whisper took him by surprise.

'I say, is it true it's all over bar the shouting? Police waiting to spring and all that?'

'I haven't heard it officially.'

Strong colour spread above and around the moustache.

'Sorry. Shouldn't have said that.' His whisper was penitent. 'Indiscreet. Sorry. Cheer-ho. Oh, by the way, and as a chum, avoid the yellow stuff.'

Mr Campion thanked him earnestly and struggled on.

The next serious obstruction wore a cardboard hat. Miss Jessica, still dressed for the street, after her walk no doubt, was chatting to the doctor. Her high voice was raised in enthusiasm.

'You admit it did him good? That's so interesting, because Herbert Boon insists that it is one of the oldest cures for cold swellings known. It's a Saxon leechdom. You pick the yarrow buds when Venus is in the ascendant – I'm afraid I didn't bother about that – and pound them in butter – I fear I used margarine – and just lay it on. Shall you try it? Oh, I should feel so proud if I thought you would.'

'Well, I don't know.' A smile curled the doctor's thin lips. 'I should like to know the cause of the cold swellings first, don't you know.'

'Oh, you think that important?' She was openly disappointed and he was suddenly irritated.

'Of course I do – vital! Be careful with these things. If the skin is unbroken you can't do much harm, I suppose, but for heaven's sake . . . Oh.' He glanced over her head and caught sight of Campion. 'Good afternoon. Nice to see you here. Is your colleague about?'

'I haven't seen him,' Campion was beginning when a small hand came to rest on his arm.

'Oh, it's you.' Miss Jessica was shyly pleased. 'Isn't this wonderful? I put a poultice on the grocer's knee and it's done it good. The doctor admits it. I made the nettle tea for the party, too, and some tansy. That's in the glasses. You'll know it because it's yellow. You *must* try it. Look, there it is over there.' She nodded her strange and dreadful hat to the far end of the room where a table, covered with a very lovely lace cloth, bore an assortment of well-filled glasses and teacups and a pair of huge enamel jugs. 'You may never taste anything like it again.'

Her tone was not altogether innocent. She was certainly laughing.

'I'll try some when I've presented myself to your sister,' he promised.

'Yes,' she said, 'I believe you will. You're very kind.'

Before he could escape Doctor Smith buttonholed him once more. He was excited and still inclined to be irritable.

'I hear they're just waiting for the right moment to arrest,' he mumbled. 'Question of proof. Can you confirm?'

I'm sorry.' Mr Campion was beginning to find the disclaimer embarrassing. 'I'm afraid I can't.' He stepped back on the last word to avoid a collision with Lawrence Palinode, who, glass in hand, had come lumbering down the room scattering the crowd. He did not stop and offered no word of apology in passing, but thrust on to the doorway and out of sight.

'Lawrence has very little grace,' observed Miss Jessica as the flow of the crowd swept her back to Campion's side. 'He never had, even as a child. He can't *see*, of course. That makes it so much more difficult for him. Did you know,' she went on, lowering her voice making it clear that one thought followed the other, 'did you know that Clytie has a *visitor*?'

He was amused to see her pleasure.

'Mr Dunning?' he inquired.

'So you knew.' She was so pleased. 'Yes, he's in the attic and she's nursing him. It has made a change in her – quite astonishing. She used to be a nondescript child, but suddenly she looks quite different. I hardly recognized her this morning. She's so alert and *defined*.'

It took him some seconds to realize that she had not observed any change in her niece's costume, but was ascribing the alteration in her appearance to spiritual causes alone. He was still slightly dazed by this discovery and all it conveyed when he came at last before Miss Evadne, who released her guest of honour to hold out the wrong hand to him.

'My right one is so tired,' she explained, smiling with all the charm of condescending royalty. 'Such a great many people!'

'It's certainly a larger gathering than usual,' put in Mr James from her side. He spoke primly as ever, his precise enunciation lending the words weight. For a moment he contemplated giving the obvious explanation but thought better of it and added, 'Much larger' with finality.

All the same, his worried glance met Campion's own and repeated the question of the evening. He saw it was not the moment for it, however, and was sadly silent as the newcomer was introduced to the actor, who smiled a weary stage-smile and asked him if he was going to have an apple.

'I hardly think so,' said Miss Evadne, laughing, and conveying that he knew quite well what she had been doing, and indeed that it was some sort of little professional secret among sleuths. 'I fear my apples have – what shall I say? . . .'

'Buttered no parsnips,' Campion suggested foolishly, and was rewarded with the silence he deserved. His descending glance fell on the occasional table at her side. It was in its customary muddle and even the saucer of jam remained much as he had first seen it, save that it was a little more dusty. But this time, he noticed, there was only one bowl of everlasting flowers amid the miscellany. He was querying the little point when Miss Evadne's remark cut into his thoughts, startling him out of his wits.

'So you didn't bring your nice friend Sir William Glossop after all?'

He was so astonished that he wondered if he really had heard the words, and he looked up to find her, wedged in among the crowd of people, amused and triumphant.

In the little pause Mr James, who was betraying a sensitiveness in social matters, came gallantly to the rescue.

'Is that the Glossop of the P.A.E.O. Trust?' he inquired importantly. 'A very brilliant man.'

'Yes, he is, isn't he?' said Miss Evadne with contented assurance. 'An interesting career. I was looking him up in the library this morning, and I see he's Cambridge. I had got it into my head that he was Bristol, I don't know why. The photograph they give is very youthful. Men are vainer than women in such matters. Isn't that interesting?'

'Was he here?' Mr James was deeply impressed.

'I hardly think,' Campion was beginning when Miss Evadne forestalled him.

'Oh, yes,' she said. 'Last night. He was waiting for this clever man, and so was I, and we fell into conversation. He omitted to introduce himself but' – she turned to Campion with gentle triumph – 'I read his name in his hat. It was lying on a chair facing me. I'm very long-sighted, you know. I found him knowledgeable, but not clever at mending kettles.' Her laugh was light and forgiving, and she turned to the actor beside her. 'Adrian, are you thinking of reciting to us or not?'

As a change of subject it was masterly. The young man addressed seemed thoroughly startled, while little Mr James's watch shot out as though by reflex action.

'I thought that was to be a treat for next week,' he said quickly. 'I'd rather hoped so because I really must not stay today. Good heavens! I had no idea how late it was. You're too perfect a hostess, Miss Palinode. A most enjoyable evening. You're going to drop in to see me tomorrow, are you, or shall I call here?'

'Oh, please come here. I'm a lazy woman,' she said, and waved her hand to him with peculiarly charming and feminine grace, as, after nodding and twinkling at the others, he hurried off through the throng.

'A thoroughly good creature,' remarked the old lady as if she were throwing a careless rose after him. 'You won't, of course, be put off by that, Adrian. He's hardly a *mind*. What do you think? Shall we or not? It's a little crowded for Ibsen, perhaps, but there's always Mercutio. Unless you feel we should be modern?'

Mr Campion, glancing round for escape, was surprised to find the doctor at his elbow.

'I understand it was you who discovered my correspondent,' he was beginning in an earnest undertone, his eyes fixed firmly on Campion's spectacles. 'I want to discuss that with you. You see, she was not a patient. That is, I didn't treat her. She wasn't ill – except mentally – as I may have told her.'

The murmur buzzed on, betraying the strained nerves of a much persecuted man. Campion was extricating himself gently, when Lugg appeared at their side. He said nothing, but a raising of the brows and two infinitesimal jerks of the heavy chins invited both men to follow him. They obeyed at once, escaping from the room with as little fuss as possible, and came out at last on to the landing, to find Renee waiting for them. She was very white and as soon as they appeared she came over and slid an arm through each man's own, leading them towards the stairs.

'Look,' she said, striving to sound matter-of-fact and achieving breathlessness. 'It's Lawrence. He's had something in there. I don't know what it is or who gave it to him, or even if they've all had it, which would be frightful, but you'd better come at once. I – think he's dying, Albert.'

CHAPTER 24

Through the Net

—

THE first wild rumour, which had hinted that refreshment at a Borgia house-warming was very small beer when compared with the Palinode counterpart, had soon been superseded by something nearer the truth. Still, no one had been allowed to leave and tension was running very high.

In the wet garden the Press had decided to swarm. They were kept out of the house and had reached a stage when they buzzed together, damp and irritable and full of unprofitable ideas.

Inside the house the excitement was even more intense. In Miss Evadne's room the party continued grimly. So far, there had been no more casualties. Names and addresses and an occasional short statement were still being taken by Inspector Porky Bowden, Luke's right-hand man from the station, and all refreshment and the vessels thereof had been removed by Dice and his poker-face assistants.

In the intervals Adrian Siddons recited.

Downstairs the drawing-room and its adjacent cloakroom had become an improvised hospital ward for Lawrence. Clarrie had taken the shades off the light bulbs at the doctor's request and the neglected apartment, which was not considered habitable by anyone in the household, had now taken on a bald sordidness of dusty boards, cruel lighting, and chipped enamel toilet-ware.

Doctor Smith was pulling down his shirt-sleeves when Renee came rustling in with a pile of fresh towels. She wore a cooking pinafore over her black finery and, now that the tragedy was averted, was inclined to be exuberant with relief.

She smiled at Lawrence, who lay on the worn Empire sofa looking dreadfully like some half-plucked black bird. His skin was wet and livid and covered with goose-pimples, but he was out of misery and an aggrieved and astonished anger had begun to possess him.

The D.D.I. and Campion were comparing their sheets of notes. They were both tired, but Luke had got his second wind.

'You see? It was quite different muck.' His murmur vibrated in Campion's ear and he ringed an item on both lists. 'This chap was handed something quite different from everybody else – different colour, different stink. We shan't get the analyst's report until tomorrow. Can't. Have to get on as far as we can without.'

His pencil point ran on down the page and stopped at a query: '*Says did not notice who gave him glass.*'

'What about that?'

'It's feasible. He'd help if he could,' said Campion. 'He takes a dim view of the entire proceedings.'

'I thought that.' His effort to be quiet made him sound like a gigantic bumble-bee. 'Everybody who knew the family at all well seems to have been helping. Miss Jessica, Lugg, Clytie even, for a time, the doc here, Mr James, Mr Drudge the lawyer chap. Renee came in, the actors, everybody.'

Mr Campion turned to confront the doctor.

'I don't want to commit myself, Luke,' he began, 'and no one can be sure without the analysis, but I think he had something more than a purely herbal poison, don't you know.'

Luke was puzzled. 'It was different stuff,' he said. 'Different colour . . .'

'Oh yes. I think the vegetable tisane was toxic, whatever it was. It probably saved his life by making him vomit. But I think he had something more.' He hesitated, his wretched eyes glancing from one man to the other. 'Something more orthodox, if that's the word. He was both stiff and drowsy – peculiar. The reaction came so quickly, too. It might have been chloral in an enormous dose. I don't know. We shall find out, of course.

I've taken specimens. Where's his glass, by the way; he had it with him?'

'Oh, Dice took that. He's got all the exhibits.' Luke brushed the question aside. He had fastened on to the new idea like a terrier. 'Hyoscine again, doc?'

'Oh no, I don't think so. It occurred to me at once and I was looking out for the symptoms, but I don't think so. If it was I shall be astounded.'

'Someone is trying to make it look like Jessica.'

The pronouncement uttered in a voice which retching had destroyed until it was no more than a rasp of dry sticks startled everybody. They moved over towards the couch in a body and Lawrence lay looking up at them, a living gargoyle, his damp hair on end and his face glistening, but his eyes intelligent as ever.

'Trying to throw suspicion on my sister.' The words were enunciated with extreme care, as if he suspected them all of being half-witted, or at best deaf. 'The intention was to make her a scapegoat.'

'What makes you think so?' Luke's interest was alive and eager and the sick man responded to it, forcing his broken voice and trying to raise himself on his pillows.

'There was a scrap of leaf in my glass. I got it out after my first mouthful – I drank half of it at one draught; only thing to do with that sort of thing. All taste unpleasant.' He was so earnest that no one smiled. 'Leaf was hemlock. Classic poison. That was how I knew. I came out at once.'

'Why did that make you sure it wasn't Miss Jessica?' The doctor put the question before either man could intervene. He spoke very simply, as if Lawrence's mind was in the same shape as his body, and the patient closed his eyes in pure exasperation.

'She wouldn't have been so crude,' he whispered, 'even if she'd been so uncharitable. Even the Greeks found hemlock difficult stuff to administer satisfactorily. She'd have known that. Someone ignorant of that is trying to suggest that she poisoned Ruth. Ridiculous, and wicked.'

Doctor Smith jerked his chin up.

'I think Mr Lawrence is right,' he said. 'It's a thing that's been bothering me without my being able to pin it down. Someone rather clever but not quite clever enough is doing this, Luke.' He paused abruptly. 'I don't quite understand the attack on that young Dunning, though.'

'But I thought you knew who it was? I thought the police had put out a net.'

They had forgotten Renee. Her invitation was as surprising as it was embarrassing.

'D'you mean to tell me you don't know *yet*?' she demanded. 'Aren't you really going to make an arrest? How long is this going on?'

The doctor coughed. 'I understood there was a certain police activity,' he began. 'The general idea seemed to be some sort of sudden swoop . . . ?'

The question trailed away. Charlie Luke's attitude had become withdrawn.

'We are anxious to interview a man called Joseph Congreve,' he said a little stiffly. 'Our search for him may have started a hare or so. Will you come along now, Mr Campion? Miss Jessica's waiting for us in the other room. You've got a midder, you say, doctor? Well, come back as soon as you can, won't you? Look after Lawrence, Renee.'

They entered the dining-room and the first person he saw, standing on the hearthrug under the portrait of Professor Palinode, was Superintendent Yeo. He was taking no part in the proceedings. He stood squarely, his hands folded under the tail of his jacket, and he glanced at them both as they appeared but did not smile.

The significance of his arrival was not lost upon anybody. Here was an ultimatum from H.Q. An arrest, in fact, would oblige.

Luke went over to him at once and Campion would have followed had not a gentle hand detained him. Miss Jessica greeted him as a deliverer. She had discarded the cardboard from her hat, but still wore the motoring veil knotted carelessly behind her head in the manner of the Victorian romantic painters. Her bag was missing, too, and her gown, which as usual was muslin over wool, had achieved some interesting drapery effects. Altogether she looked, curiously enough, rather decorative and a hundred per cent feminine.

'Something has disagreed with Lawrence,' she said superbly. 'Did you know?'

'Yes,' he said gravely, 'it might have been very serious.'

'I know. They told me.' She indicated Dice and his colleagues with a wave of her hand. Her nice voice was as intelligent as ever, but it had lost its authority, and he saw with dismay that she was desperately afraid.

'I did not make a mistake,' she went on with the dreadful earnestness of one not absolutely sure. 'You'll have to help me convince them of that. I followed Boon's recipes very carefully, except where I had to make omissions. It was a party, you see, and one does like to give one's guests one's best.'

Her little face was very serious, her nice eyes deeply troubled.

'I am fond of Lawrence,' she said, as if the admission was one of weakness. 'He is more near to me in age than any of the others. I wouldn't hurt him. But then I wouldn't hurt anybody, if I knew.'

'Look here,' said Mr Campion, 'what did you actually do?' She was only too anxious to tell him.

'I brewed two tisanes, nettle and a tansy. Evadne purchased the yerba maté and made it herself. That was a lightish brown. It's nearly tea, you know. The nettle drink I made was grey, and the tansy was yellow. But they tell me the stuff that Lawrence drank was a deep bottle-green.'

'With leaves in it,' murmured Campion involuntarily.

'Had it?' She picked him up at once. 'Then it couldn't have been anything I made. I always strain everything very carefully through old linen – clean, of course.' She regarded him inquisitively. 'Don't you remember what Boon says? "The residue constitutes a valuable vegetable addition to the diet." '

'Oh dear,' said Mr Campion, peering at her through his spectacles. 'Yes, I suppose he does. Tell me, have you got these – er – residual vegetables downstairs?'

Her reply was lost to him, for at that moment the door was opened abruptly and Clarrie Grace, looking flushed and harassed, swept in with a tray on which was an unopened bottle of Irish whiskey, a siphon and half a dozen glasses.

'Miss Roper's compliments,' he announced, addressing the room as if it were an audience. 'Everything's sealed, so no cold feet, anybody.'

He planted the tray on the desk end of the dining table, flashed his stage smile at them, and rushed out again very quickly to show he did not want to overhear any secrets.

The police ignored the entire incident and continued their muttered consultations, but Miss Jessica turned to her champion.

'A silly woman but so kind,' she observed.

'Perhaps so,' he agreed absently, and his glance strayed to the portrait over the mantel. To his amazement, for he had forgotten her gift, she behaved as if he had spoken his thought aloud. She coloured slightly.

'Oh, you know, do you?' she said softly. 'The likeness is so very marked, isn't it? Her mother danced, I believe.'

He stared at her and she hurried on, still speaking very softly but greatly enjoying the sensation she was making.

'She was also an excellent business woman, I believe. My mother, the poetess, whom I resemble, never knew of her existence, nor of the daughter, of course, but my father was a just man and he provided very handsomely for them. I think he must have known that Renee had inherited his practical ability, whereas none of the rest of us had, for he made certain that all the house property, for which he had a sentimental regard, went to her. That is why we accept so much from her.'

While he was still digesting this information she leaned close to him to whisper something which made him believe her utterly just as surely as it took his breath away.

'Please be very discreet. You see, *she does not know we know.* That way there is no embarrassment on either side.'

Her gentle voice was touched with complacency as she folded her hands on the matter, very much as the poetess must have done in the grimly practical days when Victoria was queen. Even Luke, who came striding over with a flea in his ear, did not shake her equanimity. She sat down where he told her to and answered his opening questions with complete assurance.

From the beginning, Campion found the ordeal a good deal more nerve-racking than she did. It was the old nightmare situation dreaded by all good policemen; in this case doubly unsatisfactory since it soon became obvious that she might easily have made any sort of silly mistake in her potion-brewing, while no man in the room believed for a moment that she was guilty of the premeditated crimes which had occurred.

He was on the point of turning away from the unbearable interview when Miss Jessica's voice cut across his milling thoughts.

'Oh, is that the glass Lawrence drank from? Do be careful of it. It's one of Evadne's sherries. She's only got two left. They're old Bristol.'

The words detached themselves from the immediate present and hung in front of him, very small and clear, as if they were printed in hard black type across a picture of the room.

Immediately two major problems became urgent.

Luke, who was holding the small green glass in a folded handkerchief, happened to look at him, his bright odd-shaped eyes questioning. Campion bent over Miss Jessica, surprised to find his voice shaking.

'I've seen flowers in those glasses,' he said. 'Doesn't your sister use them for flowers sometimes? Everlasting flowers?'

'Flowers?' She was horrified. 'Oh, no. They're the last of my father's sherry glasses. Evadne would never use them for anything else. They're very precious. I didn't realize she had put them out today. They are usually kept on the mantelshelf. There was no sherry. That was why we had to make something else.'

Campion had ceased to listen to her. With a word of apology he turned on his heel and went out of the room, crossed to the drawing-room where Lawrence lay and asked him a single, and, as it seemed to the sick man, utterly absurd and irrelevant question.

'Well, yes,' said Lawrence Palinode in reply. 'Yes, as a matter of fact we did. Always. It was a custom left from happier days. All of us. Yes. On every occasion. Good heavens! You're not suggesting . . .'

Campion left him. He was moving very quickly and he put his head into the dining-room looking like a bleached edition of himself in youth.

'Come on,' he said to Luke with brisk authority. 'Proof first, I suppose, and then, my lad, that net of yours had better close if we haven't left it too late.'

CHAPTER 25

Up Apron Street

—

THE crowd before Portminster Lodge had shrunk like a flannel patch in the wet. Five minutes earlier Dice had opened the front door and invited the Press inside for what he was pleased to call 'a bit of a chat with Inspector Bowden', and as the last soaked overcoat passed gratefully within, the four men, who did not wish to be observed, came quietly up the area steps and disappeared ostensibly in different directions.

They met in the mouth of the mews. Lugg and Charlie Luke went round to the front entrance of the bank and Yeo and Campion stood on the stone step of the small side door, dark and grimy under the archway. To their right was Apron Street, with the gleam of the Palinode windows making glittering pathways in the streaming roadway; to their left was the chasm of the mews, its ancient cobbles and old stable bricks catching what light there was and producing an interesting woodcut effect.

Yeo moved closer to his companion. His murmur was puzzled and a thought aggrieved.

'Why does Luke keep calling the chap "Bloblip"?'

'It will emerge, I hope.' Campion bent his head to listen at the door.

Already the shrill clamour of the bell, whose push Lugg was leaning against on the other side of the house, stole out to them through the wood. It went on steadily without pause, like the rain.

Yeo was restive. In his late middle-age he had become a heavy breather and now his whisper crept gustily through the sighing of the rain.

'Funny. Must be someone there. I'm not breaking in without a warrant, Campion, I warn you. I'm trusting you. We're all trusting and depending on you, but there are limits.'

The noise of the door-bell ceased.

A new clamour, this time of alarm bells both inside and on the front of the building, brought both men to their toes. Yeo had just time to swear violently before a shadow, jaunty and silent as an alley-cat, bore down upon them from the street.

It was Luke. Recklessness had made him offhandedly cheerful.

'Okay,' he murmured. 'It's Lugg. He's gone in through the window in a shower of glass. Damn it, he's a burglar, isn't he? He'll get the door open, hop it, and we'll rush in and protect the property. Sorry, Super. I'm working for my ticket this time, anyhow.'

Mr Campion divined rather than saw Yeo's face and could have laughed had the moment been any other than the dizzy one of failure. He could see himself opening that corner cupboard and finding it empty or full of books.

Luke pulled his sleeve. 'Time we cops did our duty and answered the bell before our efficient inferiors hear it from over the way.' He was grinning, but there was appeal and trust in his voice. Campion found them horrific. 'Come on, sir, do your bit of magic.'

They moved towards the street, but as he came out into the rain, and just before he turned the corner, Campion looked back. The sound he made stopped the others and they turned. In the centre of the mews was a sight of fantasy.

From a dark coach-house, whose doors must have been standing open unseen in the gloom, a monstrous anachronism had appeared. It was a large black horse-drawn vehicle, sinister in shape, with a high box-seat for the driver and an ominous flat body entirely enclosed, Swaying and glistening in the light of its own old-fashioned lamps, the coffin brake swung away from them and moved lightly and with surprising swiftness towards the Barrow Road exit of the mews.

Yeo's hand felt like iron on Campion's shoulder. The Superintendent was out of his depth.

'What the hell's that?' he demanded. 'Who is it? Where's he going at this time of night?'

Campion laughed aloud. He sounded hysterical.

'It's Jas,' he said. 'He's saved us – or rather, Luke's inspired general call has. He's going "up Apron Street" before our eyes. Can we get a car?'

'Can do.' Luke strode off across the road with suspicious alacrity.

Above them the burglar-alarm continued its panic-stricken cacophony. Yeo was deeply quiet for a second before he moved nearer to his old friend. Then he cleared his throat and said with a deferential restraint which lent the announcement the force of an explosion: 'I hope you know what you're doing.'

'Hope on, Guv'nor.' Campion spoke devoutly.

At that moment a long black car appeared out of the curtains of the sheeting rain.

Yeo grunted. 'What about the bank?'

'Dice and a couple of chaps are just behind me, sir. They'll take care of it.' Luke handed him into the car, and after thrusting Campion in after him, would have followed himself had not a large wet figure, furious as a startled fowl and making much the same noise, descended upon them from the soaking darkness.

''Ere, 'ere, 'ere! What's the game, eh? What's on the ivories? What are you all playin' at?' Lugg was drenched. His bald head ran water and his moustache was hung with diamond drops. He thrust Luke aside and shot into the tonneau like a cannon-ball of wet washing, to subside on the floor on the far side, where he added considerably to the discomfort of all concerned.

As the door closed after Luke, and the car started, he was still expostulating.

'Broken glass in me armpits, me finger-prints all over the door which is now ajar, and you scarpering like a pack of silly kids . . . I can believe it of some of you, but what you think *you're* doing, Mr Yeo, I don't know!'

Luke placed a large but not unfriendly hand over his face.

'Now, sir,' he said briskly to Campion, 'what's the message?'

The message, which caused comment over the entire circuit, went out in a matter of seconds.

'Car Q23 calling all cars. Chief Inspector Luke. Am pursuing black horse-drawn vehicle with single passenger driver. Technical name coffin brake, repeat coffin brake. Last seen Barrow Road, West, proceeding north. Inform all call points. Over.'

As they approached the old tram terminus at the top of Barrow Road, Yeo could bear it no longer.

'Where's the fire?' he muttered to Campion, who was jammed in beside him. 'No one on God's earth could miss an archaic contraption like that. You can't lose it. An ordinary Call must have picked him up in half an hour. What are we playing at?'

'It's imperative he doesn't stop. We must get him before he stops, that's vital.'

'All right, if you say so. Any idea at all where he's going?'

'I think to Fletchers Town. What's the address, Lugg?'

The sodden bundle heaved itself into a more comfortable position.

'Peter George Jelf's? Seventy-eight Lockhart Crescent. Going to broadcast that? You won't see him for skid marks!'

'Peter George Jelf? That's a name from the past.' Yeo sounded surprised and gratified. 'This morning Old Pullen came in to see me. He happened to mention he'd run into Jelf on Euston Station as he came into town. The man seemed quite respectable, which is a contradiction in terms, and said he'd got a little haulage business in North London. Pullen glanced in the van, the only thing the chap had on board was a packing-case marked "Conjurer's Stores" – singularly appropriate when one thinks back over his career.'

'Conjurer's Stores . . .' The lean man's lazy voice was soft with relief and satisfaction.

'So that's how they got the coffin back; I wondered about that.'

'Back?' said Luke, sitting up. 'Back?'

Mr Campion was about to explain when the loudspeaker interrupted him.

'Central Control calling Car Q23. Black horse-drawn vehicle thought to be coffin brake, seen twenty-three forty-four hours corner of Greatorex Road and Findlay Avenue N.W. proceeding north up Findlay Avenue at fair speed. Over.'

'Hullo, he's round the park,' announced Yeo, the intrinsic excitement of the chase suddenly hitting him. 'Seven and a quarter minutes ago. He's shifting, Campion. Astounding. No traffic, of course, but a dangerous surface. Here, turn up here, driver. It'll take you to Philomel Place. There's a way through right at the north end which will bring you to the Broadway. Cross the Canal Bridge there and you get out into – blow it! – thingummy street . . . I'll think of it in a moment. It's a rabbit warren just there.'

'We mustn't lose him. Mustn't miss him in the side streets.' Campion spoke abruptly. 'He mustn't get to Jelf and he mustn't stop. That's vital.'

'Why not call one of the other buses? J54 is up in Tanner's Hill.' Luke was fidgeting. 'He could get down to Lockhart Crescent and hang about for him. They can hold him till we come, can't they?'

'I suppose so.' Campion did not sound happy. 'I want him to go on feeling he's safe. All right, though. Probably best.'

Luke saw that the message went out as they raced through the dark built-up streets. Yeo, whose knowledge of London was legendary, had begun to enjoy himself, and the driver, also not without experience, became gratifyingly respectful.

The rain continued doggedly. It had settled into its stride and appeared to have achieved inevitability. They passed down Findlay Avenue and plunged into Legion Street at the roundabout where that great highroad settles down to its uninterrupted run to the north-western suburbs.

'Steady.' Yeo could not have spoken more softly on the banks of a trout stream. 'Steady now. Even if he's kept up his pace he can't be far now.'

''Im and 'is packets of fags,' said Lugg under his breath.

'Him and his lip, you mean,' said Luke.

Yeo had begun to rumble quietly. It was a sort of verbal doodling of which he was scarcely aware.

'This is the old Duke's estate . . . Wickham Street . . . Lady Clara Hough Street . . . There's a little crescent up there. I wonder . . . No, road turns back here. Wickham Place Street . . . Wick Avenue . . . slowly, boy, slowly here. Any of these little side turnings would save him a quarter of a mile if he knows. May not risk losing himself. You can go faster now. There's no turning for a hundred yards. Blast this rain! I can't see where I am half the time. Oh, yes, there's the Peculiars chapel. Come on, now, come on. Coronet Street . . . slowly again now.'

The interruption from the loudspeaker came as a relief. The unnatural voice with the metallic undertone seemed unusually loud.

'Central Control calling Car Q23. Attention. At twenty-three fifty-eight hours Constable 675 calling from Box 3Y6 stroke NW corner Clara Hough and Wickham Court Roads nor-west, reports attack at twenty-three fifty hours approx. by driver black horse-drawn vehicle thought to be a coffin brake. Acting on instructions given in your message 17GH, he advanced to intercept but was struck down by driver with heavy weapon, believed whip handle. Brake made off at fair speed, Wickham Court Road proceeding north. Over.'

'Damn! Now he knows.' Campion spoke savagely. 'He'll unload at the first opportunity.'

'Wickham Court Road – we're almost on him!' Yeo was bounding in his seat. 'He's not shifting as we are, whatever he's got in the shafts. Up here, driver. Turn left at the top. It's barely midnight now. Keep your hair on, Campion; we'll get him, boy. We'll get him. Stands to reason.'

As they turned into the wind the rain descended on the windows in a solid sheet of water. Yeo, crouching over the driver's shoulder, peered through the lunettes made by the screen wipers.

'Now right, and at once left! – oh, very good. Now – hullo! hullo! what's this? Hoardings? Wait, driver, wait. We're on Wickham Hill now. Wickham Court Road is down there on the left. It's very long and the police box must be close on a quarter of a mile down it. He must have come out here less than five minutes ago. Now then, Luke my boy, which way did he go? He didn't come to meet us. If he went left to Hollow Street and the trams, he'd be running into the next cop sure as eggs, so there's two alternatives; Polly Road, which is down there about fifty yards, or this little lane. It's called Rose Way. It goes through to Legion Street again.'

'Wait a minute.' Campion opened the door and as the car stopped, slid out into the rain. He was in a narrow hissing world of brick and water. The hoardings, standing back from improvised fences, rose up over his head on one side, and on the other were blocks of old-fashioned flats. He listened, straining his ears for a single unusual sound in a mechanized age.

Luke stepped quietly out beside him and he too stood listening, his strong chin upraised, the downpour soaking him unheeded.

'He won't risk going on. He'll unload.' Campion let the words out softly. 'He'll get away with it.'

The loudspeaker in the car sounded so clearly at their elbows that they both started. The message blared at them, the impersonal statement echoing bewilderingly through the night.

'Central Control calling Car Q23. Central Control calling Car Q23. Message for Chief Inspector Luke. Attention. Joseph Congreve, 51b Terry Street West, found dangerously ill following murderous attack. Locked in cupboard upstairs room, Apron Street branch Clough's Bank zero, zero, zero two hours. Over.'

As the message croaked its way to the end Luke came out of his stunned silence and caught Campion's coat. He was shaking with shock and disappointment.

'Apron Street!' he exploded bitterly. 'Apron Street! Bloblip's in Apron Street. What the hell are we doing here?'

Campion was standing perfectly still. He put up his hand for silence.

'Listen.'

From the far end of the lane which Yeo had called Rose Way came an unmistakable series of sounds. As they waited the noise grew louder and louder, until it seemed to fill the air. The galloping hoofs advanced towards them and behind them was the whisper and rustle of rubber-tyred wheels.

'Legion Street took him by surprise. He funked meeting the police and turned.' Campion was hardly articulate. 'My hat, we may have done it after all. Quickly, driver, quickly! Don't let him get away.'

The police car slid forward over the mouth of the lane at the moment when, with a clatter of hoofs as the iron beat the tarmac, the coffin brake appeared.

CHAPTER 26

Conjurer's Stores

—

THE undertaker pulled up the moment he saw the danger. The road was too narrow for him to hope to turn and he made a virtue of the circumstance. He let the mare stand gratefully, the steam rising up from her flanks into the rain. From the high box he looked down inquiringly, water running in streams from the brim of his hard hat.

'Why, it's Mr Luke.' He sounded both friendly and surprised. 'Terrible night, sir. Your car hasn't broke down, I hope?'

Luke took the mare's head.

'Get down, Bowels. Come on, right down into the road.'

'Why certainly, if you say the word, sir.' He managed to convey complete mystification and began at once to unwrap himself from the various layers of oilskin which swaddled him.

Campion, who had gone round quietly on the outside, swung himself up to take the heavy whip out of its socket, and the old man stared at him with enlightenment.

'Mr Luke,' he began, lowering himself cautiously on to the wet surface. 'Mr Luke, I think I understand you, sir. You've had a bit of a complaint from one of your officers.'

'Talk at the station,' said the D.D.I., woodenly official.

'But I'd like to explain, sir – it's not as if we were strangers.' The reminder was eminently reasonable and not without dignity. 'It was a goodish way back, a constable suddenly jumped out at me. He was like a lunatic, sir, though I don't want to get anyone into trouble. I didn't see 'is uniform at first in the rain, and I'm afraid that in my nervousness I struck out at 'im.

It was to save 'is life and that's a fact. The mare had taken fright and I've only this minute quietened 'er. She's taken me half a mile out of my way as it is. That's why I'm here. I ought to be on the lower road, and I would be if she'd not bolted.'

'Tell it all at the station.'

'Very good, sir. But this isn't like you. Bless my soul, what's that?'

A sound from the back of the brake had startled him. Mr Campion was closing the back of the body, which fastened with iron butterfly-bolts and opened upwards, piano-fashion. As he came back towards them Jas smiled.

'As you'll have seen, sir, I'm on my lawful occasions,' he said heartily. 'A gentleman 'as died in a nursing home and has had to be took to his son's for the interment. The firm employed couldn't see their way to shift 'im tonight and the nursing home couldn't keep 'im, so their foreman came to me. I obliged. You have to keep all the goodwill you can in my trade.'

'Hurry up, my man.' Yeo appeared in the darkness and took the horse's head. 'Take him to the car, Charlie.'

'Yes, sir. I'm going, sir.' Jas sounded hurt rather than annoyed. 'Can any of you gentlemen drive? The mare's not quite like a motor. Excuse me asking, but she's had a fright and I wouldn't trust her.'

'Don't worry about that. I'll bring your horse myself. Get in the car.' The Superintendent's voice, stiff with authority, was yet not unfriendly, and the undertaker was quick to see that he had made an impression.

'Very good, sir,' he agreed cheerfully. 'I'm in your hands. Shall I go first, Mr Luke?'

He climbed into the car in silence and sank down in the seat Yeo had vacated. As he removed his sopping hat he came face to face with Lugg. It was a shock, but he said nothing. His fine big head with its crown of white curls remained erect, but his complexion had lost some of its aggressive health and his eyes were thoughtful.

The procession set out immediately, Yeo leading with Campion on the box beside him. The wind, now full behind them, blew the oilskin rugs which they had thrown round their shoulders into tall black wings. They glistened and flapped like sails in the headlights, lending the brake the illusion of unnatural speed.

The half-drowned city swept by them, and in each vehicle the sense of urgency grew as, in silence, they made the return journey, to draw up at the Barrow Road Divisional Police Station.

Abruptly Luke handed his captive over to the startled constable who had come hurrying to meet him, and then, followed by Lugg, strode along to the brake, which had pulled up just ahead.

'He's behaving damned naturally,' he announced without preamble.

'That's what I thought.' Yeo was blunt with misgiving, and both men looked anxiously at the slender figure, now almost obscured by its cloak of dripping oilskin.

Campion said nothing. He climbed quietly down from his seat and went round to the back of the brake. As soon as a constable had taken the mare's head the others followed him. He had got the lid open by the time they arrived and his torch beam was playing on the coffin within. It was black and shining, of unusual size, and the gilding on it would have been less remarkable on a State coach.

' 'At's it, cock. 'At's the one.' Lugg's thick voice was more husky than ever and he laid a cautious hand on the wood. 'The 'inges must run along the edges, 'ere and 'ere. Can't see 'em, can yer? Artist in his way, Jas is, the old perisher. I see 'im wonderin' if ter mention Beatt the 'ole way along.'

Yeo produced his own torch.

'Looks normal to me,' he pronounced at last. 'I'm hanged if I like this, Campion, but it's for Luke to decide.'

The D.D.I. hesitated and glanced at Campion, his own doubts showing clearly in his deep-set eyes. The lean man was as expressionless as was usual when he was very excited.

'Oh, I think so, you know,' he said gently. 'I think so. Take it in and open it up.'

In the D.D.I.'s office, Campion and Lugg arranged two wooden chairs in the same pattern as those they had found in the chemist's back bedroom.

Presently, Luke, with Dice and two constables, came slowly in, carrying the coffin between them. They set its glistening length down tenderly on the chairs and stood back, while Yeo, who had followed them, his hands deep in his pockets, began to whistle a little tuneless dirge to himself.

'The weight's about right,' he observed to Luke.

The younger man glanced at him unhappily, admitting the suggestion. However, having committed himself, he did not waver. He nodded to the sergeant.

'Bring him along.'

After a moment or so they heard the undertaker and his escort coming down the corridor. He had a confident step as heavy as the police officer's own, and when he stepped into the room, bareheaded and without his heavy driving cape, he looked infinitely respectable.

Every man in the room watched his face as he caught sight of the coffin, but only one fully appreciated his remarkable control. It was true that he stopped in his tracks and the familiar stars of sweat appeared at his curling hair line, but he was outraged rather than afraid. With unerring instinct he turned to Yeo.

'I hardly expected this, sir,' he said mildly. 'It may be forward of me to say so, but this isn't very nice.' The understatement embraced the sordidness of the apartment, the sacrilegious handling of the decently dead, the rights of the individual, and the high-handedness of officials generally. He stood before them, an honest, scandalized tradesman.

Luke met his eyes squarely and strove, Mr Campion felt, to avoid anything faintly like defiance.

'Open it, Bowels.'

'*Open* it, sir?'

'Right away. If you won't, we will.'

'No, no, I'll do it, I'll do it, Mr Luke. You don't know what you're suggesting, sir.' His readiness was far more disconcerting than his shocked protests. 'I'll do it. I'm bound to do anything you say. I know my duty. I'm surprised, very surprised. I can't say more nor less.' He paused and looked round him with distaste. 'Did I understand you want me to do it here, sir?'

Once again Yeo had begun to whistle just under his breath. He seemed unaware that he was making a sound and his glance never wavered from the wide pink face with the sharp little eyes and small, unpleasant mouth.

'Here and now.' Luke was obdurate. 'Got a screwdriver on you?'

Jas made no attempt to procrastinate. He felt in his coat pocket and nodded.

'I have, sir. Never move without my tools. I'll just take my jacket off if you'll permit.'

They watched him strip to the very white shirt with the old-fashioned stiff cuffs. He took the gold links out carefully and laid them on the edge of the desk. Then he rolled up his sleeves, revealing forearms like a navvy's.

'Now I'm quite ready, sir. But there's just one little thing.'

'Speak up, man.' Yeo interfered without intending to. 'You've every right to say what you like. What is it?'

'Well, sir, I wondered if I could 'ave a drop of Lysol in a bucket of water, just to put my 'ands in.'

While a constable scuttled off to fetch it for him he took out a large handkerchief, white as his shirt, and folded it cornerwise.

'The gentleman died of a bad trouble,' he said deprecatingly to the room at large. 'I'll ask you to stand a foot or so back for the first minute or two. It's for your own sakes. You've got your work to do, but there's no need for you to run into more danger than you need. You'll excuse me, I know.'

He tied the sling over the lower part of his face and plunged his hands in the homely white bucket which the constable held out to him. Then, after shaking a shower of odorous rain over the bare boards, he got down to work.

His blunt hands worked swiftly over the screws. They appeared to be set in steel worms and moved easily, but there were a great many of them and he took his time setting them out neatly in a row beside the cuff links.

When at last he had finished, he paused and looked round, finally motioning Yeo and Luke to step a little nearer. He halted them some five feet from the casket and, glancing from one to the other, nodded briskly to show that the moment had come.

As they watched him, with the fascination which the truly horrible engenders, he whipped up the lid.

Every one in the room caught a glimpse of the body. The form was shrouded with something white and gauze-like, but the hands, folded at the waist, were unmistakably real and human.

A single note of Yeo's whistled tune sounded loudly in the silent room and Luke sagged a little, his wide shoulders suddenly less square.

A grip like a vice on his wrist took him utterly by surprise and Campion thrust him the remaining foot or so forward without effort.

At the instant when Jas Bowels was about to replace the lid it was knocked bodily out of his hold, and Luke's hand, guided by Campion's own, came down on the folded fingers in the shroud. The D.D.I. recoiled and recovered himself, and as Yeo, whose reflexes were older, came up beside him, he bent forward and took the folded hands and turned them over. The next moment he had snatched the gauze from the whitely powdered face and the entire room was in commotion. It was a most extraordinary sight.

A man clad in thick woollen underclothes was lying trussed in a contraption which, although faintly surgical in appearance, had yet something of the padded Victorian love-seat about it. A webbing corselet strapped him securely in position, and across his body just below the hands was a wooden partition securely dividing the top from the lower half of his cage. His head and the upper part of his chest were free, and ingeniously concealed holes or slits, invisible from the outside of the box, permitted the air to reach him freely. He was breathing heavily but without a great deal of noise, and his hands were secured by leather bracelets which, although they gave them little play, were yet slack enough to permit him to beat on the roof of his prison.

Yeo spoke first. He was white to the lips but still authoritative.

'Doped,' he said huskily. 'Alive.'

'Oh yes, he's alive.' Campion sounded tired but very relieved. 'They were all alive, of course. That was the object of the exercise.'

'They?' Yeo's glance wandered to the undertaker, who stood stiffly between two constables, his handkerchief-mask hanging limply round his neck like a noose.

Campion sighed. 'Greener, your Greek Street bird, was the one before this,' he said softly. 'Before him, Jackson the Brighton gunman, I think. Before that, Ed Geddy, who killed the girl in the kiosk. I haven't caught up with the others yet. They go to Ireland like this, and after, by more orthodox conveyance, to anywhere they may take a fancy. As a rule there's a mourner laid on to weep them through the Customs. She has the coroner's order-to-ship tucked in her worn black handbag.'

'This is a lovely job, worth the price of admission alone. The organization is really quite beautiful.'

'Good God!' Yeo looked at Jas Bowels's curling and venerable head. 'Who was doing it all? Him?'

'No, that's the boss.' Campion nodded to the sleeping form. 'A genius in his way, but hopeless at murder. How he managed to kill Miss Ruth successfully I really don't know. He foozled everything else concerning it.'

Yeo waited. Reaction was making him both red and irritable.

'Campion!' he burst out at last. 'That's no way to give evidence. A junior constable six weeks in the force could do better than this. What's the first thing, man, what's the first thing?'

Luke came out of his trance with a jolt.

'Sorry, sir,' he said smartly. 'His name is Henry James. He's the manager of the Apron Street branch of Clough's Bank.'

'Ah,' said Yeo with deep satisfaction, 'that's more like it. Now we're getting somewhere.'

CHAPTER 27

Farewell Apron Street

—

'IT was done out of kindness.' The undertaker spoke with dogged obstinacy. 'Put that down in writing and never let it be forgot. 'Unted animals, that's 'ow I saw them, and that's 'ow I saw *him* in the finish.'

'In spite of the fact that, on your own evidence, both you and Wilde the chemist had been forced by James, after a long period of financial pressure, to take part in this – ah – outrageous traffic?' Yeo was growing ponderous, giving his celebrated imitation of Counsel I Have Known, a sure sign that he was enjoying himself enormously.

Mr Bowels took breath. Some of his wiliness was giving place to resignation.

'Yes, we got behind with our money, me and Wilde,' he agreed. 'First to the bank and then to him privately. You'll never understand him, though, if you don't understand Apron Street. It was changing, you see, and he wouldn't have it.' He laughed abruptly. 'He tried to stop the clock.'

'For a bloke who was merely trying to preserve ancient monuments he didn't propose to do himself so badly,' observed Luke, waving a long hand towards the impressive array of packages which had been taken from the coffin. They lay on the desk in rows, treasury notes, negotiable securities, bags of coin even.

Jas turned his eyes away, no doubt out of some kind of modesty.

'The idea took hold on him,' he admitted calmly. 'I was talking about the beginning when it started, four years ago. At that time of day he was only determined that things should go on as they always had done in 'is father's and grandfather's time before 'im. It was a sort of a mania with 'im. Later on, the idea of getting rich took 'im by the throat, so to speak. It takes a lot of money, stopping the clock.' He paused and shook his magnificent head. 'He didn't ought to 'ave turned to murder. That was doing too much to it altogether. I couldn't bring meself to believe it of him, not at first.'

'Yet afterwards you did, you know,' Campion put in gently, 'because after you had made the mistake of asking your brother-in-law to get me to investigate you were terrified lest he should find out that you had done so.'

Mr Bowels's mild eyes turned to him sharply.

'Ah, you noticed old Congreve in my kitchen that night, did you? I wondered. You're very quick, Mr Campion, I'll say that for you. Congreve came round nosing and asking funny questions, and I couldn't make up my mind whether he was doing it for James or not. That's the long and the short of it, as we say in the trade.'

Mr Campion leant back. The last little tangles in his nearly level cord were pulling out.

'Why did you cosh young Dunning?' he inquired abruptly. 'Or did your son do it?'

'It was neither of us, sir. That you very well know.' Jas made an O of his tiny mouth, which, with the two teeth in the middle of it, now made him look like an enormous parrot-fish. 'It was Greener did that, Mr Campion, with the butt of 'is gun. Didn't want no noise.'

The likelihood of the explanation came as a relief to everyone in the room, and the old man continued uninterrupted.

'Greener came to my door just after dark, as was arranged. I was to hide him until Wilde, who was windy, was ready. He was pretty well out of 'is mind with fear. You could smell it off 'im. But I daren't let 'im into the house, because Magers had arrived unexpected and was setting there large as life and twice as nosey. So I sent Greener down to the shed, all unknowing that Rowley, who's only young 'imself, had let it to the boy

Dunning. I don't know what happened exactly but I can guess. Greener was a killer and he was on the run.'

He sucked a tooth thoughtfully.

'We had some strange clients.'

Yeo said something to Luke, who turned to Dice.

'You said James had notes on him from Raymond and who else?'

'Steiner, sir. That was the fence we had the inquiry about last year.'

'Raymond?' Yeo sounded more than gratified. 'If we get something fastened on him at last all this will have been worth the trouble for that alone. How very ingenious, and conventional, of James to work through the big receivers. Thoroughgoing little business man, isn't he?' He straightened himself in his chair, and lit another cigarette. 'Well, now, it's very late, Chief. Do we want any more from Bowels at the moment?' Luke eyed Campion, who seemed mildly unhappy.

'There's always Ed Geddy,' the lean man said awkwardly, and for the first time Jas Bowels grew rigid in his chair.

'Ed Geddy,' echoed Yeo with contempt. 'Well, he killed a poor little girl who couldn't have blacked his eye for him even if he'd given her the chance. He got away in this conjuring cabinet, did he? That's a crime in itself.'

Campion hesitated. 'He got away, but he didn't quite arrive,' he murmured at last. 'It was Ed Geddy who gave Apron Street its bad name among the fraternity. Either the drug was too powerful, the coffin too tight, or the journey too long. Ed died in the box. In view of the line he took when he thought Luke was going to raise the subject, Pa Wilde evidently diagnosed the drug.'

In the deep silence which followed, during which every glance in the room was upon him, old Jas Bowels took a long sighing breath. His wicked eyes, in which there was yet the saving grace of guts, met Yeo's own. He was pallid and sweating, but he kept his head.

At last he spoke softly and deferentially as ever.

'It'll be a question of proof, sir, won't it, if it's true?'

He was unanswerable he knew it quite as well as they did.

After a while they dismissed him to the cells uncharged with the more serious crime.

'I wonder how much loot he filched out of the coffin before he screwed it down,' the Superintendent remarked almost cheerfully as the departing footsteps diminished down the corridor. 'It's to his credit he didn't take the lot, I suppose. Your boys are taking his place apart now, are they, Charlie? Did you tell me you'd found the shares Campion keeps nattering about? Oh? They were with him?'

'All present and correct.' Luke patted a long envelope on the desk before him and raised his head to meet a uniformed man who had just come in.

'Message from the doctor, sir. I was to say that the drug was probably chloral hydrate.'

'Anything else?'

'It's the reporters. There's not a lot of *us* left in the front office and they're very persistent, sir.'

'Where's Inspector Bowden?'

'At the bank, sir. The main branch seems to have arrived complete. I've never seen gentlemen so upset.'

'No. I suppose not. What did they come in – hansom cabs?'

'Rolls-hire, sir.'

'I thought Inspector Gage was due from Fowler Street?'

'He's at the undertaker's. Young Bowels has just been brought in and charged. Mr Pollit has gone for Jelf with two men, and Sergeant Glover has gone to see if he can wake the coroner's department.'

Luke laughed.

'Tell 'em we won't keep 'em longer than we can help and that Superintendent Yeo will be making a statement shortly.'

'What's this?' demanded Yeo in high good humour. 'Trusting me, Charlie?'

Luke grinned at him. 'Relying on you, Guv,' he said cheerfully.

Yeo turned bodily in his chair.

'Campion, I always thought you were a clever chap,' he began, his eyes twinkling. 'All I know is that the prisoner killed the old woman for money. That's the most convincing theory I've ever heard you advance in all the years I've known you. It took you plenty of time, didn't it? It was so orthodox you nearly missed it, I suppose.'

Campion regarded him with affection.

'You give me a cigarette and I'll tell you the little I know.'

He accepted the light Luke gave him and leant back.

'There's going to be gaps in this until you fill them, and the first one was how it was that James learnt that Brownie Mines are due to produce Ingredient A in vast quantities almost at once. That is one of those burn-before-reading top secrets which have a disconcerting habit of leaking out these days. Anyway, he did learn it and it interested him because old Miss Ruth, gambler and family nuisance, not only possessed eight thousand first preference negotiable shares in the company, but, well knowing they were worthless, had left them to him in her will.'

Luke put his feet on the desk.

'When you say it like that it sounds a great temptation,' he observed seriously.

'It was. Not only that. The opportunity to kill her presented itself every other day. She was always trotting into his office on some excuse – and – this is the point – believe it or not, *whenever the Palinodes interviewed their bank manager, either at home or in his office, they expected to take a glass of sherry wine with him.*'

'Get away!' Yeo was taken off his balance. 'No bank's done that for fifty years.'

'Except this one. You know Emett's drawings of trains? Clough's is an Emett-train sort of bank. That's why I was completely fogged until this afternoon.'

'Ah, that was the significance of the green sherry glass,' put in Luke.

Campion nodded. 'The whole thing was given me on a plate – or rather, on a tray – the first time I met Miss Evadne. She and James were conferring when I went up to her room, and when I appeared she camouflaged the glasses and hid the empty bottle, presumably because it *was* empty. I had forgotten the incident until this evening, when dear little Miss Cardboard Hat spoke about the apple-green glasses. I went in to Lawrence and asked him if the family took refreshment at the bank when they called. He simply said yes. It did not occur to him that it was even unusual. His father expected it. The bank manager's father expected it. So do their children. That's the sort of people the Palinodes are. Every time the world goes thud they put their heads back in a book.'

'Well I'm damned.' Yeo seemed more shaken by this survival of past elegance than by the crime. 'So he merely slipped a dose in the old girl's glass one morning? I didn't realize he inherited the shares.'

'He didn't. Miss Ruth had changed her will since she last told him about it and had made her most irritating bequest to her latest *bête noire*, Captain Seton, with whom she was quarrelling over a room. The news did not break at once and soon after the anonymous letters started, the police came down on the street like a herd of buffaloes, and the fat was in the fire.'

Yeo permitted himself an old man's chuckle.

'You two lads couldn't have been good for his ferry service.'

'Quite. That's what Jas felt so strongly. We mucked up everything. The Bowelses had to assemble the coffin in Portminster Lodge cellar, to avoid Lugg. Greener had to be smuggled away at the last moment in a packing-case, coffin and all, and Bella had to go with him in the truck, widow's weeds notwithstanding.'

'How did Jas do that exactly?' Luke inquired. 'Did he forge the death certificates to get the coroner's order-to-export?'

'Better than that. He merely duplicated his client. I spent most of today going round to the addresses I got from the coroner. In seven of the ten cases in which Bowels had applied for an order in the last three years, the family had not arranged for anything of the sort and the relative had been interred over here. The gunmen went out with a genuine dead man's name on the lid. The Edward Palinode nameplate was made, I think, in honest error when Jas made certain he was going to get the job. Some wretched crook didn't get his passage that time. There was a long gap between Jackson and Greener. Probably no other genuine client came along at that moment. People don't die to order.'

'Very pretty,' Yeo declared. 'Very neat. Funny James was so careful over one business and so slapdash in the other. I always say a murderer isn't a crook except when he's both. He still went for the shares, though, that's the significant thing.'

'Oh yes, he got Lawrence to buy them and accepted them as part security for a small personal loan – at least that's my bet. Lawrence's attitude over them smelt that way to me. There again it looks as if Ruth's murder was somehow incidental. Otherwise I don't see why he didn't do the same thing with her in the first place. But all through there is this double motive. The hooey we made got him down and he staged today's well-nigh crazy performance, which was designed to put Lawrence out and clear up the mystery, and the street, by incriminating Miss Jessica. It was a silly, theoretical scheme, utterly unpractical.'

'Don't you be so sure, my lad.' Yeo spoke grimly. 'You'd have been hard put to it yourselves to know what line to take if he hadn't suddenly got frightened and bunked. Why did he do that, anyway?'

'Because in the middle of the party, after he had done his stuff with Lawrence, Miss Evadne suddenly informed him that Glossop had been to the house. He put two and two together and they added up to Brownie Mines. Since he had also gathered that the hue and cry was on for somebody, he assumed the worst and had to go up Apron Street.'

'Whereas, of course,' said Luke, 'the hung was on for Bloblip. He was hiding in the bank, silly sausage. We never thought to go over it; you don't with a bank.'

'Bloblip? His intention was blackmail,' Campion continued. 'But he doesn't seem to have tried it until today, probably not until after the party, when he got just about what he was asking for, the old and respected bang on head. The rest of the time

233

he appears to have been footling about trying to get evidence. I can't imagine what put him on the idea in the first place.'

A discreet cough from the other end of the table brought everyone's attention to Dice. He was unusually animated. 'You said, sir, that James had got to get the hyoscine from somewhere. He hadn't. It was there. That's what Congreve knew. I got it out of him in hospital. It's in my report.'

Yeo turned round to regard the sergeant as if he were a domestic pet who had suddenly decided to hold forth.

'What do you mean, the hyoscine was there? Where?'

'In the corner-cupboard in the manager's room, sir, along with the sherry decanter and the glasses and a lot of other objects.'

'*Hyoscine*?'

'Yes, sir. Congreve says so. It was when he noticed that it had gone that he and his sister looked it up in the family medical compendium and remembered Miss Ruth's symptoms, which the sister had heard about from the Captain.'

The silence from his audience was so uncompromisingly blank that he made haste to amplify the statement.

'Congreve had worked at the bank all his life. He was there in the prisoner's father's time. That gentleman used to keep some hyoscine in a sealed glass box to show to visitors. It was labelled and marked "Poison", of course. Peculiar, really.'

'Staggering,' said Campion drily. 'What for?'

The sergeant cleared his throat. His dull eyes developed a gleam.

'As a curio, sir. It was the poison Dr Crippen used.'

'God bless my soul, he's got it!' Yeo bounded in his excitement. 'I well remember the most respectable people behaving like that over the Crippen case. Hyoscine was comparatively new then. It's a good point too. Any judge will believe it. Excellent, Dice.'

Luke broke up the party. He was still incredulous.

'Wasn't this cupboard ever cleared out? We've had two wars since Crippen was hanged.'

'Cleaned but not cleared, sir.' Dice was almost smug. 'It's like a drawing-room piece when you get the door open. Full of what you might call relics. We found all the relevant papers in an antique wine cooler in his bedroom. We shall trace all his associates.'

'Oh, very good, very good indeed, sergeant. Nicely told and very good work.' Yeo rose and pulled down his waist-coat. 'Well,' he said, turning to the others. 'Now for the nice not-too-modest statement to the Press. Trot along and wake 'em up, sergeant, will you?'

The rain had ceased and a clear sweet dawn was breaking as Luke let himself and his friend out, and they walked round the houses to Apron Street. He was supremely happy. He walked, Campion reflected, like a proud cat. He was full of affection rather than gratitude, which was endearing, and when they paused on the corner outside the shabby old mansion, he was laughing.

'I was thinking,' he said. 'If *my* bank manager offered me a glass of sherry in his office I'd *expect* hyoscine in it. Well, good-bye. God bless. And next time I'm in trouble you'll get a wire, if not an escort.'

He hesitated and eyed the house, and his expression was speculative.

'Think they'll marry?'

'Clytie and Mike?' Campion was taken by surprise. 'I don't know. It does happen.'

Charlie Luke pulled his hat an inch farther over one eye and arched his lean stomach.

'I'll betcha,' he said. 'It's my manor. *He* doesn't know it, poor kid. But in my opinion he's just teaching her the words.'

Campion looked after his jaunty figure until, with a wave, it disappeared round the bend. He wondered.

But as he went quietly up the path he was grinning. Miss White was certainly going to have fun.

He was making across the hall when he saw he had underestimated Renee. There she was, bright as a bird, sitting on the bottom step of the staircase.

'And about time, too,' she said, flinging her arms round his neck with an abandon she kept for very special occasions. 'Oh, you are a wonderful man!'

Considered as a purely spontaneous tribute, Campion felt it was the best he had had. She tucked her arm through his and urged him towards the back staircase.

'Come and have some coffee. Oh, we have had a night! A proper Press Reception! Just like the old days at the Manchester Hipp. I don't know *what's* going to be in the papers in the morning. Jessica's been making you one of her little nasties, but I've put it down the sink, and I shall say you drank it and liked it. Come on. Clarrie has been taking special care of Mr Lugg . . . what a charming man . . . with a little something I saved. You're not to be angry with them. Just don't take any notice. They were both so *thirsty* after all this trouble.'

He burst out laughing. So far she had not let him speak and even now forestalled him.

'Oh, I was forgetting again. There's a letter for you. It came yesterday morning and nobody thought to give it to you. There it is, dear, it's on the tray. It's a woman's writing so it may be personal. You'd better read it. I'll go and pop the kettle on. Hurry up. We'll all be waiting.'

She fluttered off like a crumpled but valiant butterfly, and he took up his letter and moved under the hall lantern to read it. His wife's distinctive hand smiled at him from the single page.

Dear Albert,

Thank you for letting me know that we are not going to govern that island, I am so glad. The new Cherubim jet is almost ready for her trials so I shall be here with Alan and Val whenever you want me.

Young Sexton Blake draws all day long – nothing but mushrooms, which I thought were innocently fairylike and a good thing until I read the captions. They all consist of the same single word – 'Wham!'

I have been following your case as well as I can from the newspapers, but the reports are very sketchy, I am afraid, and I fear that any comment I might make would be so wide of the mark as to be irritating. I hope we see you very soon.

Lots of love,

AMANDA

P.S. – I can't help it. *Have* you thought of the bank manager? So *shady*.

Campion read the note through twice, and the postscript five times. He was folding the page carefully into an inside pocket when a curious smothered wailing reached him. Someone was trying to sing. It sounded ominously like Lugg.

MORE VINTAGE MURDER MYSTERIES

If you have enjoyed this book, you might like to know about the Margery Allingham Society which has members throughout the world. The Society:

- meets several times a year to explore aspects of Margery Allingham's life, work, family and interests;

- organises residential weekend conventions every few years;

- publishes a twice-yearly journal, *The Bottle Street* Gazette, with articles on Margery Allingham's life and novels and, occasionally, some of her writing; it has also published several books about her work;

- keeps in touch with members through its regular newsletter, *From the Glueworks.*

You can follow us on Facebook at The Margery Allingham Society

Or to find out how to join, write to us at info@margeryallingham.org.uk

or visit our website www.margeryallingham.org **which has up-to-date information about how to get in touch by post**

dead good

*For all of you who find
a crime story irresistible.*

Discover the very best crime and thriller books on our
dedicated website – hand-picked by our editorial team
so you have tailored recommendations to help you
choose what to read next.

We'll introduce you to our favourite authors and the
brightest new talent. Read exclusive interviews and
specially commissioned features on everything from the
best classic crime to our top ten TV detectives, join live
webchats and speak to authors directly.

Plus our monthly book competition offers you the
chance to win the latest crime fiction, and there are
DVD box sets and digital devices to be won too.

Sign up for our newsletter at
www.deadgoodbooks.co.uk/signup

Join the conversation on:

penguin.co.uk/vintage